Five Thousand Runaways

Also by Takeshi Kaiko

DARKNESS IN SUMMER

FIVE
Thousand Runaways
STORIES BY *Takeshi Kaiko*

TRANSLATED FROM THE
JAPANESE BY
Cecilia Segawa Seigle

PETER OWEN · LONDON

PETER OWEN PUBLISHERS
73 Kenway Road London SW5 0RE

First published in Great Britain 1990

British Library Cataloguing in Publication Data
Kaiko, Takeshi
Five thousand runaways.
I. Title
8956.6'35 [F]

ISBN 0 – 7206 – 0770 – 1

Peter Owen Limited gratefully acknowledge the assistance of the
Arts Council of Great Britain in the publication of this book.

Printed in Great Britain by Billings of Worcester

CONTENTS

Translator's Introduction

Takeshi Kaiko is a writer who represents contemporary Japan in a complex and varied, but honest way. He possibly deserves a Nobel Prize in Literature more than anyone else in Japan at the present time. He is old enough to have seen the prewar Japan and to retain its few good points such as honor, courtesy, modesty, self-restraint, self-discipline, and regard for others. He suffered through the Second World War as a young boy and observed human beings in extremes. And he was young enough in postwar Japan to develop as an artist in a free and vigorous atmosphere. The combination of these experiences has made him a strong, resilient writer whose work shows him to be both the conscience of Japan as well as its severest critic.

There has been a myth in Japan that artistic writers, writers of so-called "pure literature," do not sell. While Kaiko is known as a "pure literature" writer, however, he has a tremendous appeal to the masses, too. He is a best-selling raconteur of his heroic-scale international fishing expeditions, and he is a hilarious conversationalist who can entertain convivial guests for hours on end with anecdotes and bawdy jokes from various countries of the world. His face has become familiar on television commercials for fishing products. If he is not a household word, he is a familiar figure to a surprisingly broad reading public. As an expert angler, he can win trophies in any international fishing competition. As a writer, he can produce articles suitable for publication in popular weeklies as well as in serious literary magazines. While he has won many literary awards, full honor to him as a world-class artist has not yet been paid.

Kaiko is a complex man, externally a man with unusual experiences that few people in the world could claim. He is a deeply humanistic man who cannot close his eyes to crises of the human spirit. He will fly to any corner of the world to witness conflicts. Yet he is sensitive enough, once he finds it is beyond his power to do anything, to be frustrated and to turn his back in deep shame, feeling a tremendous burden of guilt for this failing. His respectable, but less than comfortable, youth may explain his untypically Japanese sense of guilt.

The oldest son of an elementary school principal in Osaka, Kaiko lost his father in 1943, when he had just entered the seventh grade. The difficulty of wartime was compounded by his responsibility as head of the family at age thirteen. Kaiko's wartime memories are dominated by starvation and its effects, going to school, not to study but to dig air-raid shelters or work at an arsenal, being bombed or strafed by American airplanes, and seeing the dead, the burned, the destroyed.

In 1949, he entered the Osaka Municipal University on a partial scholarship, but with not much hope for or intention of studying. He had to work to sustain his mother, two younger sisters, and himself. He somehow slipped through the graduation examination in December 1953, but between 1945 and 1954, he had moved endlessly from one odd job to another. He had worked at a bakery, a slate manufacturing plant, an ironworks, a herbal medicine factory (some scenes from which are used in

"The Laughingstock"), for election campaigns, and as a lottery salesman, black-market salesman, a tutor, a French fashion magazine translator, a paid pen-pal letter writer, and a teacher of English, who, only one step ahead of his students, could scarcely say, "I write a letter."

He married Yoko Maki, a poet and trained chemist, in 1952 after their only daughter was born. The experience of their initial cohabitation and the circumstances of their daughter's birth are humorously described in "The Laughingstock."

Kaiko began to work for Suntory Whiskey (then called Kotobukiya), where his wife had been employed as a research chemist. He wrote excellent advertising copy. He practically created the advertising department and instituted the much-praised PR magazine called *Yōshu Tengoku* (Whiskey Paradise), some issues of which are now collector's items. Suntory owes its success and prestige of today much to this talented copywriter and his colleague, the artist Ryōhei Yanagihara.

While struggling to sell Suntory products, Kaiko continued to write stories until the small hours of the night, and finally in 1958, he won the coveted Akutagawa Literary Prize for his *Naked King*. Shortly after that, Kaiko left Suntory and began to concentrate on his career as a literary writer. Twenty-nine years later Kaiko is a phenomenon. His output is prodigious and his position in Japan is solid. Since 1978, he has been himself one of the judges of the Akutagawa Prize.

Most of Kaiko's works have been published by Shinchosha: three volumes of essays and nine volumes of fiction. Another six or seven thick volumes of nonfiction have been published by Bungei-Shunju Co., Ltd. In a special series of critical studies of contemporary Japanese writers, *Kanshō Gendai Nihon Bungaku* (Appreciation of Contemporary Japanese Literature), an entire volume is dedicated to Kaiko's work.

A series of his books have been recent best sellers of the year: *Opa!*, *Opa! Opa!*, *Farther!*, and *Grander!* are all collections of essays on his fishing expeditions in the Amazon, off the Saint George

Island in the Bering Sea, and through North and South America.

In his mid-fifties, Kaiko remains a prolific and energetic author, although in recent years he has gone through a major operation and lost his spleen. This has provided quite an occasion for mirth since "spleen" was always considered the source of courage in the old days, and to lose spleen would have meant "losing guts." He now suffers from chronic pains in his back, which he calls his "back monster" (*onbu obake*).

It was in 1972 that the first English translation of Takeshi Kaiko's novel, *Darkness in Summer*, the second part of his trilogy, was published by Alfred Knopf. The first volume of the trilogy, *Into a Black Sun*, appeared in the fall of 1980 from Kodansha International. In the interim, two of his short stories were translated by Charles Dunn of London University and published by the University of Tokyo Press under the titles "Panic" and "The Runaway."

Still, the chances are that the English-speaking reader is not yet familiar with Kaiko because of the poor publicity and lack of promotion his books suffered. His obscurity in the English-speaking countries, despite his popularity in Japan, is a misfortune that, one hopes, will be remedied over time. His work has also been translated into French, German, Dutch, Russian, Polish, and Finnish and has won accolades in each country, particularly in the Soviet Union and Finland. In Germany there has been a proposal to make *Darkness in Summer* into a film.

Kaiko's novel *Kagayakeru Yami* (meaning Brilliant Darkness, a title borrowed from Martin Heidegger's philosophy defining the modern age), received the twenty-second Mainichi Publication Cultural Award in 1968. It was published under the title *Into a Black Sun* (translation by this writer). Its sequel and the second of the trilogy, *Natsu no Yami* (Darkness in Summer, also translated by this writer) was selected as recipient of the 1972 Minister of Education Literary Prize. Kaiko refused this prize, stating in one of his essays, "I would be happy to receive prizes given by publishing companies and by newspapers, but I have always believed that a writer should never accept prizes from the government.

I presume the Minister of Education is part of the government—so I am gratefully declining it."

A voracious intellectual curiosity and a capacity for physical activity have taken Kaiko to all corners of the world. Always drawn to problem areas wherever a war, or a riot, or an inquisition was in progress—Vietnam, Biafra, Israel, Paris, Poland, Czechoslovakia—Kaiko has observed storm centers in the closest possible proximity and has written vivid, penetrating essays. For these reports, and his extensive reportorial work on China, the Middle East, Europe, Africa, Canada, the two American continents, and Vietnam, where he made several extended visits, he received, in 1981, the twenty-ninth Kikuchi Prize of reportage literature.

Kaiko is never a political writer in the strict sense, but his concern for humanity inevitably makes him a politically and sociologically sensitive writer. An analytical eye and a dissecting pen are not scarce among contemporary Japanese writers, even among writers of *watakushi-shosetsu* (the "I-Novel" of the Japanese Naturalism strain), but such a sense of *engagement* as Kaiko's makes its possessor one of a rare breed.

From his earliest writing days in the 1940s, Kaiko has made a conscious effort to keep away from the notorious tradition of *watakushi-shosetsu*. In this special genre of modern Japanese literature, the writer's personal experience, his subjective treatment of the material, and his close identity with the protagonist are salient features. Every Japanese writer who lived through the suffocating atmosphere of the early twentieth century to the end of the Second World War was affected either positively or negatively by this pervasive major trend in modern Japanese novel writing: the writer's confession of his private life. Its roots and development are the subject of voluminous studies but, simply put, the increasing military and political repression after the Russo-Japanese War made it impossible for Japanese writers to write about society and human conditions they saw. This coincided with the dawn of modern literature, when French Naturalism had been introduced into Japan. Instead of writing about the misery of human beings, Japanese writers decided to write about their own personal misery in confession-type stories. This provided them with a political safety zone, and this genre and the lyrical and emotional tradition of Japanese literature suited each other. Before the termination of the Second World War, Japanese writers had become expert at describing details of their emotional life.

Kaiko began his writing career at the farthest point from this *wakakushi-shosetsu* tradition. His early work, from the late Fifties to the early Sixties, indicates that he was making conscious efforts to be objective and to deal with subjects outside of his own experience. But, curiously enough, beginning in about 1963 he started to use his own experience and to describe his inner-scape, permitting himself to reveal his emotional life. But his training as a detached observer never permitted him to become a *wakakushi-shosetsu* writer. As a result, Kaiko today is a much more human and interesting writer. It is as though his discipline in being an objective writer has given him confidence enough to allow some revelation of his inner groping.

For this volume, a variety of styles and subject matter has been selected, covering a period ranging from 1959 to 1979, showing his droll humor, his unsentimental treatment of more personal materials, some mood pieces, some pieces describing his poverty in postwar Japan, and some of his Vietnam War experiences.

His earlier short stories, such as "The Fishing Hole (*Ana*)" (1959), "The Laughingstock" (1963), "Five Thousand Runaways" (1964), "Festivities by the River" (1967), and "Duel" (1968), chart the path of his development as a writer.

Examples of his more recent work, "The Crushed Pellet" (1978), "Making a Shell Mound" (1978), and "Monster and Toothpick" (1979) are included. "The Crushed Pellet" received the Kawabata Prize for short stories. This prestigious prize was instituted in 1979, and Kaiko's work was the first to receive the honor in memory of the Nobel laureate. These works show Kaiko as a master storyteller, reminding me of the sixteenth-century tea-ceremony master, whose mastery of his art was so complete that he could behave in whatever way he wished, paying no attention to the rules and conventions. Kaiko has become the master of his unique story telling.

Five Thousand Runaways

Monster and Toothpick

As everyone knows, the word *tea*, with some difference in color green or red, is about the same in any language: *cha*, *char*, *Tee*, *chai*, or *thé*. In my experience, the only exception was Polish, and if I remembered correctly, it was *herbata*. And if one spoke of drinking tea or of tea time, everyone automatically associated it with rest, repose, tranquility, or relaxation. But this, too, had an exception: "Saigon Tea" could only bring an association with anxiety, uneasiness, poverty, cacophony, and fights between man and woman. Anyone who has experienced it once would show an ironic smile mixed with chagrin, and at the same time he would feel his eyes softening and a kind of nostalgia filling him like warm water.

The Saigon Tea in reality was generally some leftover juice or Coca-Cola served in a small half-filled cup. You walked into a bar, groped in the total darkness, and somehow settled down in a chair. A woman would come and seat herself beside you, and whisper to you, "Buy me a drink." This "drink" was the famous Saigon Tea. The waiter would bring a cup and a piece of paper to the woman. If the tea was 100 piastres a cup, 30 to 40 percent of that became her income. All the women were in dire straits, so they ordered tea one after another without stopping, though they did mention it to the customer. After a while, the customer would suddenly notice that the table was covered with cups and the woman was holding in her hand a large wad of paper. A feeling of panic would come over him. While the customer drank one cognac soda, the woman whispered, "Make me happy," and ordered seven, eight, ten cups of Saigon Tea. So, poor American soldiers who had been milked dry a number of times would conquer their sentiment and sympathy and pretend not to hear the women. In the beginning the women would croon sweetly, "Buy me a drink," "Make me happy," "My family beaucoup; baby-san beaucoup," entreating, supplicating, but the soldiers would continue to play dumb, knowing that they wouldn't be able to take the girls out at the end of the evening if they paid for Saigon Tea. There was even a saying that a soldier who went to a bar would come home a virgin. After a while, the women's eyes would begin to flash in the dark, and they would begin to shout, "You cheap Charlie!" Then, they would curse, "*Numbah ten! Troy oy!*" clicking their tongues peevishly. American soldiers would shout back, "S-T-I-F, S-T-I-F, Saigon Tea Is Fini!" If one raised his voice, all the rest in the bar joined the shouting match, stomping their feet, banging on the table. Sometimes the "S-T-I-F, S-T-I-F!" chanting grew into a great chorus. In the steamy darkness, hecklings, shouts, stomping shoes, noise of shattering cups and glasses, screams, perspiration, body odor, odor of alcohol, glinting eyes, chattering teeth, falling ceiling, crumbling walls . . . everything mingled and usually ended up in a chaotic extravaganza.

Sometimes, in the midst of it, a bloody dogfight between a white soldier and a black soldier broke out. Or, sometimes, somewhere in the bar, *plastique* might explode and turn the place into a miry dump of flesh, blood, glass, and shoes.

* * *

It was in one of such bars that I saw General Bao for the first time. It was the time of day when the palpitation of fresh and restless anxiety of the early evening hours had died down and night had fallen completely. I had settled down on a high stool and, resting my elbows on the counter, I was sipping Pernod. The cold and sweet scent of fennel moistened my lips, and the warm fog of alcohol had begun to diffuse slowly into my body. The waiters walked around busily, and in the dark behind me, American soldiers and Vietnamese girls laughed and cheered loudly. There was a dance floor, but it was too small and the crowd was too large; it did not allow couples to dance dramatically. All they could do was to hold on to each other tightly and sway like seaweed. There were still several hours before the frenzy of the night, but the heat was slowly filling the hall, and the evening was beginning to boil. Girls wearing *ao dai* had the dignity of court ladies and the airiness of butterflies. As one watched them walking away rapidly, their long skirts fluttering, one found in them elegance and daintiness not found anywhere else in today's world. Their gesture of giggling, hiding the mouth with small hands, was also charming, and it was only in unexpected moments that one glimpsed their strong will.

While I let my gloomy and voluminous fatigue rest on the wet counter, watching abstractly the eyes and cheeks of the girls, I suddenly noticed a man walk into the bar and sit on a stool. The first sight told me it was General Bao, and my whole body stiffened and I lowered my eyes.

Bao was protected by four bodyguards. Two sat on his left and looked around the bar, and the other two sat on the right, watching the entrance. Two had bare pistols in the holsters on their belts, and the other two had laid light machine guns on their long, muscular laps. All four had glazed eyes in the heat of the dry-season night, but anyone would have detected around their shoulders a virility that would have exploded at the slightest provocation. And in the posture of the four, also visible to any-one, was an extraordinary awe of their commander. Protected by this awe, their muscles, and by their small firearms, Bao sat on the stool with a somewhat superior air, as though he were all alone. He was small and slight, his shoulders were narrow, and his hands were childishly thin, but his face was almost grotesque. His head was completely bald, and the uneven bumps and fur-rows on his cranium were encased tightly in the breakably thin skin. His eyelids hung heavy over his thread-thin eyes, but in some moments, the hidden eyes momentarily revealed a piercing sharpness and depth—sedate, cold, and dark. His nose was there, but it appeared as though it had been crushed frontally and submerged into his cheeks. There was a gigantic and greedy mouth, and the chin that should be supporting it was almost completely lacking, so the face with only the mouth was floating in the pale light. The face itself was small, but perhaps because the shoulders were extremely narrow it sometimes appeared colossal. It was as though a monstrous, stunted hybrid, the result of a random copulation of a bald eagle and a gigantic toad in a dismal swamp, with some well-developed parts on its body, had crawled out at night onto the land. The incomparable ugliness of his face and physique was not something that had been the result of boxing or torture. It was obviously congenital.

He ordered a Pernod in an almost inaudibly low voice. When the drink was offered respectfully, he picked up the glass with a seasoned gesture and carried it to his gigantic mouth. The movement of his childlike hand had a refreshing elegance and delicacy, and I looked at him wide-eyed in amazement. The middle-aged bartender was completely cowed, stark in the up-right position, only able to steal an occasional glance at the man sipping Pernod.

It was not only the bartender. A cold wave had flowed into the bar; the waiters, the girls, the shoeshine boy, all fell silent, petrified. Some American soldiers had not noticed this change for a while and continued to laugh loudly but that, too, soon subsided. Only "Never on Sunday" wafted merrily, but the sudden silence seemed to have extracted some juice from it, and one could almost hear the noise of the winding tape. They were all frozen in the dark, alongside the wall or behind the pillars. As though sighing, they glanced up at Bao occasionally in the pale light, and immediately cast their glances downward. Bao did not show any sign of pride in the effect he had created, but sat on the stool comfortably, taking time to sip the Pernod gloomily. When he finished it, he put some money on the counter and left the bar in silence. It was a rare sight to see anyone of his high rank paying money at a bar. The four guards quickly accompanied him on both sides with genuine reverence and followed him out of the bar. Bao's steps and gestures were as soft, nimble, and light as those of his guards, which made me open my eyes in amazement once again.

After some weeks, again incidentally, I saw Bao in a French restaurant. I happened to pass in front of it at lunch time so, by chance, I entered and saw him having lunch with a woman. The moment I saw the bald head and the large mouth, I almost went out the door, but something held me back. More than anything else I felt numbed by his ominous air, and I followed the waiter to a seat in the back of the room. There were many customers but scarcely any noise, only low voices like thin smoke rising occasionally. The customers were all French or Americans, with a great number of Aloha shirts and suits, very few army uniforms. Everyone's face and shoulders seemed to be stiff, and everyone's eyes were lowered, just like those of the middle-aged Vietnamese bartender at the bar on the previous evening.

Suffocation and tension were in the air. The manager and waiters stood timidly at the entrance of the kitchen, sometimes stealing glances at Bao's seat and quickly turning their eyes away. Their eyes were not complaining of an undesirable customer or begging him to leave. The men themselves were paralyzed. Their eyes, as though only they were movable, shifted once in a while. Two guards were a little away from Bao, sipping coffee calmly;

the barrels of small firearms gleamed on their heavy and sturdy hips. The other two might have been at the front or back entrance.

Bao was lunching with a woman, and his manipulation of a knife and fork on a fillet of sole showed the same elegance and delicacy that I had seen the other night. Bao sometimes spoke to the woman softly. He acted kindly toward her, portioning the sole for her, pouring wine from a carafe to her glass, or pouring water into another glass. The woman was a rare mature beauty, unlike the usual little-girl beauties of Vietnam. She waited quietly for him to serve and, receiving her plate, began to eat the fish calmly. She did not appear to be a concubine, girlfriend, or high-class prostitute exactly, but it seemed certain that she was not his wife. She was quiet, but she was not petrified; rather, she seemed totally trusting of Bao. She was subservient and Bao was content, and he seemed to be deeply and darkly pensive, as before, but with an air of virile confidence. Having finished her lunch, the woman lightly sighed and lifted her eyes. Her blood shined in rose color around her well-tanned high cheekbones. Her calm eyes were soft and smiles moved vividly in them. Witnessing this scene, the customers turned their eyes from the hunchbacked, slimy, cold, half-rotten monster and smiled nervously. After a while, the couple went out. The moment they disappeared, a wave ran through the restaurant, a light filled the rooms, and dishes began to make noises. People relaxed all at once, took in a deep breath, and began to laugh loudly. There was even the sound of applause.

Because I saw him twice, Bao settled down and began to live in me. In broad daylight or at night, he followed me wherever I went. Holding up his gigantic bald head, his eyes under heavy eyelids followed me everywhere. In my apartment, I would be talking and laughing with some friends; a glass of cognac soda in my hand, I would be removing rice husks from the ice. Then I would suddenly notice his eyes there, not approaching, not moving away, but just gazing at me. I didn't know at all whether it would help me, but I began to listen to rumors about Bao's personal life. Around that time, he was a general in the Air Force and also sat at the top of the entire security forces. Secret police, national police, Saigon Jadin District Field Police, all other security networks completely converged on him. He was a spider highlighted at the center of his dark web.

He was born in Hué into an enormously rich family, and went to study in France. As I understand, he received doctorates in both pharmaceuticals and engineering. He disliked reporters and cameras and almost never attended official parties. He did not grant interviews or allow picture taking. So there was nothing known of him but rumors, and consequently his portrait necessarily remained hazy. As the head of a Gestapo, he was cold, cruel, merciless, and held the complete dossier of all the important men in the government, and of generals and ministers among his colleagues. So he was called "Fouché," after the ruthless French statesman of the Revolutionary period. He was also a staunch anticommunist and unyielding hawk, and he resolutely rejected American pressure toward peace. He executed all enemy captives and spies one after another on the race course, in the stadium, in marketplaces, or even on ordinary streets. In this respect, he was not an amphibian living in two worlds, so it seemed inappropriate to call him Fouché. During a street fight more recently, he shot and killed a lieutenant of the enemy forces, so the nickname Fouché receded and was replaced by a new one that made him the Beria of Saigon. The gossip that he was a skirt chaser and debaucher and drunkard went with this nickname and reinforced the idea he was a Beria. Amid varied flying rumors, persistent stories were these: in a jet plane fight or in a street battle, he was always in the forefront, charging bravely, never retreating; he took good care of his inferiors; he was content with a ridiculously low salary and was never involved in a scandal. All these seemed to come down to the fact that within his unsightly little body many contradictory personalities cohabited: at his desk, an intellectual with extraordinary brains and culture or a sadistic and bloodthirsty murderer; in the field, an upright and courageous military man. Having heard from no close observer of his private life, I had to be content with these temporary theories and conflicting images.

Since Bao's personality and the character of the organizations he controlled were generally talked about in the same jumbled fashion, it was impossible to separate the private Bao from his office and determine how far they were united or separated, all the more leaving me with a foggy impression. At any rate, none of the rumors interpreted or supported or even helped me to understand the amazing impressions I received at my two encounters with him. Not that I understood nothing, but most of Bao's mystery overflowed without being defined. It seemed that something lurked behind, but I had no way to find out what it was. I walked around aimlessly, every day, from news service to press office, from chair to chair, room to room, half melting in the glittering sunlight and heat and humidity. Bao's eyes never showed signs of disappearing.

The third time, his eyes rested directly on me at the entrance to Saigon on the My Tho Highway. This highway was an aorta connecting Saigon with the vast Mekong Delta and had a large quantity of traffic from morning to night. The area was filled at any time with exhaust gas and human noises. Usually, countless wash basins were on display by the road, each basin piled up with bananas, pineapples, dried fish, noodles, meat, intestines, gruels, ducklings, shrimp, or China fish. Women crouched by them shouting incessantly. But this was a scene closer to Saigon. Some three hundred or four hundred yards farther away, another event was taking place: numerous trucks, buses, pedicabs, and tricycles had formed a long queue on the left side of the road; on the right side in a similarly long queue were the drivers and passengers of those vehicles. Field police and military police, holding M-16s, in combat attire complete with bulletproof vests, checked one vehicle at a time, one person at a time.

Wherever you went into the Mekong Delta, you received inspections every day at both the entrance and the exit of any town, but there had never been anything so thorough as this. Both ends of the road were sealed off with tanks. So if you had been discovered having something irregular and tried to escape, you had nowhere to go but the roadside rice paddies. But the paddies were drained and dry, and the rice plants had been harvested. You would be shot down more easily and accurately than the shooting gallery's cut-out dolls. People stood silently in line, in the white flames of midday heat. When their turn came, they emptied out the contents of their suitcases, sacks, and baskets on the road and let the military police inspect them. No one spoke a word. When the inspection was over, people picked up the articles and stuffed their bags in a hurry. Keeping their eyes on the ground, they stumbled away as though making a narrow escape.

In the center of the wide road on which the tar had begun to melt in the heat and shone blue, cases of "33" beer had been piled up. A skinny little man, chinless, with a large mouth slit to the ears, stood by drinking beer slowly. His worn-out green fatigues, unsuitable for a general, were soaked in perspiration and grease, and his bulletproof vest was also sweat stained. There was nothing shiny about him. Even the gunbelt on his hip had lost its shine from handling and dirt. Two bodyguards with strong physiques, sporting rubber sandals and Aloha shirts, stood behind the mountain of beer cases. Around Bao were two or three chiefs of field and military police. Fear, respect, and obedience were visible in their eyes, shoulders, and in their demeanor. Soldiers and NCOs who ran over to report something from time to time also showed the same feelings, and their actions were crisp. Bao did not speak a word but nodded barely visibly. In the infernal sun, he emptied one bottle of beer after another. Although he was shrouded in his usual gloom, his whole body was alive with energy, filled with naked virility and danger that I had not seen at the bar or at the restaurant. Grotesque as before, nevertheless, he was not the stagnant shadow I had seen. Cold somberness was there, but he was clear as a sharpened dagger and the air of putrefaction and fermentation had disappeared. His eyes, bloodshot with beer, glinted behind the heavy eyelids and rested on one person in the line at a time. When he came to me, he lingered on my face for a while. I was stunned as though my intestine was suddenly grabbed by the rough hand of a strong man, and my whole body shuddered. Perspiration spurted as I stood against the fear. For some seconds, Bao fixed his eyes on me, as if to search his memory, then moved on to the next man. That moment, I let out a sigh of relief, and tons of fatigue fell upon me and I tottered. A military policeman approached me and signaled to my bag with his eyes, so I unzipped my Air Vietnam bag. A toothbrush, a tube of toothpaste, a towel, a bag of dried meat, a bottle of stomach pills—things I had lived with for the last five days—fell out on the road. Until then, the many layers of fatigue from my roaming around the vast Delta, seeing burned villages, torn towns, and flocks of squatting refugees, had been building up in me. This horrendous experience dissipated my exhaustion. I was stupefied.

In my Saigon apartment, I often woke up in the middle of the night. Even in the small hours, stifling heat and humidity filled the room, keeping me from sleep. Drenched in perspiration, I would smoke a cigarette, while artillery thundered outside the town and single shots sometimes cracked in the city, far or near. They were as familiar as squeaks of house lizards on the wall, and I had ceased to pay any attention to them. Even then, whenever I happened to think of Bao, I recalled a scene as though by reflex, a habit into which I had fallen unawares. It was a scene at a highland lake in the Bavarian Alps. There was a small stream that poured slowly into the lake. Early one morning, I was walking through a thicket of tall reed, drenched in dew up to my waist, when I saw little splashes in the stream. Hundreds of little fish darted and jumped in panic toward the upper stream. As I looked around, I saw a pike, about a yard long, floating like a log at the confluence of the stream and the lake. The pike was floating just below the water surface, expressionless and motionless, but the little fish were frightened into pushing and jostling toward the upper stream. I had heard about an experiment: If one pike was left in a water tank for several hours then taken out, and a small fish was put in instead, the latter would begin to swim frantically, trying to escape.

The pike is called *hecht* in German; its mouth is filled with needlelike teeth, and once it catches its prey, it will never let it escape. It will attempt to swallow without a moment of hesitation whatever crosses its path—fish, frog, rat, duckling, anything that swims, things with legs, things with wings, things with scales, anything. It is a fish that represents the meaning of gluttony. Starting from their childhood, pikes try to eat each other. I have seen many photos of a pike, unable to swallow a friend of the same size, swimming around with a half-swallowed fish dangling out of its mouth. A pike is a dangerous independent weapon that lives alone, slowly gliding along a thicket of reed near a bank or under the leaves of water lilies.

As I remembered the people with their eyes lowered hurrying away after the inspection at the My Tho Highway, and the silent figure of Bao gazing upon them, the scene at the lake vividly came back to me. Bao had shown me a slightly different side each time, at the bar, at the restaurant, and on the highway, but common in all three cases were his physical hideousness, melancholy, and loneliness—especially his loneliness. At the bar, he was buried in it; at the restaurant, it transcended his environment; on the highway, it seared his flesh. His piercing stare had etched itself into my skin, and there was no way I could be rid of it. The assassination team of the enemy force, those faceless men, who were meticulous and cold-hearted to the same degree as Bao, evidently stalked him day and night. It was obvious from the fact that bodyguards shadowed him as though they were part of his body. He was living the life of a tightrope walker every day. When he had a meal, he probably checked the table and the chair three times before he sat down, and at night, he checked his bed three times before changing into his pajamas.

In cunning and cruelty and obsession they were a perfect match, Bao and his enemies. The only difference was his having a face, whereas his enemies were without faces. The reputation that he fought bravely and always at the head of his troop seemed to be correct, and it was a point that matched his enemy. The fact that both he and his enemies were respected and feared, trusted and obeyed, gave them similar characteristics. As I canceled out the characteristics one by one, something nebulous remained. What it was, I did not know. Bao remained always a mystery. He stood alone in the desolate haze. As I remembered his melancholy eyes that hid behind heavy eyelids, I always shuddered. A cold certainty was the nucleus of my understanding him. But whether he was a sadistic killer or a gambler who was forced to fight an endless fight betting all on one desperate throw of the dice, I could not tell. Furthermore, I had begun to feel some attraction toward him in spite of my revulsion. I often admitted that he did have some character as I put a period at the end of my recurring thought. I wondered whether it was because his loneliness matched his power.

After a while, a rumor reached me that Bao was seriously injured in a battle. I heard that he was hurt in his stomach, or it was in the leg that he was wounded, but no detail was given. As usual, I went around pricking up my ears, but the news of him stopped almost completely after that. When I went to a bar or a restaurant in the evening, I caught myself looking for him unconsciously. In the light, in the dark, in the faces, my eyes searched for the uneven bald head, but I could not find it anywhere.

In the meantime, great battles were being fought one after another in the mountains, highlands, valleys, border areas, and Saigon was showered with rockets almost every night. Bars, newspaper offices, and police stations were bombed. Hospitals were all overflowing, and people slept in the corridors packed sardine-fashion. The stretchers turned black and gleamed with dried blood, perspiration, and dirt. They had the burnish of well-used leather rather than the texture of canvas cloth. The 122mm was a rocket shell designed for indiscriminate killing; once exploded, it discharged countless bits of shells. When such a rocket smashed into the slum areas with flimsy roofs and walls, a scene like that in a slaughterhouse followed.

Once the night fell and the giant American bombers began to drop bombs from high altitude miles away from the target in Saigon (I don't know what part of the Delta they were aiming at), the walls and windows of my room would shake convulsively. It was beyond my imagination to contemplate what horrors must be taking place at the point of detonation. All of the apartment houses piled up sandbags in the corridors and in the rooms, hiding all windows. People tried to guess, on their own theory, the angle at which shell bombs might jump into the room, and changed the position of the bed or moved right up to the wall. As for me, I considered the bed itself a protective wall and placed the thin mattress on the floor and slept on it. Meanwhile, the Vietcong terrorists bombed power stations, transformer substations, and electric lines night and day, so electricity was cut off, water stopped, the toilet overflowed, and the shower ceased to function. Enveloped in perspiration and dirt and suffocating in the odor of excretion, all I could do was sip cognac.

In the branch office of the news service where running water had stopped, they used temporarily a newspaper-covered bucket for defecation. A staff member looked at the bucket and muttered, "What would happen if someone set a time bomb in this?" Everybody in the room heard it but nobody laughed. *Plastiques* were set in bicycles, automobiles, pineapples, breads, ceilings, telephone poles, briefcases, shoeshine boxes, and even in coffins. Everything around our daily life was unsafe, so the joke brought a shiver rather than a laugh.

One afternoon, an unexpected opportunity came for me to meet Bao. The branch office head of the N—— Broadcasting Co., with whom I had meals sometimes, was in my room one day and in the course of our conversation invited me to the meeting. According to him, the Vietnamese interpreter who worked for his office happened to be an acquaintance of Bao.

When he went to visit him at the hospital, Bao had said that he would give a thirty-minute interview, provided that the journalist agreed to his simple condition. He would strictly forbid a camera, stenography, tape recorder, et cetera, but, depending on the interview, he might offer one or two pieces of top-secret information. The interpreter returned to the news office with Bao's message. The branch office chief was excited at the prospect of a great scoop he had never dreamed of, but he was also uneasy because of the notoriety of his interview subject, wondering what further conditions Bao would propose. He told me that he would take me as his assistant but made me promise not to take notes, to carry no ballpoint pen, no camera, nothing, and to keep absolute silence during the interview. I did not reveal to him that I had already seen Bao close up three times, and accepted his condition without argument. To show my gratitude, I took out my cognac bottle and offered him a drink. The chief hurriedly declined, waving his hand, and said he would take a rain check until after we had running water and left my room.

The next afternoon, we went to the hospital. It was the same as any other hospital. Every sick room and every corridor of every floor was filled with patients lying on top of each other. Everywhere on doors and walls, blood and dirt had spattered and poverty and disaster jostled for space. Bao was in a small private room. A bloodstained stretcher leaned against the wall, and the door was left open. There was no sign of a bodyguard or of firearms. Bao was dressed in wrinkled old pajamas and lay flat, his face above the sheet. The only thing with any bulk under the sheet was his rib cage. From this moderate height, the sheet dropped down as though his belly, hips, and thighs had disappeared. He had flattened to that extent. Bao's face was haggard. Under his eyes were black circles as though gouged, which could have been of an old man or a dead man. Because his cheeks were sunken, his nose appeared a little higher than before, but his mouth seemed slit even farther up to the ears, giving him an appearance of rapaciousness. At the My Tho Highway, his energy and danger hovered over his shoulders like gossamer, but now all had disappeared.

The chief timidly approached the bed and greeted Bao. The middle-aged Vietnamese interpreter, even more timidly but with the gentleness and kindness of a nurse, whispered into Bao's ear to convey the chief's words. Bao had remained immobile, but he was clearly awake under his ghoulish mask.

"I heard that the General was wounded in the battle in the Gia Dinh district. How has the General been?" the chief said.

"I am no longer a general, nor a commander. I've quit everything and retired. You don't have to be scared. You don't have to call me General. Don't have to call me Chief of the Security Forces. I am simply Ong Bao."

"I understand. We have only thirty minutes for an interview, so I ask you directly. I believe you have some request of us."

"Yes, I have very little time today. I am going to be anesthetized soon and operated on for the second time. My leg was hurt. It will probably be amputated below my knee. So, I have a request. I understand that there is a precision machine for making toothpicks. I would like you to send for a catalog and introduce me to a machine manufacturer."

"Toothpicks?"

"Yes, toothpicks. A manufacturing machine for toothpicks. They are small, but they are something that everyone uses every day. I won't make money with them, but I won't lose much either. From now on, that's about all I will be able to do. If my leg is cut off, I won't be able to use the piano pedal. Then I will be able to play neither Brahms nor Chopin. All I can do is make toothpicks. I've thought and thought it over. I'm not joking. I would like to ask you: Would you be good enough to send for a catalog from Tokyo?"

"I understand. I will, right away."

"When the catalog comes, I would like you to come to see me once again. Then I think I'll be able to offer you some kind of information. I am no longer a Beria, but my information is still good. Keep my name out of the paper and use the news. My country's maxim says, 'Go to the kitchen if you want to eat. Go to the graveyard if you want to die.' You can trust my information."

"Thank you very much."

"It's about time for my operation. Thank you for coming. I'll be depending on you to get the catalog. I think we will meet again."

The chief bowed deeply and retreated. Grimacing with pain, Bao said something to the interpreter, breaking off each word. The interpreter put his hand under Bao's pillow and took out a crumpled music sheet. He unwrinkled the paper and held it out. Bao mumbled, "Thank you," and he reached out his hand like a child and grasped it. On his demoniac face, a shining smile spread like a drop of oil over muddy water. On the way out, I could not help looking back. Bao was absorbed in reading the music sheet. A little distance away on the side table, I saw a Mickey Mouse comic book with its pages opened and turned down.

Duel

At the beach, two men were sitting on the coral reef. Beside them were two open lunch boxes on a spread cloth. The younger man occasionally nibbled a piece of fried chicken, while sipping local saké made from black molasses. The older man hugged his long legs, gazing into the horizon across the sea. He drank tea from the thermos bottle and ate sushi. The sky was filled with the characteristic tropical light that was clear, yet hazy at this hour, and its luminosity spread over the entire sky. The vast expanse of the East China Sea, streaked with blues, aquamarines, indigos, was at low ebb, smoothly sensuous, almost lascivious. The only sound was the water caressing and lapping innumerable tiny pores of the reef below their hips. There was no human shadow, no house on the spacious atoll. No cans, bottles, vinyl trash. No footprints, no fingerprints. The young man had been gently rocked by the lapping sound in his body ever since he reached the edge of the water.

Sea water had settled in pools here and there in the dents of the reef. The young man cautiously bent over the puddle, but the countless, tiny tropical fish fled in all directions, frightened by his shadow. Over the calcified bed of fish and insect debris, some fish emitted gleaming light, some wiggled suggestively, some others disappeared, spreading a tiny curtain of sand dust. The young man deliberately dropped a piece of chicken into the pool, instantly causing a commotion in the water. As the white piece glided down the clear aquamarine water, the yellow, the red, the violet flashed and vanished and the chicken was gone instantaneously. A tiny scorpion fish appeared from behind a rock, swaying lazily, its tentacle fins fully spread like peacock feathers. Finding nothing, the little creature swayed back to its rock, disappointed. The young man chuckled or burst out laughing each time he dropped the chicken pieces. Intermittently he threw a jigger or two of saké after them.

The older had thick eyebrows, a strong jaw, and large eyes. From time to time, he pulled out a letter from his coat pocket and read it in silence. A smile spread on his pale, hollow cheeks. His wife had written him a love poem in ancient Manyō style. As he was leaving home with his visitor that morning, she had handed each man a lacquered lunch box. In each she had enclosed a poem and instructed them not to open their lunch until they reached the beach. It seemed his wife wrote poems in the kitchen, while frying chicken or making sushi. The young man had opened his box as soon as they reached the beach and discovered a sheet of letter paper above the wrapped chicken pieces. The poem was written in antiquated but skillful calligraphy, as if challenging him. It was about the queen of all South Sea fishes welcoming the visitor to the island. The older man's lunch box seemed to have contained a love poem for her husband. "Don't read it on the way," his wife had said smiling. "You must wait until you get to the shore. Then you will want to come straight home in the evening." She had stood at the gate, waving goodbye to the departing men.

The strong, luxuriant sun began to lose its sharp edge, and a soft haze spread over the late afternoon sky. A harbinger of

evening began to flow out of the lingering clouds and to per-
meate the atmosphere almost audibly like mysterious whisper-
ing. The offshore aquamarine grew pale while the blues and
indigos deepened. Still constantly washing the reef, the sea was
somehow growing desolate. The young man stopped playing
with the fish and sipped saké, gazing into the ocean. As the
sunlight waned, the alcohol seemed to grow heavy, irritating. It
was time to stop. He had been able to maintain his freshness all
afternoon, sitting on the ancient reef. If he continued to drink
until evening, he would grow stale, troubled by words, sentences.
But he rolled yet another drop or two of saké on his already
coarsened and swollen tongue as though forcing down bitter
medicine.

The older man looked at his watch and said, "It's about time
we went. The snakeman must be waiting. You've got to see it at
least once for the experience. The man said he would choose
the best, both the snake and the mongoose. It's like a cockfight.
The battle is short but ferocious."

"Does the mongoose always win?"

"Not necessarily. Seven or eight out of ten, yes—but sometimes
he loses. This is like a *coup de main*. The duel is settled by the
point of the sword. When the swords clash, the fight is already
over. The mongoose targets the upper jaw of the snake to make
sure of his victory. His instinct tells him that the fangs are there.
He's never been taught, but he knows where the right spot is.
Once he bites into the jaw, he hangs on for dear life and chews
it up until the snake's neck is broken. If he misses the jaw, the
mongoose loses. If he bites into the body or tail of the snake,
the fangs will get him in a second."

"It's like the duel of Ganryūjima!"*

"Even if the mongoose wins, if his mouth is hurt while chewing
the snake head, the poison will get to him and he will die within

---

*The legendary duel between Musashi Miyamoto and Kojirō Sasaki in the second
half of the seventeenth century is described in the popular novel by Eiji Yosh-
ikawa, *Musashi*.—TRANS.

twenty-four hours. So, you don't know whether he is the real winner or not until the day after, so says the snakeman."

The older man continued his explanation, closing his lunch box. A *habu* snake is believed to be myopic and astigmatic. Waving his tongue, he senses the delicate stir in the air as an enemy approaches, and his unique apparatus detects the enemy's heat radiation. He strikes suddenly. He contracts his body into an *S*, and, pivoting on the third of his body on the ground, flies with the remaining two thirds. With his mouth open wide and baring scythelike fangs, he whips the air, half blind, yet with a deadly accuracy. He drives his fangs into the enemy, pours out one gram of venom, and instantly backs away. One gram of the deadly poison is said to be sufficient to kill thousands of rabbits. A *habu* can kill human beings and dogs; it can swallow eels, blue jays, frogs, black hares, field rats, long-haired rats, rocks, and occasionally, his own kind.

A *habu*'s parents disappear promptly the minute an egg hatches. The baby snake must find his own food from the day he is born, but he already possesses enough poison to kill a man. A solitary creature, a *habu* acts alone and ubiquitously. He slithers through the night, swims noiselessly across a swamp, traverses a valley, and sneaks into a town, creeps into a toilet, a boot, a kitchen, a charcoal sack, anything. Sometimes he creeps into a public bath and into a woman's clothes basket there, because he likes dark, warm, damp places. Once captured and put in a locked box, he will refuse to eat or drink, his blind eyes wide open and gaping. He will ignore a rat thrown into the box, keeping his mouth closed for six months or a year. With his eyes shining gold in the sun, or gleaming like dull copper in the dark, he will hold his head high and die of starvation.

The young man exclaimed, "What a magnificent creature!"

The older man nodded. "So, a *habu* is a desperado that can kill men and horses. As the saying goes: If his teacher comes, he will stab the teacher; if his father crosses his path, he will kill his father, too. But the mongoose is just as much of a scamp and kills snakes and rats, chickens and hens. In Okinawa, a mongoose gouged out a sleeping baby's eyes. Whether he is starved or full, he will rip the throat of an opponent. So, you might say they are a good match. The funny thing is that each one uses only one weapon. The mongoose attacks the jaw of a snake, and the snake can, if he wants to, wrap himself around the mongoose and strangle him, but he won't. A snake uses only his fangs. If the mongoose bites first, he just writhes helplessly."

The two men picked up their lunch boxes and stood. They began to trudge over the large reef toward the beach. The sky and the ocean were utterly tranquil. Only the sound of the lapping water droned. The breeze was tempered now by a few cold streaks of air. The acrid odors of seaweeds, some putrid, some fresh, hung heavily in the lagoon. The two men climbed the slope, crept through a long, low, serpentine wall of dark banyan trees entangled with a clump of pines, and entered the village. Looking back at the edge of the village toward the atoll, they found the field of rocks sparkling green and white in the softening sun. Already everything had been erased. Traces of two men eating, talking, and laughing there all afternoon were gone. The sky, sea, reef, all stood silently as they did two thousand years ago.

Walking through the forest, the older man called, "Hoot, hoot!"

Soon there was a response. Hoot, hoot! The birdcall followed the man, who continued to hoot while walking. Sometimes the hoots seemed to go astray, probably blocked by trees; still they followed the two men.

The young man stopped and cried out, "An owl! An owl is crying!"

The older man smiled. "I have a genius for doing things that bring no money."

He continued to hoot as he walked.

The owl followed him, calling from tree branches, but it finally stopped at the border of the village and, hooting two or three grudging cries, flew away to the deeper part of the forest.

There was a vacant lot in the midst of closely built matchbox shacks. Boxes with metal screens like chicken coops stood in the center of the lot, and a man in a white coat was waiting beside them, holding a stick in his hand. As soon as the two men walked up to him, he began to talk. He was a man of medium height with a ruddy face and sharp eyes. He spoke in a mellow, experienced voice, showing the differences of genitalia on several male and female snakes preserved in alcohol jars. Then, from one of the boxes, he hooked a snake with the tip of a wire and swiftly caught its narrow neck with his bare hand. The snake opened its wide mouth fully and the white, translucent, sharp fangs jutted out from the sheath folds like hypodermic needles. The man put the snake's head against the edge of the wooden box, and the viper angrily bit into the wood, grating its surface. Instantly, liquid shot from its mouth and trickled down the box. Incongruous with its gigantic, triangular head in the ugly color of dirt, and inconsistent with its ferocious gold eyes, wet flesh like the inside of a little girl's crotch suddenly exposed itself under the sun. The mouth orifice was covered with gleaming pink-white membrane. Delicate red and blue distal blood vessels ran through the virginal flesh folds inside. It was moist, clean, white, tender, and fragile. The young man was fascinated. He felt an urge to caress it with his fingers, feel the tension and wetness of the white flesh, and trace the suction of the soft resilient folds into the deep interior. He wanted to fondle the translucent, strong, sharp fangs, too.

What's wrong with me? Am I exhausted? So run-down?

The box was partitioned with a screen divider. In one section was a snake, in the other a mongoose. The snake was slithering, scraping the wooden floor, ceaselessly forming and untangling the S shape. Her head erect and darting swiftly to left and right, she flickered her black tongue continually. She crawled up the dividing metal screen and groped about the screen mesh with her tongue. Her myopic eyes goggling toward the shining mist, she seemed to wonder what this strange vibration and heat could be that came through the air. Her whiplike forebody quivered, stretching and contracting, while her hind half, swinging aimlessly, stored up energy. Beyond the shiny fog was a small quadruped with the body of a weasel and the face of a rat, making light footstep noises as it scampered to right and left. Small red eyes shining, his soft, buff-colored back undulating, the little animal pivoted on his thick tail and stood on his hind legs. Pulling his forelegs to his breast as if beckoning, he squeaked sharply two, three times as though grinding teeth. The young man bent forward in spite of himself, and the animal's small threatening face looked up. Malevolence and cruelty unimaginable from such a small, lovable body flashed in the red eyes. The single-minded bloodthirstiness made its head something mean and base. The young man involuntarily stepped back and turned away.

"Are you ready?" The snakeman's voice was ominous. "Let's go!" He pulled up the divider. A buff color flashed into the box. The mongoose had darted to the snake's head, dug into it; already his small, white teeth were crunching. Wearing the mongoose on her head, the snake rolled and wriggled and contracted her long body like a corkscrew, but she never tried to wrap around the mongoose. As the older man had described, her only weapon was the fangs, and her defeat had become decisive at the first moment. Silently, she writhed and thrashed about, trying to free herself from the animal. The mongoose's eyes flared and his small, angular, blood-covered head rolled with the snake, but he hung on fast to the slippery body of the snake with his black claws while continuing chomping.

(Forestall, give all to the first moment. Once into the enemy's vitals, never let go! Hang on to the end! Crush! Chew!) The heavy but sharp crunching noise of breaking bones continued for a while. The triangle head lost its shape and the eyes were smashed. Fresh blood spurted, and long fangs protruded helplessly from the upper jaw. Turning his face sideways, the mongoose bit into the white flesh at the root of the fangs and continued to munch. The fangs broke off and fell to the floor. They shined dully in the blood puddle in the evening sun. The mangled head of the snake gaped like a dark vermilion hole. Her body stirred spasmodically, shrinking and stretching, but finally lay long in the pool of blood. Once she lost her head, she was like a decorative cord with its tassle severed. The mouth hung gaping, crushed shapelessly. The white, voluptuous body continued to bleed slowly. His body shivering, the mongoose jutted out his angular face and began to lap up blood and munch noisily on the delicate female body of the snake. He sipped, licked his paws, tore off a mouthful of flesh, chewed.

The two men left the area in silence, shoulder to shoulder. The poverty-stricken houses, like barnacle clusters, stood in the resounding explosion of the setting subtropical sun, and the perfect moment of the day inflamed the sky and the road. The young man stopped and lit a cigarette. Although he had been drinking all afternoon, he felt no trace of the blue flame of alcohol. A thirst slowly spread throughout his body.

"They don't wrestle," he commented, his voice a little hoarse.

The older man's eyes were somber, virile. He smiled deeply. "No mercy allowed."

Trailing a long shadow on the barren road, the older man hung his head low and spoke again. "No mercy allowed."

At last, the young man thought, *I have taken my first step on this island.*

The Laughingstock

There was a man.

He lived with a woman on a farm on the outskirts of a large city. The farm was in a small valley between two smooth hills closing in upon each other. It took him two hours to commute to the city. The terrain around the farm was not quite wild enough for flying squirrels, but it was rumored that in winter badgers appeared from time to time in the surrounding copse.

They lived in a small six-mat room of a hut on the farm grounds. It was a tool shed made into a living quarter with a torn tin roof that had curled up in parts. The red mud wall that was shared with the adjacent one-room apartment had holes stuffed with crumpled newspaper. It was hard to judge whether the holes were stuffed because the young man didn't want to peep into the next room, or because he didn't want to be spied upon by his neighbors. The adjoining room, a remodeled stable, was occupied by another young couple. The husband, a cook who returned late at night from a fast-food place specializing in curried rice, had a habit of peeling the clothes off his wife and thrashing her behind. The man in the tool shed knew from his experience that raising his voice in objection would only worsen the clamor in the stable, so he remained on the torn mat and continued to read his book with a grimace. Sometimes, he heard the voice beyond the wall shouting some non sequitur like: "Don't you be cheated," or "These fish bones may get stuck in my throat, don't you know any better?"

In his own room, it was easier to count things on the floor rather than to make a list of necessary things that were lacking. Several blankets, cups, and saucers lay on the floor. Two wads of newspaper wrapped in towels were presumably pillows. Two raincoats alongside a calendar of Mariko Okada smiling radiantly, toasting with a glass of saké, hung on the wall. An orange crate in lieu of a desk, soiled beakers, chemical bottles, and various test tubes were scattered about. Crumpled pieces of paper always surrounded the orange crate.

The woman was a chemist and worked at a food-research laboratory in the city. Every evening, back from her work, she would stoop over her orange crate and work on her poems until late, constantly mumbling and clicking her tongue. Her pencil scribbled rapidly on pieces of notebook paper or on the back of advertising flyers. Sometimes she produced from her tired satchel a chemist's bottle filled with an amber-colored liquid and made her man, supine on the floor, drink it. This liquid with an indescribable taste was her own concoction of alcohol, caramel, and spices that she had pilfered and clandestinely mixed in the corner of her lab. He sipped a mouthful at a time from a teacup and timidly protested that it exploded in his head and put his eyes on fire.

Each time, she would tilt her head and make her diagnosis. "I guess the pot isn't hot enough," or "It may be too young," or "Probably it should be refined to bring out more roundness."

One day, he cried out, excited and goggle-eyed, "What's this? It's terrific!" He hurled his book and shouted. "What did you steal this time?"

Grinning, she took the cup from his hand. Smacking her lips after a sip, she admitted grudgingly, "You can't beat the real stuff after all."

Every morning he went to the city with her and returned alone late in the evening, looking totally exhausted. His hair, neck, and fingers reeked with an indescribable aroma. More than once, she asked him about the dry odor, but he stubbornly kept his mouth shut. When she pried persistently, he answered that he was making zombies, or else he knit his brows peevishly and growled that he was searching for ultimate absurdity. If she persisted, he would turn livid and begin to shout, trembling all over.

"Are you implying that there are class distinctions in profession? Don't you know there's nothing other than absurdity in this life?"

Once, he stammered out loudly, "I don't trust anybody who's never eaten bread with the salt of tears!"

She was amazed at his responses. One evening, certain that he was enjoying the stolen liquor, she suddenly pushed him over the torn mat and straddled his emaciated body. He had deep dark circles under his eyes as if gouged out with a knife.

"All right now," she exclaimed. "I'll smell and find your secret! I'm known for my detective nose, you know. Be still. I'll tell you soon enough."

She thrust her little crochet-hook nose into his hair. Sniffing around loudly, she went down from his head all over his body. This done, she shook her head.

"It's not *that*," she mused.

After another round, she shook her head again. "Not that either." She crawled on the mat around his body. Tickled by her sharp nose, he wriggled while hearing bits of long words such as aliphatic acid, aldehydes.

Finally, when she raised her face reluctantly, her large eyes appeared seriously troubled. Seeing a grin break out on his face, she shouted angrily, "I know it!"

"Well, what is it?"

"Iodine! Iodine! I know it's iodine for sure. Right?"

"Only iodine?"

With a wry smile she put the palm of her hand over her forehead and conceded slowly, "Right. Not only iodine, there's something else. I know something's mixed, but I can't tell what it is. I've never smelled anything like it. Besides, it's different from the way iodine attacks your nose usually. . . ."

"I'm making narcotics."

"No, no! Narcotics are not like this at all. They are sweeter. I know this is no narcotic. . . . Okay, you win!"

Seeing her cheerful laughter, he turned his face away. His grin faded into a forlorn look. Wrinkling his brow, he nursed his pain. When she left him to prepare their dinner, he did not pick up his book. He remained flat on the floor, tearing at the furry nap of the mats.

Some time back, he had met with a number of friends at a tavern in the city. They were all struggling to live and they had decided to get together and share whatever jobs were available. One man had rounded up a list and brought it to the tavern. The group decided to screen the jobs, wages, and conditions, and select a suitable job for each. There were jobs for a tutor, a language teacher, a poll taker for an advertising agency, a file clerk for an insurance company, and a sales clerk for a department store. Each man, while loudly complaining, shrewdly chose a job for himself, like a mouse getting hold of a piece of cheese and carrying it away. The young man remained in a corner, leaning against the wall. He had been watching them, drinking saké, not opening his mouth once until the session was over. Having chosen their jobs, the others, too, began to drink, looking somewhat relieved. Gaunt and pale and quite sober, the young man asked the friend in charge, "Is that all the jobs you have?"

"No. Why?"

"Don't you have something I can sink my teeth into?"

"What do you mean by that?"

"Something that would make me numb. Something uncouth, nothing refined. Something you can't do by mincing words and raising your pinkie. Something utterly inelegant."

They were all smart men. Sensing his ironical tone, they began to talk all at once in defense of themselves, their sharp eyes moving swiftly.

"Hey! You got it all wrong, man! Money is money. Whether you tutor or clean up gutters, money is the same."

"Right, it is. If you have a choice of tutoring or cleaning gutters, and if you take the gutter, that's your business. But if you are implying tutoring is hypocritical, that's a cause for serious contention!"

"It's sentimentalism. Pure sentimentalism! Hey, this man's a samurai!"

"I don't think it's necessarily sentimentalism," one man pontificated. "Because the concept of labor has changed drastically as we entered the age of automation. There's a school of thought that advocates returning to the starting point and recreating it all, like the Oxford School. . . ."

"Hey, that's my glass!" said someone else.

"I don't begrude saké at all, but I resent it if someone asks for a cigarette. I wonder why."

"Isn't it wrong to denounce the cleaning of gutters as premodernistic? You'll probably be unable to explain Japan if you don't interpret her by a multidimensional cognizance. Her amoebal proliferation of energy, for instance. The cognizance of machinery and that of manpower are in complete harmony with the concept of dredging the gutter. It's a bold flexibility. I think there's a definite need for creating numerous new channels of cognizance for drawing indigenous energy from the originality of the Japanese."

"Should I order a special? Should I? Should I? Oh, that's 150 yen. Maybe I'd better stick to the ordinary saké."

"The orthodox theory is uninteresting. Yet, heresy is shallow and infantile!"

All through the clamor, he remained silent, his eyes half closed. He continued to drink abstractly, looking at the bill of fare on the wall. He felt nauseous. Listening to his friends reminded him of a spitz that yelped and jumped around when its tail was ever so slightly stepped on. These boys didn't want to dirty their hands. They had no intention of paying that price from the start. They were only devoted to drinking and learning the ways of the world.

The man in charge searched through his pockets and put some pieces of paper between saké carafes. He scrutinized them one by one and soon chortled and tapped the shoulder of the young man who was smouldering in the corner. "I've found it!" He handed a piece of paper to him. "How about this one? This will make you numb. . . . This is something you can really sink your teeth into. You can't do this elegantly. It's made to order for you!"

The young man read what was given to him. He smiled, not lowering his eyes. His cheeks twitched slightly, which worried him momentarily lest it be interpreted as an abject sneer. He spoke slowly in a low voice.

"I'll take it."

When they heard the job description from their leader, the young men all burst into laughter. They stopped their discourses and came to his side, patting his shoulder patronizingly.

It had been almost a year since.

Now, early every morning, he left his hut with his woman and walked the country road through the woods to the station. They took a train to the city. At the end of the line, they shook hands casually and said good-bye. Making sure that she had vanished in the throng of workers that appeared from nowhere and disappeared somewhere, he would get on a bus, then transfer, then change to another train, and after a considerable amount of traveling, reach a slum area at the other end of the city.

The area was close to a canal and the sea. The houses were rotting green in acid, swollen with dampness. He would zigzag through the complex alleys without getting lost and reach a vacant lot in front of an old warehouse. A weather-worn sign-board hung on the door with a line, "Apothecary of the Miraculous Longevity Elixir," which had been perfunctorily crossed out. The new name written below read, "Sekiru Kompi Pharmaceutical Company." He would glance about, confirm that no one was in sight and quickly slip through a doorway, while a languid, resentful grin remained on his lips.

At five o'clock in the evening, he would creep out of the door. On his haggard, pallid face, he would still be wearing a tired, resentful grin, and he would scramble toward the station.

In this warehouse, the young man sat on the floor every day and chopped dry seaweed on the top of a tree stump. From nine to five, he minced Corsican weed, bark of pomegranate roots, prickly ash, and other unidentifiable objects. The Corsican weed seemed to be the variety that, gathered near the Formosan Strait, arrived here in crude straw sacks. But the owner of the warehouse, the apothecary, treated it with a signal reverence. Once or twice a day, he made a round of the workshop, and if *one* piece of the dry, gray-white weed was found on the floor, he picked it up carefully and then chewed the heads off his workers. He would threaten to dock their wages, or whimper as though he were on the verge of bankruptcy, or sometimes simply shriek, "Idiots!"

The young man would be silent while the apothecary stormed, but no sooner had his employers disappeared than he would take out rocks, old nails, and pieces of coke from his pockets where he had them hidden and throw them into the mounds of chopped seaweed. No matter how preoccupied he might be out on the street, if he saw something useful on the ground, he always picked it up and put it in his pocket. As though punctuating a sentence, he periodically made a point of mixing such objects into the mounds of seaweed. Older workers took care of it much more simply by spitting saliva or sputum, or blowing their snot right into the seaweed.

The job held a surprise for him in the beginning, then a sizzling fury, then laughter. Finally, there was only silence.

The plant roots and tree barks that he chopped with clockwork accuracy were gathered several times a day, measured into a huge eighty-quart tub with a scoop that looked like the bucket used at public baths, stirred, and then loaded onto a trailer and taken to a tenement house in a nearby back alley. There, sluttish housewives and young women waited in a dusky room and grabbed rapaciously at the tubs. They would stuff a pinch of seaweed in a cellophane bag, bundle twenty bags into a box, put twelve boxes into a crate.

The women worked in the dark from morning to night, gaily, doggedly, surrounded by crumbling walls, endlessly exchanging bawdy stories that would drive anyone else up a wall. The apothecary, making his round of this "Second Plant," snarled at the women and warned them to use only a pinch of Corsican weed and to fill the rest with the cheap pomegranate-root bark and prickly ash. Sometimes a woman would faint from overwork and anemia. Some of them looked like tattered rag dolls, reeking with the odor of Corsican weed.

This mixture, to be infused and taken orally, was a parasiticide called "The Miraculous Longevity Elixir" and was sold every month with miraculous certainty. The crates were shipped out of the old warehouse and regularly distributed to various parts of Japan. The young man shuddered with disgust as he worked on the straw mat on the concrete floor, which, in the pale winter sun, was like the river bottom. He tried to imagine where, by whom, and how, this quack remedy could be used. He knew that the concoction, when boiled, emitted a horrific odor and turned into a mucky brown liquid, but he could not believe that anyone in his right mind could put hope in it.

His thoughts notwithstanding, the straw sacks packed with the seaweed arrived month after month, then the contents were transferred into crates printed with a picture of fat Happy God, Hotei, and vanished. Moreover, month after month, the purchase order not only showed no sign of decline, but seemed to show an increase, if only slight. Every time he saw the picture of the simpering Hotei with his hairy pot belly, he was puzzled to distraction why other pharmaceutical companies had to spend stupendous sums of money to market their products, while this Hotei sat on the eighty-quart tub and laughed.

In the befuddled eyes of the young man, the obscene old Hotei at times appeared like a great man of conviction, whose gross pot belly was filled with scientific knowledge and capitalism. Sometimes he found the whole thing irrepressibly hilarious and put down his hatchet and laughed. Other times, he felt that nothing in the world was so audacious, insidious, and absurd as the smile of Hotei. He felt furious as though his entrails would scorch black. Stewed with hatred, he seethed as though some acid had been poured over his head. All he could do was zealously throw coke cinder and his hair into the weeds. He thought that the reason for the tremendous sale of this preposterous product must be the insecurity of the Japanese.

Once a week or so, he stopped at a friend's home on his way to the copse and filled a large wrapping cloth with books. He took these home and read voraciously. But with each book, his energy seemed to dwindle. Random words from these books of unrelated periods and subjects flooded his addled brain. These words cried out and agitated him. Unfortunately, each word, however isolated, held a genuine brilliance born out of the experiences and agony of its author. Some words were delicate and others were robust; some were inimitably impudent and others were supremely fragile. One poet smothered himself in feminine flesh, while another doted on the scent of sheep wool on sunny hillsides. A writer proclaimed that if he said two plus two was five, it was to be five. Another poet wrote an epic on his grief for a friend devoured by a monster and on the convivial merriment that followed the friend's death. There was a man who walked out of his room deranged, and stopped to ponder whether he grasped the door knob or the door knob grasped him. There was yet another man who kept shouting, "Even a man like me wants to live!" One man advocated a revolution exposing his weakness, while a woman defended human weakness and indicted the ruthlessness of revolutionaries; yet, it was the latter who died a heroic death under the political oppression. In the midst of all this was a man who spent his entire life looking at dung vermin under a microscope.

Surrounded by words overflowing with passion and sincerity, the young man, malodorous of Corsican weed, no longer knew what to do. Every written line was laden with the writer's agony. Each seemed to hold a tremendous power, one he dared not ignore. He lay awake every night near his woman, who scribbled something until the small hours. It was becoming unbearable for him to keep reading, as he would find himself deeply moved, mumbling senseless, disjointed words as a result.

The thought had occurred to him that he might not be a man but really a sea anemone. After all, he never acted or produced but just lay on the torn mat and fluttered his tentacles toward prey. Wait! Did the sea anemone have some reason for existence? The young man didn't know. He had heard that their rectum and mouth were one, that they used the same organ for eating and excreting. The crazy creature called a "hiding fish" sometimes crept under the sea anemone when feeling a danger from strong enemies, but sea anemones served no other purpose. The young man had never heard that salted or pickled sea anemones were good to eat, or that dried ones were good with saké, though the Japanese have a penchant for eating marine oddities such as sea cucumbers and sea urchins. If all things in creation had some *raison d'être*, what significance did sea anemones have?

Every day, he returned exhausted from his menial job. Scarcely held together by some glue, he barely found the energy to roll onto his musty blanket. He knew of nothing else that he could do for the time being at least. He read his books, drunk with the suspect liquor his woman brought him, and picked a quarrel apropos of nothing, catching tail ends of her statements.

"What do you mean, you *absolutely* hate Chinese noodles and love Japanese noodles?" he would yell at her. "Don't make such a sloppy statement. *Absolutely*? How dare you use such an overblown, insensitive word like *absolute*? You're a poet, aren't you?

Pay more attention to the language. Even Jesus Christ didn't make such an imperial statement."

She was used to his erratic moods and humored him no matter what.

"You are right. I am wrong. I didn't mean to say I don't like it *absolutely*. I meant to say I don't like it now, but I may change my mind later. Is that all right with you?"

Smiling, she poked her finger into his cheek. He could not agree or disagree. He only trembled, agitated, and turned over peevishly, muttering into his blanket, "You're not a purist."

He continued to fret.

He was trying to scrutinize words as if examining rocks with a magnifying glass, to capture something in the torrential flood that passed through him every day: something—one word or words with the ultimate hardness that permitted no further analysis. He didn't know what his goal was, but his wish for the present was to find a language that would be felt by his lips, mind, and brain, with a permanent hardness, sharpness, and weight like that of a steel ball bearing. These words would never rust, erode, or warp with the change of his mood as he walked, ate, made love, or worked. They would not be malleable or flexible.

Examining words with a magnifying glass or peeling them like onions enervated him. This practice, however, taught him how to see through the millions of authors' styles, hypocrisy, feigned cynicism, bluffing, hit-and-miss statements, off-the-cuff ideas, and sentimentalism à la chewing gum. Often a "novel" was an author's own life, thinly disguised. More baffling than anything else, "words" had grown too ambiguous for him. For instance, even the most concrete words such as *tree*, or *mountain*, or *wind*, or *ship* did not stand the test of repetition. Everything crumbled and vanished. *Tree, tree, tree, tree, tree, tree. Mountain, mountain, mountain, mountain, mountain. Wind, wind, wind, wind, wind.* Why the tree should be *tree*, why the mountain should be *mountain*, or why the symptoms of parched throat and cold perspiration should be called *hunger*, he no longer knew. This meant that he could not feel secure for one minute, because if he repeated any word ten times, it would fall apart.

It was a wonder that such fragile entities were dredged up, strung together in a sequence and called a sentence. People amassed them by the thousands and tens of thousands and then forgot them. People quarreled and cursed one another using words that could not survive one minute of scrutiny. Using such words they won and lost in debates. They deceived women and were deceived by them. They compromised, flattered, exploited, sold their countries, and bled to death. They starved, got fat, squeezed, and cheated. For the sake of *Jew*, a word more ambiguous and intangible than *tree* or *mountain*, they ganged up on a small country and bullied it. All of these people getting hot and cold would eventually grow old, their faces wrinkling up like a monkey's. They would not be able to say even *tree* or *Jew* and die. So, what was all this grandiloquence about?

He wanted to write stories. Sometimes, in the middle of the night, he put his book aside and sat in front of the orange crate. But he always hurled his pencil away after writing two or three lines, and crawled back into his blanket. For some reason his hands and feet grew numb. In his soft, dim brain, all words swarmed and jostled for an exit. Various opening and closing lines emerged and submerged. "A young woman came up the hilly street in front of a tearoom late one night. Bits of jazz music danced in her hair, like a brilliant sound wave." Or, "One day, when he was standing at a train station, a schoolboy he had never seen approached him. Blushing up to his ears, the boy offered him a bag. He looked into the bag and found some fried sweet potatoes. With embarrassment, the boy was perspiring and flushed to his eyes. Overwhelmed by the weight of what must have been the first act of charity in his life, the boy was speechless and looked angry. The young man mumbled something and accepted the offering. The boy ran clear across the platform as though escaping. Until the train came, the boy stubbornly kept his eyes away, looking at the sky. When the train arrived, he desperately pushed through the crowd and got on. Crouched on the platform, the young man, too, looked at the sky, while the train passed in front of him, lest the boy see him from the window and feel embarrassed."

What he wanted to write were such things. But when he sat before the orange crate, he realized that he had gone too far. The story of an intellectual vagabond pitied by a schoolboy had already been finished in his head. The opening was also set. It went, "It was spring." Having written the opening line neatly on paper, he would suddenly feel a tremendous fatigue, sigh, and roll back into his blankets. It was spring. IT WAS SPRING. His usual irrepressible dissection began. As he repeated the words, blood seemed to withdraw from his hands and feet. The meaning and warmth evaporated from the words.

It was spring. What ambiguity! Yet the effect was obviously calculated. In other words, it was a lie. The novel started as a lie from the very beginning. It was a betrayal to that flustered schoolboy. Actually, he was starved to near death that moment. While the train was passing, he had turned his face to the sky as though he had some sense. But no sooner was the train gone than his hand was in the paper bag and he gorged himself with the potatoes, didn't he? The sweetness and oiliness of the fried potatoes permeated his body, and he could feel the thin, transparent ripples of nourishment rushing to the extremities of his hands and feet.

And what was he trying to do now? Make it up in a story? It was spring? It was laughable! It was the height of audacity! So, what would he achieve by writing it? Did he think people could search out each other with such infantile attempts? No, no, this was also a lie! It was a poor excuse for not exposing his lack of talent to the world. He must be a little sick; that was why he felt so numb. He had better go to sleep. Sleep.

A month after he began to commute to the apothecary's plant, he became hungry for money and wondered how he could get a raise. The night before, she had whispered in his ear an earth-shattering piece of news. It was at that moment that he became hungry for money. After mulling over the news for some days, he went to the main store of the apothecary in the shopping center near a train station and pulled out a piece of paper from his pocket to reveal his idea to his employer. For exchange, he requested timidly a raise of 250 yen per day. He perspired as he had never before, his eyes bloodshot. He had his back to the wall. A woman's life depended on it.

The apothecary was sitting in the dark, surrounded by tree barks, plant roots, stuffed armadillo, horse's bladder stone, and ox-scrotum preserves. A dried-up, sallow little man, he could have passed for one of the desiccated objects around him had he remained silent. But it was men like him who were tough. One must be on guard against this type. These shriveled-up, small men were super-energetic, insidious, and vindictive. Brawny fat men couldn't touch them. Once this type bit into you, they wouldn't let go. There, he opened his eyes! He opened his eyes ever so slightly and is looking at me!

The apothecary jutted out his jaw and snorted. He had slits of eyes that concealed anything he saw or thought. To begin with, it was utterly impossible to look into his eyes. They were so narrow, and it was hard to tell whether they were open at all.

". . . How interesting," the apothecary said. "You have a good sixth sense. You are a layman, but you hit the right nail. This is exactly what I've been thinking for a long time. Oh, I've been procrastinating month after month. But I'd just decided to start it next month, and I've already asked the printer to design a new packing box. I have no reason to give you a raise because you were too late. It's a primitive job. There are hundreds of workers who'll gladly work for me in your place."

"I like the work. That's why I'm doing it. That's why I had the idea for improving the sales. And my wife . . ." The young man bit his lip. He could speak no more before the little man's chilly sneer. Blood curdled in his head. He knew he was cheated again. He was too naive. It was no use talking to the man. A rat;

a zombied rat; a monster! The young man's face was crimson. Hanging his head, he muffled his fury in his mouth. He hurried out of the menagerie of dried objects into the street.

Walking through the crowd, he choked and thought of his friends who had jeered at him at the tavern, of their swiftly moving eyes. He scarcely managed to stifle sobs as he walked beneath the eaves of crowded houses.

In two months, the signboard of the old warehouse changed. "The Apothecary of Miraculous Longevity Elixir" became "Sekiru Kompi Pharmaceutical Company." The packing box was printed in an alphabet with a modern typeface instead of the old-fashioned Kantei-style Japanese calligraphy. Hotei was simpering as before, thrusting his hairy pot belly. This was also his idea. The apothecary had stolen everything for nothing. His idea was to Westernize the name of the product but to retain the Hotei for a sense of irony. The exotic-sounding Sekiru Kompi was nothing but a bastardized Chinese reading for the pomegranate-root bark, which no one would have suspected.

The sales began to leap.

When she whispered that she wanted to have a baby, he let out a cry, then was dumbfounded. He felt as though he were walking on a moonless night and was suddenly kicked in the shin. For days on end, trudging along the streets with a grimace, rocking in a crowded train, chopping seaweed, he brooded over the matter. He was not thinking of how and where to scrape up the money. Rather, he was absorbed in questioning what life was all about—an effort completely futile and irrelevant. One of the characteristics of his strange illness was that it did not permit him a spontaneous reaction in any situation. As soon as the initial shock of her whisper wore off, a sense of a grotesque comedy came over him, and a wretched half cry, half smile etched itself on his face semipermanently.

He had crawled into absurdity to spite his shrewd friends who grabbed easy jobs so that they could keep their hands clean. He had believed that only blue-collar workers and sufferers were honest, so he had reduced himself to chopping ghastly roots and barks in search of purity. For this beggar who wasn't begging, the schoolboy took pity and gave sweet potatoes. He had pushed his search for purity even further and had begun to doubt words. Now he was at the point where he could easily detect other writers' complacency and self-deception. But in return, he discovered that words could not hold together under a moment's scrutiny. Books collapsed and sentences fell apart in midair.

More recently, streets began to take on the appearance of the bottom of the river, the pedestrians, objects, everything, sallow, warped, and tangled. Once in a while, he walked into a bookstore, but as soon as his eyes caught the sight of stacks of books from the floor to the ceiling, his head fogged and he felt an urge to run for his life. A moment amidst the throng of people in the smoke-filled bookstore pushing and shoving gagged him with nicotine. Sometimes he looked pityingly at this massed and unenlightened humanity of which he was a part, loving it with an inexplicable tenderness. This gentleness cleansed his body like soothing, liquid, soundless music. But a realization came to him at once that such tenderness came only when he was tired, and immediately he felt he was a hypocrite. Every time he spoke or wrote, he sounded odious and empty to himself. No sooner were the words uttered than they crumbled and flew away. The very sounds that constituted them seemed to chill and dilute with water.

And he, such as he was, had already got a woman with child!

He was tortured with shame. This supposedly cool-headed, altruistic pursuer of purity got a woman with baby, of all things! Clicking his tongue in disgust, he tried to recall when it could have happened. Some Sundays ago, he had gone down to the valley. He was irritated that fish didn't bite. When she brought him rice bails wrapped in a newspaper for lunch, he was touched by her sweet thoughtfulness and, roused, he . . . Could it have happened that time? Or, when he had brought home his minuscule wage at the end of a month (of course, not to be compared with her salary), she became playful and put a plateful of ham, sausages, and other food at the pillowside and, half naked, danced right out of the blankets. The sight of her nudity caught him; he had made love to her on the spot. Could it have been then? As he remembered the words he had whispered into her ear at different times, he began to feel hot inside and he bit his lips fiercely. Stop it! Passion was nothing but a dark delusion! Wasn't his lucidity his pride? He savagely chastised himself, then suddenly realized the absurdity of it all. He twisted his mouth in half cry and half laughter. His strange malady had progressed, but he still seemed to have retained intact a small measure of instinct, which allowed him to feel the ludicrousness of the situation.

Throughout their cohabitation, she had surprised him at quite regular intervals with her words and actions, but nothing had moved him as much as the news about the baby. When he recovered from the shock and was finally able to speak, he asked her, "But, even if your wish to have a baby is legitimate, how about the money? Besides, you know, you'll have to change diapers and nurse the baby and do all sorts of things. You won't be able to write poems."

"It's all right. To tell you the truth, I've saved up a little."

She smiled and produced a postal savings book from the orange crate. In amazement, he glanced at it and found figures that might not be called ample, but were certainly far beyond any expectation. All he had been able to do was survive, day after day. Never in a million years did he suspect that she was saving any money.

"What a shock! You fed me with dried sardines every day so that you could build a nice little nest egg!"

"Don't be funny. When did *you* ever have anything to build a nest egg with? I'd love to have your nerve. This was all scraped up from my own earnings."

"What's going to happen to your poetry?"

Dazzled and blinded, he questioned her falteringly. She sat up to her full height and looked deeply into his eyes. With unprecedented gravity, she made a judicious—almost too judicious—statement.

"Don't worry about it. I'm finally beginning to understand. Life is my husband and literature is my lover. I was mistaken before. I had believed that Rimbaud was my life and literature. But a passion for rejecting life is juvenile. It's like measles. I was immature. Of course, Gauguin went to Tahiti in rebellion after forty, but that was also a childish thing to do. Medieval stained glass made by an unknown artisan is much more sublime and beautiful. No matter how crazy they get, men are ultimately childish."

He was speechless.

"Right now, I believe in Chekhov rather than in Dostoyevsky. Chekhov was really a worldly man. But, since he knew life so thoroughly, it must have been very boring for him. This is how I feel these days."

Silence.

"Anyway, I want a baby. That's all. This is something like women's inescapable *karma*, don't you think?"

"Japan is overpopulated, you know."

"That doesn't count because it's a woman's instinct to crave for babies. Even French women are having lots of babies these days. And France is delighted, saying she's rejuvenated. We'll procreate as much as we want, and if we are stuck for space, we'll go to America and South America and open up the land. The world of men is worthless if the very basic need of women can't be met. And you know what's wrong with America? During the frontier days, they could use all the procreation and reproduction. They were nothing but a bunch of immigrants and refugees! And now, they talk about Jews, Puerto Ricans, blacks, and Italians, with their cheap nouveau-riche rationale. I don't accept that. We should all emigrate. It will be to their credit to receive all the immigrants."

"Siberia is uncultivated. So is Africa. I suppose India is overcrowded."

"It doesn't matter whether it's North America, South America, or Siberia. Wherever man's hands are needed, we should go. I'm going to bring up my child with this attitude. I won't have a baby unless I'm prepared for it. Otherwise, it will only be a lot of wasted effort for an unnecessary burden."

Again, she poked her finger into the cheek of the man who remained silent and supine on the floor. With no further speech, she crawled around the room to gather all sorts of soft rags and began to sew diapers earnestly.

This rear view of her brought him a vivid memory. The moment she confirmed that he would live with her, she transformed from a "Girl" into a "Wife." She went out and bought two matching chopstick boxes and rice bowls—one large, one small—for husband and wife. She gave one set to her "husband." Until then, she was bent on acting out the role of a rebel, threatening every day to commit suicide or to run away to the Sahara Desert. Her change was instantaneous. As soon as he sat timidly in the seat of the "husband," she plunged into sewing matching "his" and "hers" cushions. And now, the moment she discovered that "wife" was to become "mother," she set out confidently to make diapers as though she had been a "mother" for the past twenty years. After the baby in her womb crawled out of the restricting cave and another twenty years passed, the child, if a girl, would have a baby of her own. The moment this woman heard the news, she would turn into a "grandmother" as though she had been one for the past twenty years. She would unashamedly rehearse a lullaby. If he accused her of insensitivity and impurity, she would smile unabashedly and retort, "Isn't this woman's *karma*?" Thus, he would be forced into silence for the third time, averting his eyes to the earthworms creeping in the backyard. He now thoroughly understood the sentiment of the Frenchman who gave the word *nature* a feminine gender.

She diligently ate dried fish, leeks, and other cheap and nourishing food and continued to commute to her laboratory. No packed train, no crowds at the terminal, no overwork ever discouraged this young woman. Coming home exhausted in the evening, with dark circles similar to his chiseled under her eyes, she still sewed her diapers at night. From time to time, her pencil scribbled something at the orange crate. He had no idea what she was writing. Whether her creation was crumpled up in a wastebasket or, once in a while, carefully copied out in a notebook, he didn't know the content. They were bound by their pact of "noninterference in internal affairs."

Once he broke the agreement and glanced at her manuscript. She screamed as though the house were on fire. *You are a sneak! You are a cheat! You are a coward!* In the end, her large eyes fixed on him, she admonished him solemnly, "Listen, love, even Michelangelo didn't let anyone into his atelier while he was working. Even members of the Medici and the Mayor of Florence weren't allowed in. So, you be good and don't ever do that again. Understand?" He nodded at every word and muttered that Masuji Ibuse could never overcome the temptation of reading other people's love letters, but she ignored him.

For some time he had thought she was a little peculiar. Besides her bustling magnificence and her free-wheeling transformation from a "girl" to a "wife" to a "mother," and probably to a "grandmother," there was something very peculiar about her. For instance, one winter night, he was hugging a hand warmer, wrapped in a blanket from neck to toe. Sitting in front of him, she calmly stuck a hot charcoal tong right on her finger. She actually stuck her finger with a tong that had been slowly turning red on the charcoal!

"Hey! What the hell are you doing!?"

As he stared at her in shock, she said that it was quicker and better, without batting an eye. She had been vexed for some time with the infected needle wound that she had inflicted upon herself during her work at the lab. She wanted to cure it by one drastic treatment. Her theory was that this was much quicker than burning germs by acid, alcohol, or iodine. While explaining this to him, she kept the hot tong on her finger, and decided that once was not enough and began to reheat the tong.

"Isn't it awfully hot?"

"No, it's not hot. If you know it's good for you, all you have to do is to endure it a little bit. Garlic, too. I know it's good for my health, so it doesn't smell. I got rid of that sort of prejudice a long time ago."

"But you'll have a scar on your finger."

"I wonder. The skin regenerates all the time, so I think it'll be all right."

Thus she exhibited complete composure. Then, there were times when she acted just as her feelings dictated. Her emotion was often aroused by the young pervert in the next room. It was especially on his paydays that he would loudly slap his skinny wife's buttocks. He would grow excited, passionate, and start acting wild and merry. Trying to arouse the couple next door who remained silent, the cook would thrash his poor wife like a madman. Once, the young man removed the newspaper ball from a hole on the wall and peered in. Seeing the cook working away in full dress with a bow tie, he burst out laughing. After that, he decided to ignore whatever went on in the next room and to keep reading in his bed. But she could not ignore it. Their remaining quiet caused the cook to grow louder and more frantic, and his wife usually began to moan and wail in pain. The poet could not bear the sound. Sometimes the commotion made the newspaper balls roll right out of the holes. One night, she was leaning over the orange crate, but she hurled her pencil at the wall and sprang to her feet. She shouted as she hastily re-stuffed holes with crumpled paper.

"Just because you are a man, just because! Always, always . . . don't let it go to your head, you bastard!"

She was so upset by the wailing of the wife next door that sometimes tears stood in her eyes. Shoving away her blankets, she dashed out barefoot to the earthen floor of the entrance. She had forgotten how she looked in her long underwear that she was too lazy to take off. As he called it to her attention, she returned grudgingly to her orange crate and began to sniffle.

"Oh, he makes me mad! Mad! If I were a man, I would squash a man like that with my nails like a flea! I would knock him out with just one blow!" she sobbed loudly.

For a long time he mulled over how he would tell her about his job. Watching her sew baby's things and listening to her talk about what she would do for the baby, he felt paralyzed with fear and helplessness. He was also frightened by the sound of her vomiting in the middle of the night. Day after day, he lived a bubblelike existence, deceiving himself that something would turn up. But her belly swelled slowly and mercilessly.

One payday evening, when she was feeling happy enough to whistle, he decided to close his eyes to everything else and confess to her. He began to tell her slowly about the background of the "Miraculous Longevity Elixir," his daily yogalike work, his ability now to tell the time without looking at his watch but just by looking at the creeping sunlight on the concrete floor, his request for a raise in exchange for the idea of creating a new trade name, his sudden disgust and escape from the store, his employer's taking advantage of him and stealing the whole idea, and the tremendous increase in the sales of "Sekiru Kompi." He spoke seriously, trying to explain why he had so stubbornly persisted on this job, but she roared with laughter and he could not continue.

She rolled all over, wiping her tears with the back of her hand, and finally panted out, "You are such a sweet man!"

"Why?" he asked, surprised. He would have had no excuse for himself had she chastised him ferociously.

Suppressing the chuckles that continued to spring up, she said, "Because, no matter how difficult it is, you never complain, and you even try to entertain me with hilarious stories like that. You're really wonderful, you are! Your stock just shot up with me!"

While speaking, however, she grew serious and intent. She became pensive, tearful even, and her voice grew muffled. She put her fingers on her eyelids, hanging her head down. He had always thought that she was extreme in everything, but this re- action was taking an odd turn. Now that she had taken his story to be all make-believe, he could see her point of view. Moreover, he could not possibly disillusion her when she was moved to tears. He readily thought of the expression "white lies," and crawled up to her on the torn mat.

"It's all right, it's all right. It's not quite like that. Well, I don't really mean it either." He hugged her shoulders, feeling utterly forlorn.

Late that night, she let him repeat the story. It seemed to have dawned on her that it was not altogether a joke.

"Bring the elixir, I'll try it," she said to him. She couldn't possibly drink it, he protested, but again she expostulated on her theory that she could take anything if it was good for her. Reluctantly, he brought home a mound of Sekiru Kompi with the picture of Hotei with his pot belly. After dinner, she steeped it in a teapot. She spooned the uniquely viscous, murky brown concoction into a beaker and began to analyze it with some re-agents and test papers that she had swiped from the lab. For a long time she kept mumbling to herself, tilting her head, but she finally decided that it was at least harmless to the human body.

"Shall I try it? I don't know if it's good for anything, but if it's harmless I might as well try it. I might gain something."

"Don't be so frivolous."

"Yes, right." She raised the beaker swiftly and, before he could stop her, gulped down the concoction. She swallowed it to the last drop, without blinking an eye or flinching her eyebrows. He collapsed on the blanket in shock. He was too weak to say anything.

"This elixir has no body," she complained.

From the spring to the summer, she worked with an astounding vigor. She kept working until the start of her maternity leave guaranteed by the labor union. Sometimes at the lab she almost fainted from anemia, or from nausea in the foul odor of the crowded train, but she did not give up the long-distance commuting between the woods and the city. She bought fabric remnants and until late every night sewed diapers, which she neatly piled up by the orange crate.

On Sunday, she took her small wallet that had been in use

for the past eight years and walked over to a nearby shopping center to fish around for bargains. The wallet had been diligently swallowing and spitting out coins since the days when she used to say that she would go to the desert and die. Now, it was swallowing and spitting out change even more accurately and stingily.

"My training fell short," he lamented. "You are by nature hard-working and tightfisted. I completely failed to see through you. I was hooked by taking your whim seriously."

"Strength, thy name is Mother!"

She did everything by herself and for herself. She shrewdly saved her hard-earned salary for the delivery expenses. When the expected date approached, she promptly had herself admitted to a union-contracted hospital. He only puttered around with errands such as getting her paycheck from the lab and delivering it to her at the hospital, or bringing her underwear she had bought and put away. She sewed diapers even in the hospital bed, and, wrapped in her sheets, fiddled with fabric remnants. She was haggard and pale, but in her usually sharp eyes a hint of gentleness now moved.

"You act as though you got pregnant all by yourself!"

"Oh, no no. You did your part commendably."

"Stop it! You depress me!"

"Why? You were magnificent."

"I envy you."

"Why?"

"You can tame any object. A pencil, a piece of paper, anything. If you touch it, it follows you and becomes part of you and settles down beside you. It's not like that with me. Everything floats around me. Nothing is stable. Once in a while if I catch something at last, right away it gets tacky with the dirt and oil from my hand and I can't stand it."

"What did you think yesterday?"

"Well, I thought that subjectivism as such may ultimately turn into nihilism, because by denying everything in order to assert one's identity, one will only reach a dead end. But after that I got confused and I just chopped up seaweed. I'm like that every day. I just mince Corsican weed."

"Is chopping Corsican weed a sure thing?"

"Highly doubtful. Where purity ends, absurdity begins . . . something like that. I reached that conclusion, but I haven't figured out how to get out of it."

"The book has been read, but the flesh is still weak. Is it something like that?"

"That's a quotation from someone."

"Oh, right. One mustn't quote other people. It's getting more difficult. You may yet turn into a Bodhidharma if you keep thinking so hard. Pretty soon, your hands and feet will atrophy like him and you'll be a quadriplegic. You can be sure that everything has been figured out by the ancients a long time ago."

Busily she wiped her neck, throat, elbows, and wrists with an alcohol-soaked cotton ball, her method of cleansing when she could not take a bath. She had stolen a gallon of alcohol from the lab and had a jug hidden under her bed. She was an alcohol specialist. Once, she had swiped heliotrope or jasmine—some kind of fragrant herb—from the lab and dissolved it in alcohol. She splashed it all over his bed directly from the gallon jug and for a long time he had had to be embarrassed by the staring eyes in crowded commuter trains.

As she finished wiping her body, she took out some bean-jam tarts from the paper bag he had brought her and began to devour them. He had bought the sweet cakes from the vendor with a catfish face at the stand right outside of the hospital.

"Say, this is very tasty. It's got a lot of bean jam in it. The vendor was in a generous mood today. Something good must have happened to him!" She licked her fingers like a cat and ate one tart after another. He had watched her gloomily until finally he was seduced into eating one. The bean-jam tart was delicious, soft and hot, and the sweet smell of the cheap bean jam dispelled the odor of phenol in the room. Blowing on the hot tart with his puckered lips, he wondered what this state of mind should be called: *élan vital*?

He was in an unprecedented predicament. With her in the hospital, he now cooked for himself in the woods and commuted to the workshop. All the while, his strange sickness progressed tenaciously. The schoolboy who gave him fried potatoes and the piece of music that danced in the young woman's hair often returned to him. On the other hand, he kept convincing himself that there was nothing new under the sun, that too many books had been already written. Every time he picked up a pencil to write, the words of numerous writers and poets ancient and modern, of East and West, that he had read at random swarmed around him and clouded his brain. Yet, he thought at the same time, he had only one life to live, and the triteness of the subjects notwithstanding, he should be entitled to write his own lines in his own way. The life observed only by words is nothing but a complete vacuum. After chopping seaweed for half a year in the warehouse, he finally reached this conclusion. No matter how passionate or moving, other writers' words were not his; it was not necessary to take off his hat and pay homage to every word. He should be free to do anything, to say anything.

He felt he should write. He was permitted to write. Even if his written words turned out to be completely the same as someone else's, it didn't mean he had plagiarized them in broad daylight. Yet, picking up a pencil, he found that he could not write one line. In his head, words lost their blood, warmth, flesh, scent, and were dehydrated. They tumbled down the emaciated forest of his rib cage with a dry sound and disappeared. Whatever the word, if he repeated it ten times, it faded and fell apart the moment he shifted his eyes from the orange crate to the round rock in the yard. He didn't know why and when it began to happen, and he didn't know how to stop it. This was some kind of delusion, some sickness. It was similar to the fact that he couldn't stop pimples. It indicated no lucidity of mind. Lucidity itself was a word game of some kind, only a variety of delusion. As a matter of fact, no one could lucidly explain the work of a mind that purports to have lucidity, not even one's own mind.

If this was so, the womanly bustling of hers, her constant,

nimble transformation from one moment to another, might be considered as the only wisdom. Oh, she would sink into introspection from time to time, but if she saw a stepladder, she would immediately jump on it in order to leave the depths. A springboard; perhaps that was all one needed. It was probably a matter of one's ability or inability to get hold of it and climb on it. He had denounced it as self-deception, but who, with no confidence in his criteria and judgment, had the right to call it "deception"? What did he have as his own? Only twitching pallid cheeks and cowering posture, that was all. How could he criticize her bustling or her self-delusion? This was like the idiocy of pompous critics ranting about the cat not having the characteristics of the tiger.

He felt numb from the fear of not knowing what was to come. He was forlorn and felt gutless, almost as though his intestines had been extracted. Overwhelmed, all he could do was to stamp helplessly on the ground like a child throwing a tantrum, but his eyes, hands, and head were not functioning. Every day, the city was yellow, stagnating, warped, and the pedestrians and buildings ghastly and chaotic. He was jumping around in it like a flea, a flea that was on the verge of tears.

As the expected day approached, her eyes sometimes showed an appalling darkness, and he drooped his head in remorse. She comforted him like a big sister and pretended cheeriness, but it was obvious she was scared to death. With her swollen belly, she looked like the ceramic badger that usually stood in front of a pottery shop as a trade sign. Clad in a thin summer kimono and covered in perspiration, she was panting in a dirty sickroom filled with the heat of July and the stench of phenol.

The concrete walls of the hospital were moldy, damp, and rain-spotted. Along the wall, women deformed by their men lay, softly moaning, enduring, and sleeping. They were all poor. Sometimes husbands came and stood at the head of their beds, preoccupied and disconsolate. Not knowing what to do, they just watched, their hands hanging uselessly. There was incontestable solemnity and innocence in the ignorant women who were swollen to disfigurement. The men saw it in their women's eyes. They were like the eyes of a dog that, bleeding internally, looked up to plead that something had hurt it. Every time her eyes suddenly took on such an expression in the midst of a seemingly gay conversation, he had to avert his own. He was killing this woman. Stubborn and compulsive, he had dragged her out and locked her in the hut in the copse. He had forced upon her a life without music or theater, and their future was a total hazard. Yet at this juncture, he still indulged himself shamelessly with inconsequential gibberish such as "Absurdity is born where purity ends" and "Subjectivism is nihilism."

His thoughts became unbearable and he ran away from the hospital, but the gnats of shame pursued him into the hut and gnawed into his dreams. More than once he was awakened, startled in the middle of the night, his arms and legs trembling. The perspiration that soaked his body was hot and cold, sticky as oil. As he stared into the darkness, his past, future, indiscretion, insecurity welled up and engulfed him. Damn, damn! He gnashed his teeth and fell back on the blanket filled with the odor of Corsican weed.

It came at last. At the end of a long darkness, it came.

One July evening, he returned from his workshop and built a fire. He was broiling wreath shells in the woods when a telegram delivery man came pushing his bicycle. He was indulging in a little game of pouring soy sauce into the crackling and sizzling shells, enjoying its sight and aroma, when the delivery man confronted him with a telegram. His heart leapt. He put down the sauce bottle and jumped to his feet. This was an unprecedented event. He had neither written to anyone, even a postcard, nor received any mail from anyone, ever.

"I had a hard time finding this place. Why don't you put up your name at least?" the delivery man said with a stern face. The wrinkles in the tails of his eyes said he had weathered many seasons. The young man was impressed and frightened. He opened the telegram under the naked light bulb in the hut.

"Operation tonight at eight."

There was no signature. Something had happened to her! She must have asked the nurse to send a telegram before the general anesthesia. He was about to kill a woman! He felt faint. Crawling back to the fire, he nevertheless ate the flesh of three wreath shells. He then ladled out water with a large bowl and poured it over the charcoal fire. At this hour there were no more buses. He had to walk over the pitch-black mountain road, but he knew every blade of grass and every rock like the palm of his hand because he walked to the station daily. He ran and walked alternately, increasing his speed more and more as he approached the town. Through the dark that was filled with the scent of summer foliage, scenes and characters from various novels came back to him: a man who prayed constantly while he ran; a woman who prayed until she was overcome by fatigue; a man, exhausted, from praying, who began to feel that nothing mattered, yet continued to pray.

He felt vexed with himself while running. What a tramp he had turned into! Even at this point he could not escape from the book poison! But what did he really feel? Did he want her to live or think it better if she died? Or didn't he care? Was he just running because he felt better running? He felt rotten to the core and grew disgusted with himself.

Young men and women were giggling in the thicket of the park. In the brightly lit fish store, the middle-aged spinster he saw every day was poking about the stretched legs of an octopus. Her teeth were smeared with lipstick.

The station's ticket taker stopped reading a sports paper and clipped his ticket, yawning. The night train was a run-down, noisy box with rubbish strewn all over the floor; it was a running trash bin. Across from him, a civil servant seemed engrossed in thought, withdrawn into his wrinkles. He was probably calculating his installment payments. What would the response be if he told the old man his woman was about to have a baby? In a corner of this city with its ten-million population, several people were now working in a certain dingy room because of him. They were perspiring, bleeding, moaning, hating, or counting up their overtime hours.

The hospital's dark wall was silent and solid as usual, emitting an acrid odor in the night. The woman at the reception window picked up her tea cup from among medicine bottles, and, sipping tea, turned the pages of the patients' directory.

"What is your name?"

He answered fretfully. "I'm her family. I'm in a hurry."

The woman picked up the phone. He waited in the corner of the waiting room as though trying to hide. Soon a nurse appeared and told him to come out of the dark. She spoke languidly as they walked through the corridor, as though reading the hospital schedule on the calendar.

"It was an easy delivery," she said.

He drooped his head and wiped perspiration from his brow. "Yes . . . ?"

He did not realize where and how he was walking but just followed the nurse, who turned dark corridors to right and left and climbed stairs. Suddenly they were standing at the entrance of the operating room in the blinding light of astral lamps. The nurse led him into the anteroom. The white tile walls and floor of the operating room were wet. The room resembled a large freezer in a slaughterhouse. Scalpels, scissors, medicine bottles, and bloody cotton wads lay on a metal wagon. Under the tile wall stood a bucket containing a mound of a purple plum color, an inert, bloody object, looking like a horrid giant salamander. Shame and fear struck him and he stood petrified. At last, the outer world burst open the thick wall and avalanched over him. The book poison dispersed. His hands and legs numb, he barely stood, quivering.

In the middle of the room was the operating table. Coming out of her anesthesia, she moved her ghastly sallow face slightly and saw him.

"I don't even have the strength to cry," she whispered.

"Um . . . ," he murmured.

Suddenly she groaned. "Ouch, ouch, ouch! It hurts! I've got

to take care of this baby. I've got to send her to kindergarten and college, too. It hurts, it hurts! I won't have her kidnapped!"

It was an odd thing to say.

A physician, masked to his eyes, silently pushed the operating table with the hoarsely wailing woman on it into the adjacent room. The young man looked at the table covered with white cloth, his eyes filmed with perspiration. Her scream rose over the doctor's shoulders.

"Ouch! It hurts! Doctor, give me some morphine! I won't let the kidnappers take my baby!"

Her voice shrieking in his ear, he grew intent on one thought: He would quit Sekiru Kompi.

A voice called out, searching for someone.

"Father, the baby's father, is he here? It was a baby girl. It was an easy birth. Father of the baby . . . ?"

He raised his face.

The head nurse was standing, holding the baby.

"I'm the . . . ," his faint voice faltered, ". . . father."

Amazement came over the solemn face of the nurse, and he watched it with a mounting irritation until he could bear it no longer. He turned his face. In her attempt to hide her fluster, the nurse suddenly thrust the baby under his nose.

"It was a baby girl. Congratulations! How darling she is! She looks just like you. She's really darling!"

He backed away desperately and murmured.

"It's all right. I know that. . . ."

The head nurse, holding the baby, retired quickly into the anteroom.

As he watched her, perspiration and red haze clouded his eyes, and everything grew foggy. Through the glass window, he could see the white figure of the head nurse bending over. She must be putting the baby in a crib. She rose. She looked this way. She smiled. She turned away. She talked to other nurses. He began to back out inch by inch. He almost stumbled into an oxygen pump and slipped on the wet tile floor. As he slowly passed the anteroom, several nurses' faces peered through the glass window, their heads close together. As soon as they saw him glaring at them, they disappeared and, the minute he stepped out to the corridor, a sudden loud burst of laughter broke out behind him. It was an explosion of laughter, convulsive and confoundedly open, without a shadow of restraint. It was a dazzling laughter.

"Damn it! They laughed! They laughed at me! They laughed! They laughed at me! Damn it all!"

He ran down the phenol-filled dark staircase like a rolling ball, and not knowing where he meant to go, darted into the night town.

He was nineteen years old.

Building a Shell Mound

Car Vunlau are a species of catfish. They live in sea water as well as in the aerobic sediment of a muddy estuary where the sea water ebbs and flows. The cat face and barbel are features of this fish that resemble any other catfish, but in addition, they are beautifully colored in silver, gray, and blue. In the wet dusk of morning they leap and splash, gleaming like large machetes. They are the most delicious and therefore the most expensive kind of catfish among many species. After I first heard of them, it took me ten days to find two master fishermen known as expert Car Vunlau catchers. One was a young gunman, a bodyguard to a company president, and the other was a taxi driver in his late middle age who was always looking for a customer in front of the Caravelle Hotel in Saigon. I invited them to a restaurant to learn more about this fish. I was told that Car Vunlau were clever bait snatchers and hard to catch, and that everyone was after them for this very reason. They said that the best bait was cockroaches. You would keep them in a box in a kitchen corner and feed them with bits of bread with lots of butter until they were nice and fat. You pierced three or four juicy cockroaches on the fishing hook, pulled out their legs and threw the line in the river. Delicious odor and juice would flow out of the leg orifices and attract the fish. The next best was chicken intestine, ideally stuffed with green feces. Soak this in the cheap fish sauce that Vietnamese soldiers like. A terrible-smelling stuff. The third best was beef. A cheap cut would do.

One could fish at a number of locations, but right now the best was Nha Be. This was at the confluence of two tributaries into the Saigon River, and the three watercourses, forming a large triangle, attracted a traffic of many fishes.

After I parted with the two master fishermen, I returned to my apartment, called a Japanese press office I knew well and explained my plan. I told the man who answered the phone to be ready for a catfish banquet, to purchase some "spring rain" noodles, tofu, lime, *shungiku* (aromatic green), fish sauce, and white wine. The fish sauce should be the best kind, the maroon-colored product of the Island of Phu Quoc, and the wine should be Montrachet '71, which I had seen the other day at the Tie Tack on Boulevard Tu Do. From the other end of the line came a vulgar snort. The man had the temerity to chide, "It's a big effort for a fish you'll end up buying at the market."

The next day, I marinated some fat green chicken intestine in a fetid fish sauce, my face turned away while I carried out the task. I went out with a plastic bagful of this aromatic preparation, but I didn't catch any fish. I waited all day, but they didn't even come close. As soon as the curfew had ended at six o'clock in the morning, I had left the apartment and sat under the incandescent white flame of the sun by the yellow river for the next twelve hours, but not one fish was caught. I changed the bait diligently, holding my breath and turning my face away each time. But no matter how many times I let the fresh stench drift down the river, no fish came even to tease. When I returned to my apartment and looked into the cracked mirror, my eyes were completely bloodshot. I reeled into bed and slept like a log, wrapped in the sickening sticky odor. My head burned and my entire body, irradiated by a glittering red light, sank and floated intermittently. Late in the evening, three or four separate times, the telephone rang for a long time, tenaciously, but I let it ring.

Several days later, when an employee of a Japanese commercial firm happened to visit the press office, I broached the subject of Car Vunlau. "There must be a devoted angler among your customers: a Vietnamese, a Chinese, anyone will do. Could you possibly introduce me to him?" In a few days, an excited voice at the other end of the line told me that such a man, a VIP, had been found. He was a bigwig among the Chinese in Cholon, president of three or four companies. He was an angler par excellence and would be glad to take me on a fishing expedition. But first, he would like to see me at a restaurant. It was morning when I received this telephone call. In the afternoon, when I was taking a nap, a knock was heard at the door. I answered and found a smiling boy, who handed me an envelope and disappeared. The invitation to dinner was written in a beautiful hand on a thick, red, Chinese paper, requesting the pleasure of my company at seven in the evening the day after tomorrow, at Yun-yüan on Boulevard Tu Do, and it was signed "Ts'ai Chienchung." Later, I was told that before inviting me, Mr. Ts'ai had gone to Yun-yüan and ordered several dishes to check on the chef's skill. Satisfied, he made up a menu immediately, had the chef look at it, and, confirming that all the preparations would be ready in five days, went home to write the invitation.

As I observed during our get-together and later, Ts'ai seemed to be a quick decision maker but extremely prudent and thorough, and once he made a decision he did everything to achieve what he set out to do. I had never seen him conducting his business, but at banquets, at the beach, or on the open sea, he was voracious, impetuous, lascivious, and a true gourmet with exquisite demands. He had a plastics factory as well as companies for loans, real estate, and canning, but his four businesses in Saigon could not exhaust his energy. He would appear in his office at eleven o'clock in the morning, go over his business mail and give instructions in an hour, then spend the rest of the day dining with friends and playing mah-jongg. The mah-jongg was apparently a business venture rather than a game, four to seven million piasters changing hands at a throw. Still, he had time to kill, so he devoted the rest to women and fishing. He had been rather bored, seeing the same faces all the time, when I happened to appear on the scene. He rose from his slumber. His curiosity piqued, he seemed to have renewed himself in all aspects of his life, quality- and quantity-wise, his voraciousness and his exquisiteness, all. Fishing was his avocation and addiction, and he had had many years of practice since his childhood. He welcomed me like a wasp soaring to meet a challenger.

The Ts'ai I met at Yun-yüan was a middle-aged man of medium height, plumpish, his face tanned and swarthy, with thick lips and glaring eyes. He was rather quiet, but responded to jokes quickly with loud laughter, though his eyes rarely smiled. When he guffawed, his chin jutted in the air and his brows and cheeks relaxed, yet his eyes remained sober. On occasion, if his eyes smiled momentarily, they immediately returned to their usual solemnity and watchfulness.

After hearing the account of my debacle at Nha Be, he diagnosed the situation immediately.

"It's the tide. The tide was bad," he declared.

"The tide?"

"Yes. The wrong time. I fish pretty often at Nha Be, which is a good place. But if you have the tide against you, you can do nothing. There are four or five meters of difference between the flow and ebb, you see. The day you went was during the worst week this month."

He spoke confidently in a slow, accurate English that didn't come out disjointed as others' often did. Later, this slow English mixed with occasional French words became our lingua franca. He inserted French in his conversation quite often because he had worked for the Indo-Chinese Bank for some years, but he did not use his mother tongue, Chinese, as often as one might have expected. As far as I could remember, he used Chinese only twice. He referred to the steamed fresh fish as "ch'ing ch'ing," and I asked if it was not "ch'ing chêng" in Pekinese. He looked at me sharply and snapped, "We don't speak Pekinese." On one other occasion, when we were sipping tea in the dusk under the large tamarind trees of Phu Quoc Island, he commented that the way the Communists acted was *Pa-tao* (tyranny) under the guise of *Wang-tao* (the "righteous way," the perfect way of the ancient kings).

Two insects meeting on the road grope for each other's antennae twice, three times and, understanding each other, they go on their ways. The magnificent dinner at Yun-yüan lasted two hours, but it took less than thirty minutes for Ts'ai and me to accept each other as fishermen. Each of us advanced our chessmen discreetly. He told me in a whisper about his barracuda fishing at Vung Tau, swordfish chasing on the sea of Indonesia, and bumper fishing offshore at Phu Quoc Island. Since I'm a river fisherman, I whispered to him about the king salmon fishing in Alaskan rivers and the pike fishing in the Swedish mountain villa of the Abu Company that I had experienced. He listened to my stories, glaring at me, but his eyes momentarily softened and wavered when I mentioned the mountain villa in Sweden. He resumed his listening, his gentleman-gangster's face down, his head nodding sometimes like a little boy. After the story, I began to tell him about the trout fishing in the Tyrol, but he no longer listened.

He nodded irritably and said, "Good, all right. Let's go fishing together. First in the sea of Vung Tau. You find good barracuda there, you see. Night fishing. Then, we'll fly to Phu Quoc. Fishing there is still good, though fish are now fewer and slightly smaller. There's real fishing, a man's game. Just bring a raincoat and a pair of slippers and leave the rest to me."

He spoke rapidly. His sharp eyes were confident, and impatience and excitement had replaced steely coldness. I wasn't trying to instigate him, but my remarks seemed to have triggered his enthusiasm unwittingly.

Trying to be polite but hardly able to wait for me to finish the meal, Ts'ai rose from the table and nudged me on the elbow. We moved onto the steaming street. He pushed me into his chauffeur-driven Chrysler, which carried us smoothly to No. 609, Nguyen Chai Boulevard, in Cholon. It was not very far from the entrance to Cholon, yet somewhat protected from the noise of Chinatown, where traveling Peking opera troupes beat the drums and gongs obstreperously. Ts'ai had his Chrysler park along the dark sidewalk and took me into a house that seemed three or four stories high. I climbed up the steps of barren concrete, feeling the grittiness of the gray-white surface under my feet. After climbing and turning a number of staircases, we finally stepped into a door that opened suddenly, and the fragrance of fresh flowers and deep forest engulfed me. We entered what looked like his bedroom. A gigantic double bed, large enough to use as a trampoline, was at the center. The walls were covered from the floor to the ceiling with thickly woven gold fabric, and the ceiling was a deep-set lattice of hardwood. Here and there, heavy, red "double happiness" banner decorations hung, shining in a dim light. On one side of the bed was a black ebony mirror, a weight in itself, and a vanity on which dozens of perfume bottles stood like the towers of a miniature city. The fragrance of flowers and the forest seemed to rise from them secretly, moving and filling the room languidly.

Ts'ai paid no attention to the bed or to the mirror, and took me straight to the fishing poles and knapsacks that stood along the wall. I observed them carefully. At a glance, I knew that the poles were all for ocean fishing, their metal parts oxidized to gray-white. Judging from the appearance of erosion and blisters from salt water, they had been used by the owner over many years. With three or four exceptions, I saw that they were all products of Garcia of America and Abu of Sweden. Now I understood why his eyes had gleamed when I mentioned my visit to the mountain villa. Next to the numerous fishing poles, many well-used and soiled U.S. Army knapsacks were lying. Ts'ai pointed to each one and told me this was for reels and that was for lines, hooks, and sinkers, and another sack was for a lamp and sleeping bag. He was not satisfied until he opened every drawer of the intimidatingly grand-looking ebony desk by the wall, showing me lines, sinkers, and hooks. In each drawer, tools were neatly wrapped in plastic bags or cased in cardboard boxes, stacked snugly to the brim of the drawer. Bedazzled, I looked up and realized that this bedroom was equipped only for sleeping and fishing, save for the double happiness hangings on the wall.

With a weary but probing look in his eyes, Ts'ai picked up a Garcia boat tackle that was leaning against the wall and examined the pole and reel. He began to mutter in his slow, accurate English, "Long time ago, there was a poet in China. There were many poets, of course, but this man was outstanding. He wrote many poems on flowers, birds, fish, and animals, but especially on methods of cooking them. There's a poem about a delicious fish caught in the Pine River, a fish with a large mouth and small scales. Who was the poet? What was the fish?"

This I knew. I fumbled in my shirt and pants pockets but couldn't find a piece of paper, so I wrote with a ballpoint pen on my palm, "Su Tung-po" and next to it, "perch."

Ts'ai pulled my hand by the fingers to his eyes. Faintly smiling, he nodded and snorted, "Hum!" He moved slowly to the next pole and, picking up a sturdy medium-sized trolling pole, mumbled again, "There was a philosopher in ancient China. One day, he went for a stroll with his disciple, and when they came to the river they saw a big fish swimming. The philosopher commented that the fish was having a good time. His disciple said, 'How do you know that the fish is having a good time? You are not the fish.' Then the philosopher said, 'You are not me. So how do you know for sure that I don't understand the fish's pleasure?' The disciple said, 'I am not you, therefore of course I don't know what you know. But you are not the fish, therefore you don't know the joys of the fish. That much is for sure.' Who were the philosopher and his disciple?"

Good. I knew that, too. The story was almost too well known. It was long ago that I had read it, but Ts'ai's questions had brought back my memory. I crossed out what I had written and wrote on my palm, "Chuang-tzu," and on the side, "Hui-tzu," and stuck my hand out. Ts'ai again lifted it by the fingers, pulled it close to his eyes and said, "Hum!" Then he turned his attention to a fishing pole on the wall.

"I want to wash my hand," I said.

"There's a bathroom behind you."

Hidden behind a door covered with thick woven cloth was a bathroom with impeccably clean, shining tile walls, bathtub, and tile floor. Again I found a city of small towers—bottles of eau de toilette and perfume. The bathroom was completely European, and the luminous, mysterious towers clearly smelled of women, as did those in the bedroom. Furthermore, it was not of a single woman, but of a number of women. Such things could not be erased, no matter how neatly the bed was made or the tub scrubbed.

After I came out of the bathroom, I happened to see a small, beat-up magazine on the ebony table. He must have read it many times. The front and back covers were missing and the soiled pages were thick with fuzz. A little excited, I thumbed through it. As I had suspected, it was *Tight Lines*, a magazine in English published annually by Abu Company. As it happened, it was the 1971 issue. I turned the pages smudged with fingerprints and a picture of a fisherman appeared. The background was a forest in early morning, towering over a river misty with white vapor. Myriads of gnats were aflutter like golden powder in the air, and a man in a white shirt stood winding his reel at the edge of the white pier that protruded into the river.

I showed the picture to Ts'ai. "It's me," I said.

Ts'ai, who was seated on the edge of the bed, winding the fishing reel, looked at the photo and at me, and a childlike surprise replaced the sharpness in his eyes. It was easy to imagine that a man devoted to the tools made by Garcia and Abu would be presented with this magazine at a tackle shop, say, in Hong Kong. But that this issue, the only one in which I appeared, was in the Cholon bedroom was an astonishing coincidence. I was probably more surprised than Ts'ai. It was 1969 that I was invited to the mountain villa of Abu, and the cameraman who accompanied me had sent the photo to Abu Company, giving them permission to use it in any manner they wished. The only issue of the magazine that carried it was this.

"Really?"

"This man's back is turned. Look. It's me. After I return to Tokyo, I'll send you my book. My book on fishing. It carries the same photo. Look." I turned around and showed him my back, then I sat next to him on the bed. He was completely baffled, and kept looking at the photo in amazement. He was not about to test me again by quoting Su Tung-po or Chuang-tzu. I had been secretly afraid he might ask me more difficult questions.

I teased him a little. "According to what you told me at Yun-Yüan, you had decided that Saigon was bad for the education of your children, so you made your wife and children live in Hong Kong. But I see you have a lot of perfume bottles around you."

I meant it to be a light joke, but Ts'ai was ruffled a little and frowned. He glared around the room and grunted, "I do smuggling sometimes."

Far off the Cape of Vung Tau, a broad reef rises from the bottom of the sea, creating billowing waves where, at midnight, gigantic barracudas float up in search of food. Once hooked, a barracuda will dart through the sea surface, jumping and leaping. In the small, round spotlight of the Coleman lamp, the fish appears like a vision of a silver tower, showering sprays of water.

"You can't catch this fish until midnight, you see. You might as well have a siesta at the hotel on the beach," said Ts'ai, but no sooner had we arrived at the beach than he hurriedly took out the lamp and poles and rushed me out to the boat, under the blazing sun of three o'clock. The boat was a shallow sampan, the surface of the water almost reaching the low rim. With every movement of the tide, the boat pitched and rolled like a piece of wood in the surf near the reef. There was nothing we could hold on to, so my backbone began to complain immediately and loudly. We were up all night and caught three barracudas, each two meters long, and then returned to the shore under the morning glow of cumulonimbus clouds flaring red and gold like some prehistoric conflagration.

Back in my Saigon apartment, without bothering to shower off the sticky salt on my body, I fell right into bed and into a comalike sleep. At ten o'clock the next morning, Ts'ai telephoned me and told me to come to his office at No. 35, Ben Tuon Down. I went there and found him sitting in his glassed-in office. He took out two plane tickets and apologized for having made plans without checking with me. We would be going to Phu Quoc Island. "Fishing at Phu Quoc is truly a man's game. I want to do this with you, just the two of us for about a week, you see," he said. I asked when he expected to go and he said, "Tomorrow. Wait in front of your apartment about six o'clock in the morning. I'll come and pick you up." He was proposing that I bathe in the water of the Bay of Siam two days after the water of the South China Sea showered all over me.

I was a little taken aback, but I said, "OK, will do!"

Ts'ai laughed, crinkling up his nose, and made some unintelligible noise. He came rushing around his magnificent teak desk and took my hands and jumped up and down several times like a child. "Good! We'll have a party tonight! Come to my house on Nguyen Chai at six o'clock. Good? OK?" Upon leaving the president's office, I glanced back. He was already in his chair, leaning over the desk and going through papers with an absorbed air.

I went to his home in Cholon at six o'clock in the evening and was shown to the roof garden. There, a banquet was in progress just like the night before we left for the Cape of Vung Tau. In the center of an immense table was a brass stove filled with burning charcoal. On another gigantic table were mounds of beef, pork, venison, as well as piles of crab, shrimp, squid, red-spotted fish, noodles, fish bladder, pork lard, aromatic green, tofu, coriander, all neatly arranged. There were many medium-sized dishes with spices and condiments, such as clear fish sauce, red fish sauce, pepper, salt, shrimp oil, sesame oil, soy sauce, mustard, ketchup, vinegar, pimento, bell pepper.

Surrounding the table was an array of VIPs, Ts'ai's colleagues in business, gambling cronies, fishing partners, all of them eating and drinking nonstop, manipulating chopsticks elegantly. The curfew started at midnight in Saigon, and one could not complain if after that hour one was caught on the street and shot at by one of the vigilante boys with a carbine. The diners had to finish the banquet before twelve, but had there been no curfew, they might have continued talking, wining, and dining for several nights. Yet, no amount of consumption made them lose their self-control; no one loosened his necktie or moved a notch on his belt. No matter how late the hour, these men maintained the cheerfulness and decorum of the beginning. This atmosphere might be what the ancient Chinese described as

> *Good eating is what makes Heaven,*
> *the expanse of great blue Heaven.*
> *The mounds of beef and the forest of dried meat,*
> *the complete menu of Great China.*

These four lines that I had seen on the walls of restaurants in various cities flashed in my mind. Ts'ai kept his watchful eyes on his guests, moving his chopsticks sometimes, lightly nodding at his friends' jokes, speaking a few words from time to time and pouring into my glass the rare cognac from the bottle that said simply *sans l'age*. Whether I said anything or not, drank or not, I felt no need to worry. I was completely relaxed and comfortable. Was it because they were all accomplished men?

"A long time ago, many crocodiles lived on Phu Quoc," Ts'ai began to say. "But they are all gone now. There, they used to catch crocodiles with an interesting method. The usual way is, you put a lot of rotten fish or pork on a large hook and leave it on the bank. A crocodile will come up from the river and swallow it in one gulp, you see. Two or three men will pull it by the rope connected with the hook. This is the way they catch a croc on

the Malay Peninsula, you see. It's different on Phu Quoc. You
dive into the river holding a wooden stick in the right hand and
a sharp pointed iron stake in the left. You jut out the stick right
in front of the croc's face, and the croc will bite into it. He won't
let go once he bites, you see. Water gets in his throat but the
crocs are too dumb to let go. He can't breathe, so he starts to
wiggle. Then you tickle the armpit of the croc a little with the
iron stick. It's tender there, you see. He's ticklish and he can't
stand it, so he starts to swim and you chase him, tickling him in
the armpit, and little by little, he will wriggle and wriggle right
out of the water onto the shore. That's the way they used to
catch crocodiles. It used to be a lot of fun."

His eyes solemn, smiling faintly, Ts'ai spoke in a low voice,
savoring the cognac with his tongue.

We left Saigon's Tan Son Nhut Airport in a double propeller
plane with a leaky engine and waddled over the Mekong Delta.
Phu Quoc written in Chinese characters means "rich country."
The island belongs to Vietnam but it is on the border line of
Cambodia. The notable feature of this elongated triangle is the
prison on the north side. The entire island is covered with bush
jungle inhabited by gigantic deer, and until a short while ago
crocodiles lived in the river. Delicate and fragrant peppercorns
and a fish sauce with a smooth, soft, rich taste are the specialties
of the island. Fish sauce can be made from any fish, but here it
is famous because it's made only from *car com*. Interestingly
enough, *car com* means "rice fish," and it coincides with the fact
that Japanese fishermen call the same sardines "sea rice." The
island is not in the South China Sea but in the Bay of Siam,
which is known for its calmness and rich bounty. Casting nets
can haul absurd amounts of small sardines, so the fishermen of
this island hardly bother to catch other kinds of fish. They don't
go after the deep-sea fish that would have to be caught one by
one with a line and hook. They are satisfied with sardines, squid,
and shrimp, which they can haul in large quantities by casting

a net. Ts'ai benefited by the situation and went after the ignored deep-sea fish. What he was interested in especially was the red-dotted fish, or *hata*, of Japan. He was totally devoted to ch'ing chên, the steamed fish dish made from *hata*.

We arrived at the Phu Quoc Island airport with its single cracked runway in the middle of a field of wild grass. A friend of Ts'ai's had come to meet us in a pick-up truck, and we loaded it with the knapsacks we had brought from Ts'ai's golden bedroom and went to the inn by the fishing harbor. The inn happened to be a big empty warehouse, and all the guests hung hammocks between the walls and pillars for sleeping. The hammock was tacky with the oil, perspiration, and dirt of numerous past customers, but Ts'ai said nothing. No sooner had he let out a long, big sigh and turned over than he was snoring soundly. When I woke to go to the toilet in the middle of the night, Ts'ai was lost to the world, a mere lump of mud, his loud snore resounding throughout the room. House lizards were squeaking in the dark. Their voices made something in me vibrate like small avalanches. The ups and downs of Ts'ai's protruding round belly with his rhythmic respiration gave me an insight into the man's droll innocence and vulnerability.

Outside, the steamy, sultry night of the Bay of Siam, laden with grass and trees, was crammed with monstrous energy that almost burst out. I felt the night pushing against the mud wall, packed with energy so heavy and dense that a needle could not go through.

The next morning, after eating hot porridge in the fishermen's hut, we loaded a boat with water, food, fruit, and all the knapsacks and poles Ts'ai had brought, and started down the river. The boat was larger than the one we had hired at Vung Tau, but had no cabin of any sort, so we just had to sleep on deck. As before, the draught of the boat was very light. So we faced the constant danger of rolling right into the water whenever we shifted our weight. The boat went slowly down the smooth yellow river. From the riverbank, we heard the cries and laughter of women in small fish markets constructed of poles and thatch roofs. We saw half-naked old women in river huts holding babies in bamboo baskets, their kimma-dyed red mouths agape in laughter. Sunshine splashed like water on the fronds of coconut palms, cycad palms, and banana trees.

An aging but strong-bodied fisherman and his wife handled the boat, giving directions to two boy helpers. The younger of the boys, clad in tattered shorts, was skinny and small, but on looking at his small-featured face, I discovered that his eyes and nose were beautiful. He worked hard and laughed easily, but he was so small I was afraid he might fall into the water when he handled a big rope. The fisherman's wife, her head wrapped in an old turbanlike cloth, brought us local absinthe in an empty Johnny Walker bottle. I sipped it in a flyblown glass. The clear drops burned into my tongue, and a strong fragrance of anise rose through my nose and enveloped me. It reminded me of arrack, which I once tasted in a tree shade at a park in Istanbul.

Following the coastline northward, one could reach the tip of the island, where the vast sea was dotted with atolls and reefs that resembled a barrier reef. The islands and the atolls were all connected at the ocean floor, at the roots of the rocks. Ts'ai knew exactly which nooks of which reefs were treasure troves of fish and directed the fisherman. We wandered around, three hours here, four hours there. There were spots with absolutely limpid water and others with muddy water. In some parts, the sea bed was covered with mollusks and elsewhere with sea urchins. As I gazed into the transparent blue-green water, following with my eyes the large, brilliant tropical fish as they floated and swung slowly to left and to right, I felt as though I were adrift in the air.

During the day the heat was intense, and the catch included mostly small- or medium-size fish. We moored in the shadow of an island for a siesta, awoke toward evening, had dinner, and began to fish about nine o'clock when the tide started to flow. At high tide we took a rest, and when the sea began to ebb, we resumed our fishing. It was difficult to fish by the light of a Coleman lamp, yet night fishing was often absurdly bountiful.

The bathyal fish, medium-depth fish, and shoal fish all bit indiscriminately, and often a whole school jostled to the surface, fighting for bait, splashing, skittering, darting. As soon as we unhooked a fish and tossed it on deck, we would throw the line in and again unhook, and in no time we had no space to stand, let alone lie down. The fish were red, blue, gold, green, silver, green-gold, star-dusted, all gleaming wet, sparkling, twinkling. It was as though all the imaginable colors were released from a chaotic subterranean unconsciousness and let loose at every flashing moment. *Car chem, car kem, car Singapore!* Every time a fish was hooked, the fisherman's wife cried out its name and tittered. The Vietnamese language has an intonation climbing to a high pitch at the end of every phrase that reminds one of a bird call or a girl's cry, regardless of the speaker's age or sex, but when the middle-aged fisherwoman cheered like a sixteen-year-old girl, I sometimes had to turn around and look, even after I had become accustomed to her.

Ts'ai exclaimed, "Felicitations!" when a strong-pulling fish like barracuda or a flat horse-mackerel bit, but whenever a red-spotted fish was hooked, no matter what size, it was always a special occasion for him. This was the *hata* of Japan. There is a red-patterned and a black-patterned variety, but he preferred the red. Each time we caught either of these, Ts'ai called out excitedly, "*Seppan, honpan!*" and carefully took it into the boat and put it in a separate pile. When the dawn approached, he had the boat rushed to an uninhabited island and moored. As we landed on the rocks, he picked out one of many knapsacks and ordered a boy to carry it. He built a fireplace with several rocks and put a pot over it. The knapsack contained a complete battery of kitchen tools. As I watched, rubbing my eyes, Ts'ai removed the cooking tools one by one: a pot, a knife, a knife sharpener, a grater, sets of bamboo chopsticks, small dishes, medium dishes, large plates, soy sauce bottles, lumps of ginger, garlic, coriander, bottles of hot pepper, fish sauce, shrimp oil, oyster oil. He arranged them all on the beach and started a fire. He put a wok on the fireplace and from the catch of the night before scrupulously selected a red-spotted fish and began to clean it. He displayed an impressive skill, meticulous and expert, in handling fish and knife.

I asked, "What are the best parts of this fish?"

Without a word, Ts'ai pointed to the head, eyes, lips, belly, and intestines in that order, then at last, the back and the side. Looking at my grin, he grinned, too. Soon, the fish was steamed. He called me, the fisherman and his wife, and the two boys, and made us all eat. He reached out with his chopsticks, too, now and then, and nodded and smacked his tongue lightly.

I could not help shouting, "Delicious! Absolutely delicious!" I was delighted by the taste of this white, fragile fish, so noble and subtle, with just a hint of the flavor of wine. I have always believed that all the fish of the southern seas, other than small shrimp and crabs, were bland, even unpalatable, sometimes with strange oily odors. But these red-spotted fish, especially when steamed this way, were exceptionally delectable. Since then, I have noticed that better-than-average restaurants always had steamed red-spotted fish on their menus. Looking at all the tools and spices neatly arranged on the beach and seeing that the tools were worn out and oily from the use of many years, tamed like pets rather than objects, I was really impressed by the thoroughness of Ts'ai's culinary ambition. Had it been in another country . . . But this was Vietnam, war-torn for many years without respite. No doubt, he only thought of fishing on the beach, ignoring the noise of battles, absorbed in cooking and eating. This complete dedication to "Good eating is what makes Heaven, the expanse of great blue Heaven," reduced me to silence.

After a while, I put down the dish and said, "You can open a restaurant, Mr. Ts'ai."

He nodded slowly and said, "So says everybody."

The sea undulated at the flow and ebb of the tide, but when the tide stopped the sea was as calm as a lake. Once the lapping sound at the boatside quieted down, the vast stretch of water under the moonlight assumed the appearance of a soft plain without grass, trees, or sand. We could almost go for a stroll.

But if you looked into the dim circle of water lit by the Coleman lamp hung at the edge of the boat, you could see clearly the frenzy of tempestuous commotion all around you to left and to right in the water. It was a furious battle of organisms and in-organisms. It was a howling blizzard. It was a kinetic chaos of myriads of fish, shellfish, eggs, seaweeds, larvae, plankton, ma-rine snow, each of them rejecting each other, eating each other, swallowing, ingesting, struggling, exterminating. If a small fish happened to charge through this bedlam of organisms with its mouth open, its stomach would explode with the thick potage before it could move fifty centimeters. It was a great turbulence of astronomical quantities that could only be comprehended in the denominations of trillions and zillions, composed with an-tennae, claws, talons, hooks, fangs, tongues, eyes, noses, mem-branes, fat nutrition, and rich juice of membranes, all pushing and jostling, eating and being eaten, chasing and being chased, acting and reacting. From the beginning of life, the quantity had not changed, nor had the quality. Absolutely nothing has changed. Only the forms and shapes have been transformed. Urged by a whim, I wound the reel and shook the pole. Sixty yards beyond, a cold flash ran through the dark, but the glowworms clinging to my fishline resubmerged in the water, melting into the great chaos, and the tender, tranquil plain showed neither spot nor scar.

One night, when we were drifting on the current near the borderline, anchor down, a battle suddenly broke out on the land. The noises were single shots and running shots, the guns were 105mm or 155mm. Amid the chirping of portable arms, heavy machine guns roared with throaty groans, and mortars crumped like fireworks and shot up flares. I saw the sharp, short fire lines tearing through the dark, and the wet, pale blue light of the flares light up the contour of the great wall of jungle in relief and then disappear. The uproar lasted for some thirty minutes, but I felt no direct explosion in my belly. I knew that a carbine was no more ominous than a firecracker if pointed away from me, but it took on a more threatening sound when the gun nozzle was pointed in my direction. Then, no matter how far away, no matter how small the firearm, the sound would come directly to my belly. The unmistakable, frightening pressure of the exploded air would travel and hit me. The awareness that I was aimed at would register momentarily and send a current of electric shock through my whole body, amplifying the impact. The power of imagination would be let loose, opening some floodgate, and the whole mass of fear and hallucination would engulf me.

But that night the incident was brief. The Bay of Siam returned to its quietude. Only Ts'ai and I were awake in the boat. The fisher couple and the two boys didn't even stir. The boat drifted secretly, swaying, dragging anchor. After a while, Ts'ai's hand reached from the darkness beyond the lamp and handed me a piece of paper. Something was scratched on it. I read it in the lamplight.

The moon was down, the crow cawed and the frost was sharp;
With sadness in my heart I fell asleep,
While maple leaves and fishing lights could be seen dimly.
Soon the bell of Han-shan Temple beyond Soochow sounded,
And its deep booming was carried to my boat,
*Yet it still seemed midnight.**

I thrust my hand into a pocket and found a crumpled ball of the toilet paper that I had torn off before leaving my apartment in Saigon. I spread it and borrowed Ts'ai's ballpoint pen and wrote down "Anchored at Maple Bridge." I handed it through the darkness above the lamp, and Ts'ai's coarse fingers grabbed it. In a while, I heard him say, "Hum!" After that he said no more and sent me no more messages in the dark. Sometimes I heard him sigh or spit; he seemed to be eating durian. I lit a cigarette in the shade of the lamp and leaned out from the rim

---

*A poem by Chang Chi, a ninth-century poet.—TRANS.

of the boat to enjoy the phantasmagoric blizzard of life in the circle of light.

"Tell you something. There's an island near the place we are going to fish today. There, the son of our fisherman, a thirty-year-old man, is living alone. All alone. He ran away from the army, went AWOL, you see. He was an infantryman in the Fourth Army District, but during the Tet vacation last year, he got away. He can't live on the land because of the police and the MPs. So they decided to hide him on this island, you see. He earns a living making charcoal. When the parents carry some rice and fish sauce to him every three or four months, they pick up and sell the charcoal at Phu Quoc and buy the next batch of rice and fish sauce for him, you see. That's the way they've been doing it for a year and half. It takes half a day to get to the island, so, we fish tonight. Is it OK with you?"

"OK. Absolutely and completely OK!"

"It's going to be hot."

"I don't mind, I've gotten used to it."

"It's nice where we fish tonight. It's going to be wonderful fishing. A first-rate location, I guarantee you. It's going to be terrific. Nobody knows the place, you see."

"Good, I'm looking forward to it."

This conversation took place in the boat the third morning, when we went back to Phu Quoc to get a supply of water, food, and fuel. He tapped my shoulder and pointed to the shore, and I saw the fisherman and his wife and the two boys returning to the boat, carrying rice and white jars on their shoulders. They loaded the boat and disappeared, then appeared again, carrying large baskets of chickens, bananas, durians, and absinthe. Ts'ai had them put down the bamboo basket of durians and picked up the fruit one by one and smelled one end of each, looking like a slave merchant. He put one back in the basket and handed two to the fisherman's wife and told her sternly to bring better ones. After a while, she came back with two new durians, and again Ts'ai smelled each one solemnly and put them in the basket with a grudging assent.

With great reverence, he said, "Durians are difficult to pick, you see." Then, "As difficult as choosing dogs."

Thanks probably to his thorough scrutiny and expertise, at Cape Vung Tau and also at Phu Quoc, I was able to enjoy durian every day. In the past, I had savored the magic taste of this fruit in my apartment or at restaurants but always indoors. Ts'ai taught me the magic of tasting this fruit on the open sea at night. He had left the results of his fastidious scrutiny lying at the rear of the sampan. If we were in the lee, the fragrance wafted toward us all night, at every breeze, every movement of air, on and on. Just before completely ripening, the fruit carried a rich aroma with a streak of coolness that flowed like a cold, narrow stream. The fresh combination of this richness and coolness was so exquisite that I wanted to savor it forever. Because of this fragrance, I was able to forget the torture of the salty stickiness that covered my body, the squeak of my backbone, and the pain of my muscles that hardened into planks at times and tangled into ropes some other times. I was able to imagine that I had wandered into a greenhouse of spring flowers. In the morning, I reflected upon it and realized that sensuality was nothing more than stringent intellectuality. I had begun to see in the voracious Ts'ai a glimpse of a steel-cold sage.

After crossing the Bay of Siam slowly in the swaying flames of white noon, sighting no shadow of seagull, boat, or waves, we arrived at last at the island about three o'clock in the afternoon. It was an ordinary small island that had no sand beach but a tree-covered rocky shoreline, no different from any other island and reef that dotted the sea around it. The fisherman stopped the engine offshore and approached the land cautiously. There were only the white, incandescent horizon, the cumulus clouds, and the cheers and laughter of the two boys reverberating from the bow as though we were in an echo chamber.

Minutes after the cries died down, a face suddenly appeared

over the large white rock on the shore. Momentarily the face disappeared, and then a barefoot youth in green jungle fatigues leaped upon the rock and began to wave his hands wildly and jump up and down. As the boat made its slow approach, the young man could wait no longer and bounded into the sea. Holding over his shoulder the rope thrown from the boat, he swam back to the shore and expertly pulled in the boat and moored it to a nearby rock. The mother and father handed the rice bag and fish-sauce jars to the two boys, and the boys handed them to the young man. All the supplies unloaded, each of us carried something on his shoulders or under his arms, swiftly leaping from rock to rock, scrambling up the cliff behind deep foliage, holding onto tree roots and branches.

It was not so difficult to jump from one rock to another, but it was not easy to climb the bluff. The earth had been stamped down to form some runglike dents, too few and far apart, and one had to hang onto the roots and branches to make use of them. As I climbed the steep slope, dragging my shapeless middle-aged flesh that now sagged pallidly due to nicotine, opium, liquor, and internal soliloquy, my breathing became turbulent, my lungs fluttered, while oil and perspiration gushed out from my pores. By the time I reached our destination halfway up the mountain, my lips were parched to agony. Soaked in sweat, hanging out our tongues like a couple of dogs, Ts'ai and I panted heavily, unable to speak. Looking at us, the fisherman's family chuckled gently. They climbed the bluff with total effortlessness, carrying rice bags and fish-sauce jars. The supplies had been put neatly away, the rice bag in the hut, the jars lined up under the eaves of the hut. The father was sitting on the pile of firewood, smoking. The mother, chirping away in her girlish voice, was already slitting the chicken's neck that she had wrung, ready to bleed it. The young man had built a fire in the small fireplace of rocks and placed over it a pot completely black with soot. The two boys romped around the hut.

"I'll interpret. Ask him anything," Ts'ai offered, panting.

I wanted to take him up on it, but both Ts'ai and I were still breathing heavily, our shoulders heaving. I could not even lift my hand to brush off sweat dripping from my cheeks and chin.

The walls and the roof of the hut were woven with long, dead leaves. Inside was a cot made of tree branches bound with vines. Leaning against the entrance was a machete, its handle shiny with oily dirt. A crude shelf on the wall had on it several cracked bowls, plates, chopsticks, and a thin aluminum spoon. There was nothing else. No shirt or trousers, no old newspaper or magazine. Outside the hut was the well-burned and well-used fireplace constructed with two or three rocks and a makeshift chicken coop. The coop was woven with branches and roughly peeled with a machete, bound by vines. Several shrewish chickens were pecking the ground. No door or threshold graced the hut. The young man's kiln was not far off, a simple small oven made of mud. Ts'ai explained that a special trick was necessary for baking charcoal here. If you always cut down trees for charcoal from the same side of the mountain, there would soon be a naked patch that would be spotted by the government patrol boat that occasionally skirted the area. The trees had to be felled in various parts of the jungle. Lest the thick smoke from the kiln should invite suspicion, the young man had built two or three conduits to the chimney so that some smoke could be channeled into the boughs on the other side of the mountain. Smoke on a moonlit night would be conspicuous, so he baked charcoal only on dark nights. Fish were abundant in the sea, but he could fish only at night, so he could not depend on it for subsistence. On the other hand, he could dig out any amount of clams and mussels. He would go down to the beach at night and get as many clams as he wished, and sometimes even crabs. For a year and a half, he had subsisted almost entirely on clams, rice, and fish sauce.

"Don't you ever catch cold?"

"Never."

"Don't you ever have stomachaches?"

"Never."

"No poisonous snakes?"

"Not on this island. There are large rats. Rats are delicious. It's not easy to catch them, but once you catch one, there's a lot of meat on it. It's better than chicken. Rat is good."

"Malaria?"

"No."

"What are you going to do if you do get sick?"

"I don't get sick. I've been a fisherman since I was born. I've never been sick and I haven't been sick since I've lived on this island, either. I even prefer living on this island to living anywhere else. I can't eat delicious things and I'm always hungry, but I don't have to work like a dog. It's easier than being a fisherman."

When I asked about cold and stomachache, his family laughed heartily. The young man was also amused. And when he answered that he liked the life of the island better than the life of a fisherman, Ts'ai and the others laughed loudly, but the father grinned wryly and turned away and dropped his chin. The young man was wearing the worn-out jungle fatigues on his naked, skinny body, but his muscles and bones were the picture of strength. His toes, all ten of them, were widely spread, and each toe could grasp the boat's edge or the craggy rocks on the shore like a hook.

He went into the hut and brought out a sling made of a forked branch. It had a strong rubber band, but he said he had never caught a bird. The handle had a profile of a bird crudely but lovingly carved out, probably with the large machete he had. A flat-bottomed plant pot with a cracked edge hung under the eaves of the hut, and a clump of coriander thrived in it. Wire must have been very valuable here, and he could have used it for a number of more pressing needs, but he chose to use it for the purpose of hanging a plant, and sometimes picking the coriander leaves to flavor his rice and fish sauce, enjoying it just as a Japanese would a pot of ferns.

"How about drinking water?"

"I can get as much as I want. There's a spot on a boulder near the beach where I found water running down from the mountain. I wash my face with it. I wash my clothes and body with it. No matter how much I use, I have a full supply in the morning. I decided to live on this island when I found the supply of fresh water."

Later, when we went down to the beach, we saw that water trickled steadily into the dent of a large boulder just as the young man had said. Heated by the sun, the surface was like hot water. The dent had the depth and length of a tub in which he could lie down. If he was soaking in this natural bathtub between the rocks, no one could detect him from the sea, but from his side, he could take in the entire seascape at a glance. Close to the bathtub, the side of the bluff was hollowed out and charcoal was stored in it. As in the hut, a bed made of tree branches and vine was provided. If he lay down, resting his head on an arm, he could watch the sea through the hanging tree branches and leaves. When he carried down charcoal from the mountain, he probably entered this cave and lay down and rested, while keeping a watch on the sea. Ts'ai lay on the bed and exclaimed, "This is a wonderful pavilion!"

Ts'ai and I were admiring the cave, when the father walked over and murmured something to Ts'ai and went away. Ts'ai was silent for a while, then asked me a question that was probably translated exactly as it was asked.

"You must know everything because you are a newspaperman. When is the war going to end?" Having put the question, he glanced at me and ambled away without waiting for the answer. I stood there for a while. When I thought I heard someone calling, I left the place finally to join the others.

In the evening, we all had chicken soup with coriander prepared by the mother under the supervision of Ts'ai, and we climbed down the cliff again, holding onto one branch after another. The two boys carried the charcoal from the cave and loaded the boat. The mother and father each embraced the young man and whispered to him, then we boarded the boat and started the engine. The boat moved away slowly from the shore. The father was at the steering wheel, and the mother and the boys stood at the stern, waving, crying out, and laughing, for a long, long time. The young man stood on the rock, responding to them, waving and calling, but finally disappeared. The precursor of the sunset glow, suggestive of a prehistoric fire, had begun to descend on the island. My arms and chest began to shine in red, purple, aquamarine.

I sat on the deck, smoking, and watched the now-distant island that had become a stroke of brush painting, and I reflected on something I had noted outside the young man's hut. He had made use of everything completely, so there was no waste inside or outside the hut, but he could not make anything with shells. They were discarded next to the hut. The view of the mound made me realize what a quantity of hand-dug clams a man could consume within a year and a half. There were rolled shells, double shells, mollusks, and wreath shells, but most were the ordinary double-shell clams. On the top of the pile, you could distinguish the shape of each shell, but the middle layer had already begun to dissolve, and at the bottom, the lime had melted and the shapes of shells had disappeared, leaving only coarse, strong folds. You could see that the rains of the monsoon belt dissolved shells like diluted sulfuric acid, melted and transformed them into a material similar to rocks and walls. To me, it appeared to be more than the transformation of waste. It was like a secretion squeezed from the pungent and bitter flesh of the young man. He was secreting a ruin in his efforts to stay alive, and he would continue to secrete a ruin to stay alive.

"How about a durian?" Ts'ai asked me, his eyes shining gloomily.

I threw away my cigarette and answered.

"A good idea!"

The Crushed Pellet

Late one morning, I awoke in the capital of a certain country and found myself—not changed overnight into a large brown beetle, nor feeling exactly on top of the world—merely ready to go home. For about an hour I remained between the sheets, wriggling, pondering, and scrutinizing my decision from all angles until it became clear that my mind was made up. Then I slipped out of bed. I walked down a boulevard where the aroma of freshly baked bread drifted from glimmering shop windows, and went into the first airline office I encountered to make a reservation on a flight to Tokyo via the southern route. Since I wanted to spend a day or two in Hong Kong, it had to be the southern route. Once I had reserved a seat and pushed through the glass door to the street, I felt as though a period had been written at the end of a long, convoluted paragraph. It was time for a new paragraph to begin and a story to unroll, but I had no idea where it would lead. I felt no exhilaration in thoughts of the future. When I left Japan, there had been fresh, if anxious, expectations moving vividly through the vague unknown. But going home was no more than bringing a sentence to a close, and opening a paragraph. I had no idea what lay ahead, but it aroused no apprehension or sense of promise. Until a few years ago, I had felt excitement—fading rapidly, perhaps, but there nonetheless—about changing paragraphs. But as I grew older, I found myself feeling less and less of anything. Where once there had been a deep pool of water, mysterious and cool, I now saw a bone-dry riverbed.

I returned to the hotel and began to pack, feeling the familiar fungus starting to form on my back and shoulders. I took the elevator to the lobby, settled my account, and deposited my body and suitcase on the shuttle bus to the airport. I tried to be as active as I could, but the fungus had already begun to spread. On my shoulders, chest, belly, and legs the invisible mold proliferated, consuming me inwardly but leaving my outer form untouched. The closer I came to Tokyo, the faster it would grow, and dreary apathy would gradually take hold.

Imprisoned in the giant aluminum cylinder, speeding through a sea of cotton clouds, I thought over the past several months spent drifting here and there. I already felt nostalgia for those months, as though they had occurred a decade ago instead of ending only yesterday. Reluctantly, I was heading home to a place whose familiarity I had hated, and therefore fled. I went home crestfallen, like a soldier whose army has surrendered before fighting any battle. Each repetition of this same old process was merely adding yet another link to a chain of follies. Unnerved by this thought, I remained rigid, strapped to my narrow seat. I would probably forget these feelings briefly in the hubbub of customs at Haneda Airport. But the moment I opened the glass door to the outside world, that swarming fungus would surround me. Within a month or two, I would turn into a snowman covered with a fuzzy blue-gray mold. I knew this would happen, yet I had no choice but to go home, for I had found no cure elsewhere. I was being catapulted back to my starting point because I had failed to escape.

* * *

I entered a small hotel on the Kowloon Peninsula and turned the pages of my tattered memo book to find the telephone number of Chang Li-jen. I always gave him a call when I was there; if he was out, I would leave my name and the name of the hotel, since my Chinese was barely good enough to order food at restaurants. Then I would telephone again at nine or ten in the morning, and Chang's lively, fluent Japanese would burst into my ear. We would decide to meet in a few hours at the corner of Nathan Road, or at the pier of the Star Ferry, or sometimes at the entrance to the monstrous Tiger Balm Garden. Chang was a prematurely wizened man in his fifties, who always walked with his head down; when he approached a friend, he would suddenly lift his head and break into a big, toothy smile, his eyes and mouth gaping all at once. When he laughed, his mouth seemed to crack up to his ears. I found it somehow warm and reassuring each time I saw those large stained teeth, and felt the intervening years drop away. As soon as he smiled and began to chatter about everything, the fungus seemed to retreat a little. But it would never disappear, and the moment I was the least bit off guard, it would revive and batten on me. While I talked with Chang, though, it was usually subdued, waiting like a dog. I would walk shoulder to shoulder with him, telling him about the fighting in Africa, the Near East, Southeast Asia, or whatever I had just seen. Chang almost bounded along, listening to my words, clicking his tongue and exclaiming. And when my story was over, he would tell me about the conditions in China, citing the editorials of the left- and right-wing papers and often quoting Lu Hsün.

I had met Chang some years back through a Japanese newspaperman. The journalist had gone home soon afterward, but I had made a point of seeing Chang every time I had an occasion to visit Hong Kong. I knew his telephone number but had never been invited to his home, and I knew scarcely anything about his job or his past. Since he had graduated from a Japanese university, his Japanese was flawless, and I was aware that he had an extraordinary knowledge of Japanese literature. And yet, beyond the fact that he worked in a small trading company and occasionally wrote articles for various newspapers to earn some pocket money, I knew nothing about his life.

He would lead me through the hustle of Nathan Road, commenting, if he spotted a sign on a Swiss watch shop saying "King of Ocean Mark," that it meant an Omega Seamaster; or, stopping at a small bookstore to pick up a pamphlet with crude illustrations of tangled bodies, he would show me the caption, "Putting oneself straight forward," explaining that it meant the missionary position. He also taught me that the Chinese called hotels "wine shops" and restaurants "wine houses," though no one knew the reason why.

For the last several years, one particular question had come up whenever we saw each other, but we had never found an answer to it. In Tokyo one would have laughed it off as nonsense, but here it was a serious issue. If you were forced to choose between black and white, right and left, all and nothing—to choose a side or risk being killed—what would you do? If you didn't want to choose either side, but silence meant death, what would you do? How would you escape? There are two chairs and you can sit in either one, but you can't remain standing between them. You know, moreover, that though you're free to make your choice, you are expected to sit in one particular chair; make the wrong choice, and the result is certain: "Kill!" they'll shout—"Attack!" "Exterminate!" In the circumstances, what kind of answer can you give to avoid sitting in either chair, and yet satisfy their leader, at least for the time being? Does history provide a precedent? China's beleaguered history, its several thousand years of troubled rise and fall, must surely have fostered and crystallized some sort of wisdom on the subject. Wasn't there some example, some ingenious answer there?

I was the one who had originally brought up this question. We were in a small dim sum restaurant on a back street. I had asked it quite casually, posing a riddle as it were, but Chang's shoulders fidgeted and his eyes turned away in confusion. He pushed the dim sum dishes aside and, pulling out a cigarette, stroked it several times with fingers thin as chicken bones. He lit it carefully and inhaled deeply and slowly; he then blew out the smoke and murmured:

" 'Neither a horse nor a tiger'—it's the same old story. In old China, there was a phrase, '*Ma-ma, hu-hu,*' that meant a non-committal 'neither one thing nor the other.' The characters were horse-horse, tiger-tiger. It's a clever expression, and the attitude was called Ma-huism. But they'd probably kill you if you gave an answer like that today. It sounds vague, but actually you're making the ambiguity of your feelings known. It wouldn't work. They'd kill you on the spot. So, how to answer . . . you've raised a difficult question, haven't you?"

I asked him to think it over until I saw him next time. Chang had become pensive, motionless, as though shocked into deep thought. He left his dumplings untouched, and when I called this to his attention, he smiled crookedly and scratched something on a piece of paper. He handed it to me and said, "You should remember this when you're eating with a friend." He had written "*Mo t'an kuo shih,*" which means roughly "Don't discuss politics." I apologized profusely for my thoughtlessness.

Since then, I have stopped in Hong Kong and seen Chang at intervals of one year, sometimes two. After going for a walk or having a meal (I made sure we had finished eating), I always asked him the same question. He would cock his head thoughtfully or smile ruefully and ask me to wait a little longer. On my part, I could only pose the question, because I had no wisdom to impart; so the riddle stayed unsolved for many years, its cruel face still turned toward us. In point of fact, if there were a clever way of solving the riddle, everyone would have used it—and a new situation requiring a new answer would have arisen, per-petuating the dilemma. A shrewd answer would lose its sting in no time, and the question would remain unanswered. On occasion, however—for instance, when Chang told me about Laoshê—I came very close to discerning an answer.

Many years ago, Laoshê visited Japan as leader of a literary group and stopped in Hong Kong on his way back to China. Chang had been given an assignment to interview him for a newspaper and went to the hotel where Laoshê was staying. Laoshê kept his appointment but said nothing that could be turned into an article, and when Chang kept asking how the intellectuals had fared in post-revolutionary China, the question was always evaded. When this had happened several times, Chang began to think that Laoshê's power as a writer had probably waned. Then Laoshê began talking about country cooking, and continued for three solid hours. Eloquently and colorfully he described an old restaurant somewhere in Szechwan, probably Chungking or Chengtu, where a gigantic cauldron had simmered for several centuries over a fire that had never gone out. Scallions, Chinese lettuce, potatoes, heads of cows, pigs' feet— just about anything and everything was thrown into the pot. Customers sat around the cauldron and ladled the stew into soup bowls; and the charge was determined by adding up the number of empty bowls each person had beside him. This was the sole subject that Laoshê discussed for three hours, in minute and vivid detail—what was cooked, how the froth rose in the pot, what the stew tasted like, how many bowls one could eat. When he finished talking he disappeared.

"He left so suddenly there was no way to stop him," said Chang. "He was magnificent. . . . Among Laoshê's works, I prefer *Rickshaw Boy* to *Four Generations Under One Roof*. When Laoshê spoke, I felt as though I had just reread *Rickshaw Boy* after many years. His poignant satire, the humor and sharp observation in that book—that's what I recognized in him. I felt tremendously happy and moved when I left the hotel. When I got home, I was afraid I might forget the experience if I slept, so I had a stiff drink and went over the story, savoring every word."

"You didn't write an article?"

"Oh, yes, I wrote something, but I just strung together some fancy-sounding words, that's all. I wouldn't swear to it, but he seemed to trust me when he talked like that. And the story was really too delicious for the newspaper."

Chang's craggy face broke into a great wrinkled smile. I felt as though I had seen the flash of a sword, a brief glimpse of pain, grief, and fury. I could do nothing but look down in silence. Evidently there was a narrow path, something akin to an escape route between the chairs, but its danger was immeasurable. Didn't the English call this kind of situation "between the devil and the deep blue sea?"

Late in the afternoon of the day before my departure for Tokyo, Chang and I were strolling along when we came to a sign that read "Heavenly Bath Hall." Chang stopped and explained.

"This is a *tsao t'ang*, a bathhouse. It's not just a soak in a bath, though; you can have the dirt scraped off your body, get a good massage, have the calluses removed from your feet, and your nails clipped. All you have to do is take off your clothes and lie down. If you feel sleepy, you just doze off and sleep as long as you like. Obviously some are better than others, but this one is famous for the thorough service you get. And when you leave, they'll give you the ball of dirt they scraped off you; it's a good souvenir. How would you like to try it? They use three kinds of cloth—rough, medium, and soft. They wrap them around their hands and rub you down. A surprising amount of dead skin will come off, you know, enough to make a ball of it. It's fun."

I nodded my consent, and he led me inside the door and talked to the man at the counter. The man put down his newspaper, listened to Chang, and with a smile gestured to me to come in. Chang said he had some errands to do, but would come to the hotel the next day to see me off. He left me at the bathhouse.

When the bathkeeper stood up I found he was tall, with muscular shoulders and hips. He beckoned, and I followed him down a dim corridor with shabby walls, then into a cubicle with two simple beds. One was occupied by a client wrapped in a white towel and stretched out on his stomach, while a nail-cutter held his leg, paring skin off his heel as though fitting a horseshoe. The bathkeeper gestured to me, and I emptied my pockets and gave him my billfold, passport, and watch. He took them and put them in the drawer of a night table, then locked it with a sturdy, old-fashioned padlock. The key was chained to his waist with a soiled cord. He smiled and slapped his hip a couple of times as though to reassure me before going out. I took off all my clothes. A small, good-looking boy in a white robe, with a head like an arrowhead bulb, came in and wrapped my hips from behind with a towel and slung another over my shoulder. I followed the boy into the dark corridor, slippers on my feet. Another boy was waiting in the room leading to the bath, and quickly peeled off my towel before pushing the door open onto a gritty concrete floor. A large rusty nozzle on the wall splashed hot water over me, and I washed my body.

The bathtub was a vast, heavy rectangle of marble with a three-foot ledge. A client just out of the tub was sprawled face down on a towel, like a basking seal. A naked assistant was rubbing the man's buttocks with a cloth wrapped around his hand. Timidly, I stepped into the water and found it not hot, nor cool, but soft and smooth, oiled by the bodies of many men. There was none of the stinging heat of the Japanese public bath. It was a thick heat and heavy, slow-moving. Two washers, a big muscular man and a thin one, stood by the wall, quite naked except for their bundled hands, waiting for me to come out. The large man's penis looked like a snail, while the other's was long, plump, and purple, with all the appearance of debauchery. It hung with the weight and languor of a man with a long track record, making me wonder how many thousands of polishings it would take to look like that. It was a masterpiece that inspired admiration rather than envy, appended to a figure that might have stepped from the Buddhist hell of starvation. But his face showed no pride or conceit; he was simply and absentmindedly waiting for me to get out of the tub. I covered myself with my hands and stepped out of the warm water. He spread a bath towel quickly and instructed me to lie down.

As Chang had told me, there were three kinds of rubbing cloths. The coarse, hempen one was for the arms, buttocks, back, and legs. Another cotton cloth, softer than the first, was for the sides and underarms. The softest was gauzy and used on the soles of the feet, the crotch, and other sensitive areas. He changed the cloth according to the area, tightly wrapping it around his hand like a bandage before rubbing my skin. He took one hand or leg at a time, shifted me around, turned me over, then over again, always with an expert, slightly rough touch, which remained essentially gentle and considerate. After a while, he seemed to sigh and I heard him murmuring "*Aiya* . . ." under his breath. I half opened my eyes and found my arms, my belly, my entire body covered with a scale of gray dead skin like that produced by a schoolboy's eraser. The man seemed to sense a challenge and began to apply more strength. It was less a matter of rubbing than of peeling off a layer of skin without resorting to surgery, the patient task of removing a layer of dirt closely adhering to the body. Talking to himself in amusement, he moved toward my head, then my legs, absorbed in his meticulous work. I had ceased to be embarrassed and, dropping my hands to my sides, I placed my whole body at his disposal. I let him take my right hand or left hand as he worked. Once I had surrendered my body to him, the whole operation was extremely relaxing, like wallowing in warm mud. Soap was applied, then washed off with warm water; I was told to soak in the tub, and when I came out, again warm water was poured over me several times. Then he wiped me thoroughly with a steamed towel as hot as a lump of coal.

Finally—smiling, as though to say "Here you are!"—he placed a pellet of skin on my palm. It was like a gray ball of tofu mash. The moist, tightly squeezed sphere was the size of a smallish plover's egg. With so many dead cells removed, my skin had become as tender as a baby's, clear and fresh, and all my cells, replenished with new serum, rejoiced aloud.

I returned to the dressing room and tumbled into bed. The good-looking boy brought me a cup of hot jasmine tea. I drank it lying in bed, and with each mouthful felt as though a spurt of perspiration had shot from my body. With a fresh towel, the boy gently dried me. The nail cutter entered and clipped my toes and fingernails, trimmed the thick skin off my heels, and shaved my corns, changing his instruments each time. When the work was completed, he left the room in silence. In his place, a masseur entered and began to work without a word. Strong, sensitive fingers and palms crept over my body, searching and finding the nests and roots of strained muscles, pressing, rubbing, pinching, patting, and untangling the knots. Every one of these employees was scrupulous in delivering his services. They concentrated on the work, unstinting of time and energy, their solemn delicacy incomparable. Their skill made me think of a heavyweight fighter skipping rope with the lightness of a feather. A cool mist emanated from the masseur's strong fingers. My weight melted away and I dissolved into a sweet sleep.

"My shirt."

Chang looked at me quizzically.

"That's the shirt I was wearing until yesterday."

When Chang came to my hotel room the next day, I pointed out the dirty pellet on the table. For some reason, only a twisted smile appeared on his face. He took out a packet of tea, enough for one pot, and said that he had bought me the very best tea in Hong Kong; I was to drink it in Tokyo. Then he fell silent, staring blankly. I told him about the washer, the nail clipper, the boys, the tea, the sleep. I described everything in detail and reveled in my praise of these men, who knew one's body and one's needs so thoroughly, and were devoted to their work. One might have called them anarchists without bombs. Chang nodded only sporadically and smiled at whatever I said, but soon fell to gazing darkly at the wall. His preoccupation was so obvious that I was forced to stop talking and begin packing my suitcase. I had been completely atomized in the dressing room of the bath-house. Even when I had revived and walked out of the door, there seemed to be some space between my clothing and my flesh. I had felt chilly, and staggered at every sound and smell, every gust of air. But one night's sleep restored my bones and muscles to their proper position, and a thin but opaque coating covered my skin, shrouding the insecurity of stark nakedness. Dried up and shriveled, the ball of dirt looked as if it might crumble at the lightest touch of a finger, so I carefully wrapped it in layers of tissue and put it in my pocket.

We arrived at the airport, where I checked in and took care of all the usual details. When only the parting handshake remained before I left, Chang suddenly broke his silence. A friend in the press had called him last night. Laoshê had died in Peking. It was rumored that he was beaten to death, surrounded by the children of the Red Guard. There was another rumor that he had escaped this ignominy by jumping from the second-floor window of his home. Another source reported that he had jumped into a river. The circumstances were not at all clear, but it seemed a certainty that Laoshê had died an unnatural death. The fact seemed inescapable.

"Why?" I asked.

"I don't know."

"What did he do to be denounced?"

"I don't know."

"What sort of things was he writing recently?"

"I haven't read them. I don't know."

I looked at Chang, almost trembling myself. Tears were about to brim from his eyes; he held his narrow shoulders rigid. He had lost his usual calm, his gaiety, humor, all, but without anger or rancor. He just stood there like a child filled with fear and despair. This man, who must have withstood the most relentless of hardships, was helpless, his head hanging, his eyes red, like a child astray in a crowd.

"It's time for you to go," he said. "Please come again."

I was silent.

"Take care of yourself," Chang said and held out his hand timidly; he shook mine lightly. Then he turned around, his head still downcast, and slowly disappeared into the crowd.

I boarded the plane and found my seat. When I had fastened the seat belt, a vision from long ago suddenly returned to me. I had once visited Laoshê at his home in Peking. I now saw the lean, sinewy old writer rise amid a profusion of potted chrysanthemums and turn his silent, penetrating gaze upon me. Only his eyes and the cluster of flowers were visible, distant and clear. Distracted, I took the wrapping from my pocket and opened it. The gray pellet, now quite dried up, had crumbled into dusty powder.

The Fishing Hole (Ana)

A crowd appears at authorized rivers on the first day of legal fishing for sweetfish, known and loved by the Japanese as *ayu*. On all opening days one needs a kind of psychological armor to brave the mob, but this occasion is special. Throngs of angling maniacs rush to the river before dawn, and snakelike queues, longer than those at bicycle races, form in front of the license window for admission to the river. Nothing can be seen in the predawn dark, but once the sun is up, a scene like that of a flea market for old clothes unfolds.

Men wearing hunting caps, mountain climbers' hats, beanies, headbands, dirty old suits, wrinkled jackets, leather jackets, rubber boots, straw shoes, moccasins, swarm all over the river bank. These smudges in the landscape line up and begin to throw lines, lower their tackle. It is hardly a fishing scene. Engrossed in what they are doing, they scarcely notice their neighbors; shoulders jostle against each other and lines tangle in the air.

This is only one example. There are fishing holes in seas,

rivers, everywhere, all year around. In spring, Crucian carp, in autumn, goby. Whatever the season, crowds like those in second-hand clothes shops appear on river banks. The railroad companies are prompt to cash in. Posters go up all over the cities, spot radio announcements advertise special-rate trains and long-distance buses for the season, all pouring fuel over the flames of fishing enthusiasts. Everyone should know that fresh fishing holes are impossible to find since angling has become so improbably popular. But, no, fishermen never give up and for good reason. Every fishing-tackle shop, for a ten-yen purchase of worms, hands out a map of all the river systems with details that would shame an Army Ordnance survey. The banks for goby fishing make one wonder when they will collapse under the weight of the piscators.

And what about the quality of fish? Seas are contaminated more and more each year with industrial wastes, and rivers are polluted with agricultural chemicals to the point that one can't see guppies—one has to go to fish tanks at a department store to see them. Occasionally, one may find a pollution-free river, but it will be spoiled as soon as a dam is built upstream. The fish's escape routes will be cut off. They will be caught in nets or numbed by electric shock, and that will be the end.

What about fish ponds? Yes, there are those, if you don't mind the murky water and the exhausted carp coming up at the end of fishlines, dangling numerous hooks around their mouths like some kind of decoration.

But I had a plan. I'll tell it only to you.

It took me almost half a year to prepare—no, even longer, because it was based on the total experience of my fishing life. In preparation, I visited all the tackle shops and travel agencies one by one and bought up the damned brochures called "Fishing News." And I bought all the new publications on fishing and traveling—completely. I need not tell you that my purpose was to find a valley no one knew, no one had been to, and no one had written about. I made a list of rivers and calculated how far they were from Tokyo and how far they were from other major cities. Then I researched the possibilities of pollution, defoliation, typhoon, flood, and landslide that might have occurred in recent years. I eliminated rivers one by one. Finally, there remained one river.

No, I won't tell you where.

Then, shut up in my room, I studied this river from every angle for many, many days. With all the maps and books around me, I painstakingly analyzed all the details. I also went to the library and got a map of the freshwater fish distribution on the archipelago of Japan. I couldn't go wrong with this sort of preparation.

I finally arrived, by my sixth sense and by the process of elimination, at one area where there was no factory, no dam, no hot spring, no rice field, and no typhoon or flood in recent years. So on a seventy to eighty percent chance, the river could not have been damaged.

The river originates in one of the mountains in the Japan Alps and gathers numerous tributaries as it flows downstream. Growing into one of the largest rivers in the region, it finally pours into the Pacific Ocean. I was primarily interested in ravine fishing, and the valley I spotted was one of the upper stream tributaries of this river. Just to get there would take the major part of a day. It was 4,705 feet above sea level. That's a fact.

It was also a fact that this could be a real treasure trove of chars! The riverfish distribution in the order of appearance from upper to lower stream is generally like this: salamander, char, trout, dace, carp, eel, and uninteresting ordinary fish. But in these days of pollution, areas where chars used to live would be no longer habitable for them. The only species that interests me is chars, but these fish will never, absolutely never, go downstream, choosing to remain among rocks and snow. Naturally, not too many exist today. But the ravine I found is 4,705 feet above sea level. No matter how greedy Keita Gotō* might be, he would not send special fishing trains and buses to this area.

In the clear, cold water, chars watch out like hawks. They are frightened by the shadow of a falling leaf—not to mention human shadows—and they flit away immediately. Once a char hides behind a rock, he will not come out all day. Okay, they could keep their own idiosyncracies, but in the river I finally found by the process of elimination, they could not have experienced much of human disturbance in the past. They should be fat, resilient, and strong enough to return a sharp shock through the line and pole directly to my heart. When a lizard, surprised by wind, scurries along the shore, a char will spring up and chase the reptile, twisting its body and spraying white water. The fish is close to two feet long, and when it springs from the torrent and bites, the line will tighten, spray water, and tremble. The reel will clatter, the pole will squeak and arch, and my throat will be parched. At this point, even I, a veteran of many years, will lose my senses.

I had to dress myself like an Alpine climber. In addition to my fishing tackle, I carried a rucksack on my back, a climbing pick, a rope, a lantern, and all my provisions. In total, the load easily weighed one hundred twenty-five pounds. God knows whether chars were actually there. Still, I would carry complete housekeeping paraphernalia and climb and crawl to find a fish hole come hell or high water. It was obvious that no hotels or hot springs were up there.

So, what was I doing this for? Well, simply because chars must be there, because I wanted to feel that pristine shock, that heart-thumping sensation. Do you know Poe's words? "A lucid spirit is incapable of clarifying itself." As I polished my fishing tackle and oiled my climbing tools, tightening my plan, I became com-

---

*Keita Gotō is a financial tycoon who started his multifaceted industry with the Tōkyū train system.—TRANS.

pletely enthralled by the megalomaniac fantasy that any veteran piscator knows during the preparation period. I had never seen the river or the land around it, yet I felt like the feudal lord who had owned this entire territory from way back, who was going to visit his land for the first time in years to indulge himself with all the pleasure that would be offered to him. I even answered my own question about the feelings of such a lord of the manor, "I know, I understand, I know it very well!"

You mean the name of the prefecture and county? Don't rush me. Listen to my story.

Well, finally I arrived at my destination.

I was standing in the cold darkness. There was no moon, no stars. Apart from two bare lamps, one over the sign plate for the station on the platform and the other over the window of the ramshackle ticket office, it was completely dark. As soon as I got off and hauled out my housekeeping gear, the train let out a toy-horn toot and rumbled off. Left behind were me, my bundle, and two bare lamps. No, there were a couple of other things. Something odoriferous passed me and I saw a peasant woman carrying a bamboo basket full of salted dried fish on her back. Behind her, an old man wearing a worn-out *haori* coat appeared. He may have been on his way home from a Buddhist memorial service. After these two characters disappeared, leaving the smell of dried fish, saké, and incense, there was no one but me on the platform. In the blackness, mountains towered closely and the forest surrounded me with oppressive solidity. As I listened, somewhere deep down, I heard the sound of water. It was the sound of a torrent in the valley dashing against rocks.

I smiled in the dark, congratulating myself on a propitious start, and threw my rucksack on my back and began to walk.

An old clerk was waiting at the exit gate. He took my ticket and looked at me over his small, round specs, as if he had been standing there for the last twenty years.

"Mountain climbing, eh?" He inspected me all over and noticed the pole sticking out of my sack.

"Dace fishing, too, eh?" Then he added, "Nice getup you have on." And once more before he disappeared in the hut, he turned around to look at me and muttered something, shaking his head.

It was completely dark when I went out of the gate. The path lit by the dim light formed a considerable slope disappearing into the tenebrous unknown from which I had heard the sound of water. There were a few shops—a bean-paste store and a general store—around the little square in front of the station, but everything was closed. There was nothing else except the mountains. This was a station for monkeys.

Had I gone too far in planning? I stood there, with my sack on my back, looking around forlornly, when I heard heavy footsteps behind me and a voice call, "Hello! How goes everything?"

I turned and saw a heavy, muscular man in a mountaineer's outfit handing his ticket to the clerk in the hut. Quickly I hid in the shadow and watched him. He was wearing an old snowsuit, climbing boots, and held a climbing pick in one hand and portable tent under his arm. But my eyes immediately caught the conspicuous fishing pole—detectable even to astigmatic men— that protruded from a mountainous rucksack packed full. Swiftly counting the differences between him and myself, I found only three: his snowsuit and my jacket, his connecting pole and my reel pole, and his portable tent and my sleeping bag. All the rest was the same. I understood at a glance and averted my eyes. When was the next train going deeper into the mountain?

"What a lousy place this is," he said to the station clerk in a loud voice. The old man must have answered from the hut, maybe while drinking tea. I couldn't hear him.

The man spoke, retying cords on the tent. "I had to change the train three times to get here from Tokyo. It's terrible. Only two trains a day on this single track and if I miss it, I have to sleep at the last junction. I'm crazy to do this."

The clerk in the hut said something inaudible. The fisherman answered in a loud voice.

"No, not dace. Chars. The usual."

Then, when the clerk responded, the man did not answer.

I was watching from the shadow and saw him put his rucksack on his back and push up the tent under his arm. He stepped away from the ticket gate and stood there, staring suspiciously through the dark, and, before his eyes made out anything, I stepped out in full view of him. He was standing there with the bare lamp behind him. His face was in the shadow and I couldn't see his expression, but I detected a tension in his shoulders as he saw me.

"Hello," I said.

"Did you come from Tokyo?" He was a quick one. Before I could say anything, he tried to control the conversation. I decided to pretend naiveté.

"Well, this is my first time and I am completely lost."

I sighed, jacking up my heavy rucksack on my shoulders. To be honest, the shoulder straps of the sack had locked tightly into my collarbone and I couldn't move my neck. Unfortunately, as I shoved up the backpack with my hip, the fishing pole stuck out and revealed itself. I couldn't help it. The man saw it at once.

"Un-ha, this is a professional job. Let me see." He came close and touched the pole. "It's a little scarred, but a nice pole. It's well taken care of, a real pro's job. Surely this isn't for dace?"

I closed my eyes. With the one hundred and twenty-five pounds on my back, I couldn't brush off his hand. He continued to handle and examine my tackle. "Absolutely not," he said. "This is not a dace pole."

I mumbled with my eyes closed. "I would appreciate it if you didn't touch the pole. I've trained it, you see."

"Sorry."

The man quickly stepped away.

Immediately I recovered and challenged. "Now that you've seen me, let's shake." I was straightforward. I smiled generously. "We are two foxes in a hole. You don't mind, do you? Won't you show me where you camp usually?"

It was my turn to inspect his tent. It was a dirty one. He instantly pushed it behind his back and guffawed in a shockingly loud voice. He arched his strong neck and laughed openly.

"Good. Two foxes in a hole," he said. "Okay, let's go. It's this way."

He tapped my shoulder and, still chuckling in the back of his throat, began to walk rapidly. He crossed the small square in front of the station in long strides and, just as I had suspected, followed the path toward the valley. I walked behind him, hunchbacked. His backpack seemed to be lighter than mine, and he kept his back straight with ease. I had to stop stealthily from time to time to shrug up my sack and stretch my back.

"It's slippery here . . . careful of this rock . . . it rained about three days ago . . . here's a sharp rock sticking out . . ."

He called these obstacles to my attention generously. Evidently able to see like an owl in the pitch black, he stooped down and stepped sideways nimbly. In the beginning, I tried not to pay any attention to his warning, but soon enough I found that not only were his words accurate but also the path grew narrower and steeper so that I could not help but follow his instructions. He was laughing cheerfully in the beginning, but now he had fallen silent except to warn me as he groped in the dark. I was silent, too. Who would be pleasant to a man who'd stolen his wife? Drenched in perspiration, we went down without a word. The old fox!

Once down on the riverbed, we immediately got ready for sleep. My adversary—for so I regarded him—guided me behind a large boulder and told me here would be a good place to sleep, relatively free of rock. I took my sleeping bag out and laid it on the ground. The other pitched his tent right next to my bed. He was expert at it and set it up in no time without light. I finished my bedtime preparations, lit my lantern, and took a bottle of whiskey to his tent to show him my gratitude. My enemy saw the bottle, swiftly hid the tackle he had been examining, and crawled out of his tent.

"Well, well, thanks!" he said.

While I went back to my backpack to look for some cheese,

he had polished off almost half the bottle. I hurriedly finished the remaining half in three gulps. Part of the third gulp went into the wrong pipe, and I gagged and coughed as though my lungs were on fire.

After that, we nibbled the cheese and talked. We soon put out the lantern to save oil. In the dark, we hugged our knees, facing each other and peering into each other's eyes. To tell you the truth, I wanted to look at his face. I was sorry I couldn't see what sort of expression lay on it. He said he was the managing director of a small company in Tokyo, that he came to this area on vacation since his business was slow at the moment. I didn't ask what kind of company or what the name of it was. I commented on his drinking capacity; he seemed to be unaffected by the volume he had consumed. He answered that he couldn't boast about it because his was a capacity developed by freeloading at business parties. I baited him and let him talk about fishing. He knew all the rivers and valleys worth knowing, and thoroughly. So I touched upon the main subject—though it was a little premature—why he came to such a hinterland when he had the skill to catch *ayu* or rainbow trout anywhere.

"Well . . . to put it simply, I don't know about you but I feel *ayu* and trout are artificially raised fish. They have some merits, too, but somehow I don't feel like fishing them. They are like netting goldfish at the department store, and there's no thrill. Our natural environment is disappearing, so it's hard to find real fish. I'm a little stubborn, I guess. But to come to the point . . ." He broke off his sentence and leaned forward. "I've been meaning to ask you. How do you know this place?"

"Just by chance. I asked a friend, who is a fishing aficionado, for a good place to fish and he told me about this valley. He had heard about this river from someone else. He had never come here himself, you understand. So here I am, but whether I can find any fish . . ."

"You mean char?"

"Well, yes. Whether chars are here, whether I can catch any fish here, I have no idea."

"What's your friend's name?"

"You wouldn't know him."

"Does he also work for a company?"

"No, he's not much of anything."

"You say he likes to fish?"

"Well, yes. He likes it as an amateur, you understand? He's the kind that says if he's going to waste a Sunday, he might as well waste it at a fishpond. His appearance is professional, but there's no fish dopey enough to get caught by him."

I don't know how my enemy took my story, but he sighed after a while.

"There's no keeping a secret any more," he said. "Everything leaks. This valley's no good if people know about it. There's nowhere else I can go but the mountains of Hokkaido. Japan's crowded to the point of hopelessness. This is the end."

"I agree. The population is too large, the country too small, there's no unknown fishing hole any more. Railroad companies hustle and send special trains."

"I know."

"The fish die of pollution. Men build dams so fish can't get away. Men catch young fish indiscriminately, so fish become scarcer every year."

"I know!" my enemy shouted irritably. "You don't have to tell me! That's why I come to a place like this. Damn it!"

"We can't do anything about it."

"Mmm. . . ."

"We've got to accept the reality. . . . By the way," I spoke cautiously. "How about chars in this river? Do they bite?"

"Yeah."

"Are there lots of shades?"

He did not answer my question but mused. "I'm really puzzled."

"By what?"

"You've found this place and I can do nothing about it. But for about a year, I saw no one here. I was absolutely the only one who came all the way from Tokyo to this valley, and it couldn't have been known to anyone else. As a matter of fact, I asked Gen the Fool at the station and he said nobody else had ever come. Of course I never talk, so I don't understand. Who could have known it?"

"Some people go poaching, looking like hikers."

"To come here?"

"That is, just for instance." We were sparring like boxers in the ring. "There's no reason why a thief should look like a thief," I added. "You never know what sort of clothes people put on to do what and where."

"Um?"

"What's it like? The distribution of fishing holes on this river?"

"So-so."

"Yes?"

"*Comme-ci comme-ça*," my enemy spit out and crawled into his tent. He seemed to have decided to get his tackle ready at this midnight hour. He hung a flashlight from a pole of the tent. I grinned and crept into my sleeping bag. I zipped myself in from toe to chest.

"Good night," I called out, careful not to sound too cheerful, but there was no answer. He was angry. Really angry. That was all right. Most fishing maniacs are short-tempered and quick to jump to a conclusion. Another characteristic is that they are often notorious womanizers. Of course there was no way to prove this last statement.

Our game up to this point was just about half and half, fifty-fifty. We were both unprepared for each other. My enemy saw through me at first glance, but I hoodwinked him completely after that. That was a ten-point advantage for me, but he brought me to the camping site, so I would make the match fifty-fifty.

The next morning, I woke up under a twilight sky. Around me were deep, sheer cliffs. How could I have climbed down? It had been dark and I had been completely engrossed. I couldn't have done it alone, that was for sure. I stuck my neck out from the sleeping bag and looked around. I saw the tent and an open rucksack but couldn't see him. I got up immediately. His fishing pole was gone. I understood and crept out of the bag like a pupa and, rubbing my eyes, ran over to my backpack.

I pulled out my fishing pole and tool box, and hastened to thread the ring and reel, to attach a hook, a sinker, and a ball float. My baits were vine bugs that I had bought at the tackle shop near the Ueno Station where I usually went. Vine bugs are small, sluglike larvae that live inside grapevines. You split a grapevine with a pair of scissors just before baiting so that the bug is still alive. This is a favorite food of daces and chars. As soon as I got the pole ready, I stood quickly, grabbed five or six dry grapevines and thrust them into my pocket. Then I caught sight of a piece of white paper. On it were some notes I had made over the past six months on the cost estimates, locations, maps, all the detailed information and plans. When I had dug out the cheese on the previous night, I must have pulled it out by accident. Quickly, I stowed it in my pocket.

I was absorbed for the next half-hour in fishing and didn't even think about my companion. Then I went back to the boulder and saw him. He was in his snowsuit, crouching under the boulder, building a fire. His pole was beside him, and seven or eight fine-looking daces were on the ground, perfunctorily pierced through their mouths with young bamboo sticks.

"How was it?"

"It's a nice valley," I answered.

I placed the basket containing my catch at my foot, and he quickly glanced at it, pretending a casual interest.

"Ah-ha, you are pretty good!" he said and turned away.

The boxing gong sounded for this round.

I put down my fishing pole and took out the daces from the basket and put them on the sand one by one. They were all close to a foot, and the scales still shone with the fresh iridescence of mother-of-pearl in the light of the dawn. I was overwhelmed. My heart was still palpitating.

"Five! Five fish in thirty minutes!" I was ecstatic. Holding my hands above the fire, I eulogized in rapture. "What a fine valley! Five fish in thirty minutes! There are deep coves and still pools, one hole after another. There's no brush on the other side so there's no worry about the hook getting caught. I can swing my pole as much as I want. If I swing from the depth to the rapids, it's a hundred percent hit. I've never seen a place like this! This is the best, made to order. What luck!"

Suddenly I remembered him and looked up. He wore a grimace as though he had bitten into something bitter. He had stubbornly kept his mouth shut, his eyes averted.

I could not stop talking. "It's completely understandable why you would want to come out here from Tokyo no matter what. It's a magnificent place!"

He picked up a twig angrily, pierced it through a dace's mouth, and thrust the fish into the fire. He raised his eyes and said disgustedly, "You'd better not tell anyone else!"

An almost violent gleam flashed in his eyes. He was a real maniac. When a man begins to show this sort of gleam in his eyes, you cannot reason with him. These are the eyes that have been exposed to the rain, wind, and sun for many years. A veteran among veterans, this sort of man has no wife, no children, no home, no work. Even a rain puddle suggests to him a torrential mountain rapid, and once the idea gets hold of him, he is obsessed to go seek. Neither trouble nor expense will bring him back to his senses. He and his kind are a suicidal lot.

I closed my mouth. While he was broiling the fish, I put enough rice for two in the rice cooker, washed it in the brook, and collected kindling from the riverbed. When I returned to him with an armful of firewood, he was digging a hole near the fire. I took a piece of aluminum foil from my sack and handed it to him. Realizing that I had guessed his intention, he said sullenly, "You even brought this, and last night you had the nerve to tell me you were a complete amateur."

"No, it's just by chance."

"Yeah, you brought a char rod by chance, a sleeping bag by chance, and put aluminum foil in your sack by chance!"

It was better not to argue.

I helped him. I sprinkled salt on the fish and wrapped them in the foil, put the packages in the hole, covered them with a layer of dirt, piled kindlings over them, and started a fire. I put the rice cooker over it. While we were waiting for the fish to bake, those on the other fire began to sizzle, dripping oil from the burned skins, and a delicious aroma began to waft toward me.

"Would you like a drink?" I asked him.

"No, I don't want it. . . . Take a sip in the morning and my legs will start wobbling."

". . . Well, I'm going to have one."

"A lot of men have died fishing chars. They fell from the rocks. It's that dangerous, you know."

"Yes, I know. . . . May I have some of that fish?"

After a while, he said, "Is it good?"

"The dace is delicious."

". . . Give me just a sip."

I threw the flask toward him and he caught it deftly in one hand, and the first smile of the day appeared on his swarthy leatherlike cheeks. Under his snowsuit, he seemed to be hiding formidable muscles, but the smile made him look like a child. It was short-lived, but it was still charming. He opened his big mouth and, showing horsey white teeth, poured whiskey down his throat with a lush gurgling noise. The golden sun splashed on his chin.

"Say," I called.

"What?"

"Let's make a pact."

"What for?"

"Well, there's only one river and there are two fishermen. Our object is to catch those sensitive fish. If we frighten them, that hole is lost to us for the rest of the day. So . . ."

"So, what?"

"Let's make a pact here and decide our respective territories. One of us will take upstream just above here and the other will go farther up. The one going farther up will not walk up the river because fish will be frightened, but take a detour over the cliff."

"Yeah, then?"

"Each of us will fish as much as we want, and will return here in the evening. It'll be all right to leave our things here, won't it?"

"I suppose so, as long as we don't have poachers in hiking outfits."

"Let's make this our base camp. Do you agree?"

"I have no choice. Do you want up or down?"

"It's my first time here, it doesn't matter."

"I agree," he said.

"Which would you like?"

"I'll take the closer," he said.

"All right."

That was settled quickly.

Soon the sun came up. We finished our meal in a hurry and prepared to leave. Whether I went by way of the rocks or up the cliff, it was just as dangerous. It was best to go out light. I decided to take only the reel pole, a few necessities, and the climbing pick. This was still dace territory, both where I was to go and where he was to go. To reach where chars might be found required much walking upstream.

"Are you all right? Rocks, rapids, and cliffs. If you miss one step . . ." Suddenly my adversary clapped his hands. "Bang! You go. It's all right to use a pick, but your energy is limited. If you exhaust yourself, you won't be able to return. I won't be responsible for you."

"I'll be all right. If you can give me a general picture of the holes, I won't push too hard."

He tightened his belt, retied his shoelaces, examined his pick thoroughly, and nodded.

Upstream, the water from many small but deep ravine tributaries joined the main stream of this river. The ravines were sheer, blinding abysses. If a fisherman should wander into one of the ravines after sundown, he would never get out alive. So,

I had to have a general idea of the holes and act accordingly. My adviser said there were ideal holes everywhere, but he told me about one that was the best, safest, and nearest.

"Never repeat this. All right? From here, you leave the river and go up to the top of the cliff. Follow the path and you will leave the river eventually, but turn right at the single cedar in the shape of a mushroom. After a while, you'll see a big boulder in a bamboo grove. Look around carefully, there's a small path I've made. Turn left and go down, and you will find a small brook; that is not the same river. That's one of the tributaries. I don't know the name and most maps don't show it. But if you hide behind a rock and throw your line, you'll get the thrill of your lifetime. You will feel a tap going straight up to your heart, one after the other. Why don't you try around there?"

"I climb up the cliff, turn right at the single cedar, turn left on the path beside the rock that's in the bamboo grove. Is that it?"

"Yes. Turn right at the single cedar."

"Right at the cedar."

"Take your map just in case."

"You told me the river isn't on the map."

"Just in case. It won't weigh you down. Take it. I won't be around if you get lost."

"Okay," I said, and parted with my rival at the riverbed.

I walked to the cliff and began to climb. It was almost a monolith, a gigantic rock as large as a building, and it was difficult to find footholds. The trouble was that my hands were occupied, a pole in my left, a pick in my right. I couldn't use the pole like a cane because it would crack in a second, so I was actually one-armed for climbing. I flattened myself against the wall like a lizard, and driving the pick into the rock, climbed up step by step. Somewhere midway, I turned my neck and saw, far below beside a large boulder, a tent that looked like a handkerchief. I moved my eyes and saw a small green spot hopping along upstream from one rock to another.

Once up, it was easy enough to walk over the cliff. There were boulders, bushes, and groves, but I reached the target tree without getting tired. He had said there was a mushroom-shaped cedar, but the tree looked more like a spear. I searched around but didn't see any other cedar. I opened a map just to be on the safe side. Of course, the map had no marking for the cedar. Such things just don't appear on a map. There was no path anywhere.

I listened and heard the sound of water to the right and to the left, but I didn't know the tributary from the main stream. After a moment of hesitation, I turned left. The path again grew very steep.

An hour had passed.

I peeped from behind a rock and saw at the end of a sheer drop a clear, blue pool. The opposite side was a clean, smooth rock wall like a block of sliced butter. Even a monkey would not be able to climb on it. A small waterfall blocked by a boulder at the top poured into the pool, splashing. Sparkling foam swirled in a slow whirlpool. I watched the blue water, holding my breath, and saw shadows well over twelve inches long, shadows that darted one after another from the dark bottom, jumping and plunging in the foam and ripples. They were chars.

I had found chars! I didn't know what they were eating, but they seemed to be in the midst of breakfast. I held my pole tightly in my left hand, and with my right clung to the top of the precipice. As I began to climb down, I found footing only deep enough for the tips of my boots. As though sneering at me, the sound of streaming water continued coldly and loudly.

Two hours later.

I was hanging on for dear life. I couldn't move an inch. I couldn't even look down at the pool any more. I was just clinging like a desperate housefly. Perspiration spurted from my whole

body, and my legs shook like aspen leaves. The wall was a one-
way route; I had somehow managed to come down this far but
I couldn't go up. I had descended, stepping half a shoe at a
time, on the wrinkles of the wall, with my face flat against it, but
I could no longer proceed. The precipice was slippery like a steel
bearing. I could not change even the direction of my body. I
had my pick in my right hand, but it was useless for going up
or down. What was I to do? The sun was beating down ferociously, blindingly. Energy was dwindling from my shoulders
and hips like a water keg that had a crack. I decided to give up
my fishing pole. The moment I opened my left fingers, something collapsed inside me. My precious tackle dropped at a sharp
speed.

He slithered down inch by inch facing the wall and stopped right
at my head. The strength of his whole body was summoned
under his snowsuit. His muscular shoulders were tense, and his
hips and legs were trembling—I could see them clearly. I wiped
my sweating brow with a shoulder and lifted my face with a
forlorn hope.

"How . . . ," I wheezed, "how did you know where I was?"

"I knew."

He was spread-eagled against the wall, looking like a bat. "You
didn't follow my direction, did you?"

I did not answer.

"You didn't turn right at the cedar, did you?"

Silence.

"I know everything."

Panting, he pressed his face against the rock and snickered.

"You were only thinking of double-crossing me. If I'd told
you to go right, you'd go left, and if I told you left, you'd go
right. I had it all figured out, so I told you the reverse of the
reverse."

He chuckled in the back of his throat, hearing me click my
tongue in fury. He inched down a step and spoke quietly.

"Be still. . . . Wait till I hold my hand out. Don't get smart ideas."

"Umm. . . ."

"You shouldn't have lied to me. You said you heard about this valley from your friend. I saw your notes while you were sleeping and found out everything. I realized you wouldn't listen to me anyway. So I decided to tell you everything—the real truth. If you had followed my direction and turned right at the cedar, you would have reached a fishing hole that would have flabbergasted you. My very special secret hole."

"You're lying."

"Don't be so positive about things you don't know. That's your bad habit. Keep still, I'm coming down for you."

"What would you do if I held your hand and didn't move?"

"If you meant to do that, you wouldn't have asked the question."

"You are a know-it-all. That's your bad habit."

"Shut up! Sour grapes!"

He worked painstakingly and put a foot down on a crack of the rock about three inches lower than where he was. Only half his shoe rested on it. I almost bored a hole through the rock staring to see whether there wasn't any dangerous fissure in it. My heart almost burst out.

"I'm asking you just once again," he said, panting. "Why didn't you follow my direction?"

"If I were going to listen to anybody, I wouldn't have come to a mountain like this."

He bent slowly, his belly adhering to the rock wall, and he lowered his arm. I stretched as far as possible and still could not reach him. He started to stoop even lower.

"Stay there!" I cried. "I'm coming up."

I put the pick under an arm. There was a tiny protuberance above me that I had not considered a possibility before. Now I reached for it, clasped it, and with both hands and all the effort of chinning-up, I raised my body slowly and stretched my left arm. I almost lost my balance in midair when I felt his hand. I let my pick go from under my arm and held onto him with both hands. I was dangling in the air above the blue depth of the pool. I looked up at the blinding precipice cutting across the steel-blue morning sky.

"Can we get out of here?" I cried out.

"We'll manage," he answered, pulling me up with all his might. "I was here alone before, but I managed to escape."

He suspended me by his right hand. With his left and his two feet he held onto the slick wall that was as elusive as a greased frying pan, and began to creep upward. His movement was tortoise slow, but as accurate as the movement of the sun.

At length, I managed to find a foothold. As I let out a sigh, the man above me continued to pull me up with his whole body, his shoulders and legs tremulous.

And still, he threatened me over my head:

"If you breathe one word about this ravine in Tokyo . . ."

Five Thousand Runaways

1

Why do bridges draw your heart so irresistibly? No matter how tired, you are tempted to give them your attention. In fact, it seems the more tired you are the more attracted you feel. From a single log bridge over a village brook to the steel-suspension structure of California's Golden Gate, all bridges hold something that fascinates, that stirs the human heart. In Parisian cafés, entertainers sing a song likening each of the Seine bridges to a type of love. One bridge is a timid yet eternal first love; one bridge is a jaded, middle-aged love; another is a secret rendezvous threatened by the march of time; one is a Saturday-night rapture drenched in perspiration; yet another is a distant firework in the memory of an old philanderer—one by one, the song pays tribute to the bridges of Paris.

Walking through a dark, deep canyon of walls, if you suddenly come upon a bridge, you feel as though a sheet of white paper has been turned over. The sky and water emerge and you stop and lift your eyes. It is not often that you encounter such a moment in a city. Does the simple transport of people and freight from here to there, from one quay to another, refresh your eyes? Unlike banks, office buildings, and department stores, the bridge is exposed under the sky, baring its hunched back, its limbs. The frankness and boldness of it refresh and soothe your eyes as you come wandering like a jellyfish in water, through the canyon of walls, the fog of gasoline, and waves of pedestrians. If there were no bridges, many, many tales and plays would never have been written.

The following events occurred because of a bridge.

There was a bridge.

One May evening about five o'clock, an executive of a firm, Mr. Teruichi Ashida, came up from the Ochanomizu subway station with a briefcase in his hand. Mr. Ashida stopped at the top of the steps to catch his breath and looked at the pale evening haze drifting to the sidewalk. The numerous automobiles reminded him of schools of fish following a rising tide into an estuary. There was a feverishness in the air. Throngs of students and office workers were ascending the station steps, pushing each other. Mr. Ashida bought a weekly magazine from an old woman at a newsstand, and after carefully brushing some sandy dust off its cover, he put it into his briefcase. His briefcase was of a fine, black, genuine leather and had in it a lunchbox, a fountain pen, tobacco, and five or six not-so-important documents.

Mr. Ashida began to cross the bridge against the human waves that moved toward him. Every time an automobile passed, the bridge shook under him, and he felt the recurrent spasms of its thick, concrete flesh. Endless waves of footsteps and shoulders surged constantly from a network of exits. At such hours, young men, irritated by their lost individuality, hardened their angry eyes and purposely bumped into strangers in an effort to arouse pleasure and excitement from unpredictable reactions. But the middle-aged, amiable Mr. Ashida chose to avoid any contact. Stepping to the side by the bridge railing, he let his eyes wander for a while. The bridge did not suggest first love, which is timid and yet may be fatal, nor the middle-aged philanderer's sensual love, neither a secret rendezvous threatened by time, nor the Saturday-night rapture drenched in perspiration. It did not recall the scent of faded perfume, as in the reminiscence of an old roué. If one really had to compare it to love, one might call it that of a jilted tramp with her eyes closed, crouching there. Mr. Ashida, carefully avoiding dust, placed his hand on the railing and looked around. On one side was a cliff covered with green grass, under which a yellow river stagnated, dotted with rubbish. Dirty flat-bottomed dinghies floated on the river. The roof of the train station, covered with red iron dust, stretched beyond, and hundreds of people swarmed underneath it. The trains came and went, blue-white lights gleaming in their windows. On the cliff were matchboxlike tearooms, noodle shops, pawn shops, and book stalls, all making their living from students. The May evening with its pastel color hovered over the squalor—greasy walls, cracks, and warped windows that resembled nests of gutter rats. Neon lights sparkled through the blue haze.

"I suppose so. . . ."

"That man's unbelievable . . . !"

"And then if you cash the check . . ."

"Kari is really working hard, isn't he?"

". . . Yes."

". . . No."

"I made it really tough for them."

"Yes, that's right, yes."

"And that's when I buckled down to . . ."

". . . gorging on fruit and bean cocktails . . ."

"Gosh, I don't like that!"

". . . Yes."

". . . No."

"The only thing you can read in that magazine is the reportage."

"I threw it into a double wait.* Damn!"

"I wrote, peach blossoms bloom on peach trees. . . ."

"Thanks, thanks,"

"Then, see you again, bye-bye!"

". . . Yes."

". . . No."

A bridge is a bridge is a bridge even if it is like a tramp. The pastel haze of twilight disappeared and the evening of a dark oil painting now surrounded him. The yellow river, green cliff, soiled flatboats, the dirt, grease, and warped windows of students' eateries alternately faded out and then suddenly appeared with a flash. Mr. Ashida looked at the small figures of men and women in the windows or on the cliff, eating, talking, pondering, or busily walking. He looked at the crowd waiting under the long roof of the station. The pedestrians on the bridge had thinned out. Only a few minutes ago, the crowd had had the vitality of salmon swimming against an upstream current, an air of insurgency; but everything had vanished. Meanwhile, the bridge had stopped trembling, and its thick concrete flesh had stiffened and chilled. Through his skin, Mr. Ashida felt the slow but mercilessly accurate rotation of a gigantic axis somewhere.

It had been many, many years since he had last noticed the hidden charm of an evening city. He felt a liquid softness suffuse his body while he looked down on the station, people, and river from his vantage point. He did not know what part of the bridge created such a feeling, but it seemed to generate an irresistible power without passion, poignancy, or determination. He was no longer able to use excuses for waiting, such as avoiding the crowds or taking breath. He felt a mysterious lightness. His buoyancy and cheerful serenity puzzled him. Where could it have come from—in this city filled with noise, irritants, dirt, obscenity, this shallow and energetic, polluted, flat city that would taste like the

---

*A double game in mah-jongg.—Trans.

inside of an empty tin can? This new mood teased Mr. Ashida
with its little finger, luring him away.

Tomorrow I have a board meeting.
Saturday, there's a PTA meeting.
Must go to the bank tomorrow afternoon.
Must work on the lawn in the garden.
I have no raincoat with me.
I have only my lunchbox.
I have no map.
Do I stay at an inn?
Where do I stay?
Without a reservation?
I hope there's a seat in the train.

At last, he thought of his home in the Suginami district. There
was a tiny lawn garden, with a surrounding wall made of Ōya
rocks* covered with climbing ivy. The rocks seemed to swell
modestly like a sponge when they absorbed rain. In the short
time since the ivy had been planted, it had spread all over, re-
sembling the bulging veins on a young man's hand. A mercury
lamp stood in a corner of the garden. In summer, a movable
stove was brought out under the lamp and barbecue dinners
were served, after a fashion. Perhaps because a section of the
Musashino woods still remained in the vicinity, once a long-horn
beetle flew into the house. His little daughter caught it nervously
and pinned it down in her entomic collection box. His wife bought
an illustrated entomological encyclopedia and, glued to her
daughter's side, taught her the beetle's Latin and Japanese names
and made her write about them in her school diary. His wife
was completely devoted to such matters. She would make her

---

*The light blue-green tufa that comes from Ōya in Tochigi Prefecture is used
as garden and construction material.—TRANS.

daughter sit at the piano in a corner of their Western-style room and practice for hours on end. She would strike chords, and the two females would shout to each other, *"cheh, deh, hah!"* (C-D-H) or *"eh, ghe, hah!"* (E-G-H). Mr. Ashida didn't know anything about the piano. He seldom listened and he couldn't play. Sometimes when he was annoyed, he hurled the newspaper from his sofa and blared out the silly parodies he used to sing in his childhood, but the females of his household only laughed at him.

After the piano, his wife would start a watercolor, her daughter's homework. At one or two o'clock at night, she would complete a picture that looked too finished for a child, but too clumsy for an adult, and put it quietly by the pillow of her soundly sleeping daughter. Then, filled with the pleasure of complete physical exhaustion, she would creep into her bed. Mr. Ashida slept alone on the second floor. Clad in pajamas of red and blue candy stripes that his wife had bought for him at Isetan, he would examine a balance sheet or read a novel about the art of becoming invisible for exactly one hour, and after drinking exactly two glasses of whiskey and a glass of water, he would creep into his bed. In the morning, his wife would send her daughter to school and then polish Mr. Ashida's shoes. In a while, the company car would arrive to meet him. His wife would cheerily take a cup of tea flavored with roasted rice to the driver.

In his office, Mr. Ashida alternately used the dialects of Osaka and Tokyo. He spoke the Osaka dialect to bankers and government officials and the Tokyo dialect to subcontractors and other businessmen. With his subordinates, he used the Tokyo accent in the office, and the Osaka accent at bars and restaurants. When applying pressure, he used the Tokyo accent, when relaxing, the Osaka accent. For some reason, the system seemed to work for him. He had begun to use it a long time ago, not consciously knowing when.

He was the director in charge of finance. His was not a large firm, but he had a large teak desk, a side table, and a capable-if-not-pretty spinster secretary. He had carefully stayed both outside and inside of all the political factions of the company, manipulating his Osaka and Tokyo accents as needed. The company manufactured paint and had its main office in a Nihonbashi building. It had a consistent record of neither a huge profit nor a huge deficit. Among the trade journals and newspapers, the company had a reputation as a well-bred, quiet, honor-roll concern. It had never been written up in a roman à clef of business-world scandal.

Mr. Ashida always walked the corridors with deliberate slowness. With intellect revealed in his forehead, generosity in his chin, and a tender smile rounding his cheeks, he regarded people kindly. He told a few off-color jokes at bars, never got involved with women, read only the headlines in the newspaper, never listened to the radio, never watched the television. When others let him, however, he showed amazingly broad knowledge, and he professed to be a Hanshin fan in baseball. He never bought serialized collections of world literature or art books and never read best-sellers, but he was remarkably well informed.

He bathed every other day. He copulated with his wife once a week (his prophylactic was a condom), the required time ranging from five to twenty minutes. On Sundays, he sometimes played golf. The club fees, as well as the bar expenses, were charged against the company account. For sushi, he ate only the hand-rolled tuna; his tea was the kind mixed with roasted brown rice; he liked a simple stir-fried vegetable dish cooked with fried tofu; when he became very drunk at Western-style bars, he sang an old French popular song; at Japanese restaurants, he moaned out an old popular Japanese song. His favorite saying was: "There's nothing new under the sun." The company's young secretaries thought he was a real gentleman, and the young men thought he was a regular nihilist as intellectuals of his generation all were at one time. Other directors trusted that he would take care of them through the evening no matter how drunk they became. The banks had confidence in him because he was the kind of man who would strike a stone bridge with a cane before crossing, and then again after crossing to make sure he hadn't broken the bridge. Sometimes young critics in trade journals scorned him as a "happy sea-anemone," and middle-aged critics described him as an "overworked third-class executive." Mr. Ashida paid them absolutely no attention, thinking that they would change their tunes in several years.

I must go to the bank about the loan.
  A board meeting tomorrow.
  PTA on Saturday.
  A half day at the office.

Standing in the dark, Mr. Ashida looked pensively down at the station and the river. He remembered again that he did not have a raincoat with him but only a lunchbox in his briefcase. He thought about a map, hotel reservations, train tickets, and all kinds of things. He patiently waited for these problems to turn into a sharp rasp that would scrape away this cheerful, inexplicable buoyancy and force him back to his sensible daily self. The small figures moving behind the distant, shining windows on the cliff insisted on returning to his eyes. His wife, daughter, mercury lamp in the garden, teak desk, and mounds of documents for some reason also appeared in the far distance and remained silent. Mr. Ashida remembered his secret savings account of about 200,000 yen in a Shinjuku bank. He looked at his watch and noted it was six o'clock. Banks had closed a long time ago. But he remembered also that one particular branch had widely publicized its special evening hours. After leaning against the bridge rail for a while, he began to walk casually. He stopped at a small drugstore in front of the Ochanomizu station and bought a toothbrush, toothpaste, towel, and soap and put them into his briefcase.

2

After withdrawing his 200,000-yen nest egg, Mr. Ashida returned to the Tokyo station. Since he had earlier gone through the station to take the subway, and he had commuted, he had gone through the Tokyo station altogether three times on this day. Wearing a gray flannel suit that fitted elegantly, he went into the station calmly, with an air of a middle-aged executive commuter from the Shōnan summer-home area. He bought a novel based on the art of invisibility at the newsstand and put it into his bag, and he paid sixty yen to a shoeshine woman for giving his shoes a specially good shine. He had added a ten-yen tip to the fifty-yen charge. The shoeshiner was a buglike old woman, but, upon receiving the money from him, she began to work on his shoes with an apparent determination to split every seam. Even through the thick leather, the vigorous massage was pleasantly felt, and the waves of sensation spiraled up his calves to his hips and buttocks. His shoes polished, he made his way to the ticket window and asked for a sleeping-car ticket to Osaka. No second-class berth was available, so he bought a first-class ticket. He had not spent his money with such pleasure in many, many years. He was surprised that spending could give him so much pleasure. It was a strange discovery for a director of finance who handled billions of yen every month. The buoyancy that had seized Mr. Ashida by the shoulder, the back of the head, and especially behind his ears on the Ochanomizu bridge continued to bubble and to obliterate all physical fatigue. While he had been waiting on the tacky vinyl sofa in the Shinjuku bank for his turn to receive cash, and after he had left the bank and was walking through the crowd, and even in the roaring noise of the subway, he felt a kind of light hovering over his head like a nimbus. It never faded away. If it had gone out, Mr. Ashida's modest odyssey would not have materialized, but it did not. He did not turn into a beetle or a bedbug, nor did he shine in glory or change into a brick in order to assert his rebellion.

You might say that a slight transformation did take place in his appetite. He bought a box of rice balls sprinkled with sesame seeds that came with another box of vegetables and meat, as well as a pot of tea, at the Tokyo station. He bought Chinese dumplings at Yokohama, and planned to buy sandwiches and milk at the Ōfuna station, but the train failed to stop at Ōfuna. So he gave up the sandwiches grudgingly. Instead, he jumped out in his underwear at the Shizuoka station platform and bought a pickled-horseradish lunch and tea. In Hamamatsu, he was sleeping but suddenly woke up and ran out to buy an eel lunch. He piled up these lunchboxes by the new, stiff white pillow in his compartment and slowly but continuously consumed the contents of box after box, alternating a mouthful of rice with a mouthful of tea while he read his story about the art of invisibility. The story exerted a formidable magnetism when read in the complete vacuum of a night train.

In the novel, a boy magus is dueling with an old magus. After exhausting all the techniques of invisibility, they have come to throwing knives at each other. The boy's knife pierces the right eye of the old man; the latter pulls out the knife and hurls it back, stabbing the boy's right shoulder; the boy draws it out and lances the old man's left eye; the old man pulls it out and flings it at the boy's left shoulder. The boy loses the use of his arms; the old man loses his eyes. After stalking each other briefly, the two begin to fight again. The boy blows the knife out of his mouth and stabs the right arm of the old man, who throws it back with his left. The boy's right eye is pierced; he extracts the knife with his mouth and ejects it; the knife plunges into the old man's left arm. He pulls it off with his feet and throws it back. Thus, they continue the pulling and throwing and turn into two bloody, sluglike creatures. The boy finally strangles his opponent with his right arm. What? Wasn't his right arm stabbed? Well, the story has a surprise ending in that he turns out to be an illegitimate son of the famous one-arm Tange Sazen, and his left arm is lost but the other is artificial and as good as a natural arm.

On the dust cover was a critic's recommendation: "The tales of this writer, filled with fantastic imagination, will catapult modern men, who have turned into mice of the office district, into a flurry of action, and, transforming reality into an instant chaos, pervade the universe with the heroic but vacuous laughter of its protagonists!" Mr. Ashida was very much puzzled by this statement. But, surrounded by the green curtains of his berth, he continued to read the tale without paying much attention to it. The antiquated style of writing added spice that made the nonsense of the story more palatable. For several hours he forgot to look at his watch. He finished reading about half the book at the same time that he had finished eating the rice, dumplings, pickled horseradish, and eels. He stretched out, moaning with a pleasurable fatigue, and realized that his stomach, which had been as lean as a dried herring at the Tokyo station, was now blown-up like a pregnant salmon. As the train pulled into the Osaka station in the morning, he felt around his face with a hand and found it very greasy and sticky, unsuitable for one who might be called a "solitary atom in flight."

The station washroom was filled with men with puffed eyelids who were shaving and washing. Looking into the mirror, he found in the smudged pale fog of the mirror with peeled-off mercury the vague face of a man who looked sixty years old, bloated and with deep circles under his eyes. After he had washed his face with cold water, the wrinkles finally tightened and the puffiness reduced, and there appeared something close to the face that he customarily presented at his office.

Mr. Ashida knew Osaka well. He was born and had been brought up here, and after graduating from the university he had gone to Tokyo and joined the present firm. His age had doubled since then. In the interim, he had made many business trips back to Osaka. His firm had a branch office and important clients throughout Osaka. He had made enough business visits to know the city well. He could have rattled off several addresses and telephone numbers. But coming out of the washroom, he did not attempt to call anyone or to catch a taxi to go to them.

This elegant gentleman in the light gray flannel suit watched men and women of all ages emerging from the station and swarming toward the office districts. He walked slowly into a crowded back street of eateries behind the station and sneaked into one of the stalls with a sign for rice, soup, et cetera, and ordered noodle soup. While the noodles cooked, he leaned his elbow against the warped table and read a sports newspaper. The noodles served, he vigorously shook red-hot pepper from a rusty tin can over them and began to eat, blowing the steam off with puckered lips. Then he opened his mouth unashamedly and picked his teeth with a toothpick as he watched the dogs sniff around the alley gutters and the sunshine beaming playfully on the tin roofs of tenement houses. He paid, looked at his watch, and walked over to a movie theater. The first show of the day was just starting, and only a handful of customers were scattered about the theater. The film rattled noisily and ceaselessly in the projector. It was a weird experience to sit and chuckle by himself in an empty movie house at this hour of the day. Mr. Ashida watched a romantic comedy involving well-nourished American men and women on Miami Beach and chuckled, but soon the melancholy of a man drinking alone in an empty house began to envelop him. He decided to close his eyes and sleep. He was not used to English speech and, once his eyes were closed, he could not tell lovers' whispers on a summer evening from the noise of automobiles. He fell sound asleep from the fatigue induced by reading the night before.

When he awoke, he was in his seat, bent like an old nail, his shoulders and hips aching. The first show and the intermission had just finished, and the commercials were on the screen. A girl and a dog were fighting for a piece of chocolate on the gigantic silver screen. Palm trees soon appeared, the surf, a colossal white hotel; the long, long hotel bar where a one-hundred-yard dash might be possible; beautiful girls flashing white teeth; the back muscles of water-skiing youths that looked like maps; corny jokes told in expensive nightclubs; tuxedoes with Chesterfield collars; kisses exchanged hastily behind a statue in the bush. . . .

The moment Mr. Ashida stepped out of the movie house, a million needles coming from the May afternoon sun pierced his eyes. The intestinelike food alley was exposed to the brilliant light. Vegetable pancakes, skewed pork cutlets, boiled vegetables, fresh buckwheat noodles, "The Second Best Steak House in the World," sukiyaki, a classical-music tearoom, "Pachinko House for Consciousness Raising," "Suigetsu-Seafood Cuisine," . . .

As he walked on the narrow, cracked pavement sprayed with water, Mr. Ashida felt the scenes of Miami Beach peel off from his retina one by one. Somehow he felt left behind in desolation. Why was it that seeing a movie in the morning made him feel as though he had taken part in a terrible debauchery? All organs slipped out of his body, melted and disappeared. He felt as though all the fluids in his body had been drained and his bones were scarcely held together by the skin. Then he felt his body vanish, leaving only his eyes and feet moving. Automobiles, trains, department stores, men, women, old folk, children, he wondered, why do they all look as if they had some secret energy stored somewhere? They seem to have iron intestines, while I feel like a snail dissolving in salt. No one turns around to look at me, a man undergoing a metamorphosis in broad daylight.

Walking through the intestine, Mr. Ashida saw an inn with a sign reading COUPLES WELCOME—ALPINE VILLA and stepped in. The cheap building was styled after a European castle in children's storybooks, with a stained-glass rose window. The single glass door at the entrance was heavy, and he pushed it with some difficulty and entered the dim foyer. The rug and the velvet on the corridor wall were vermilion red. It was as though he had stepped into a puddle of blood at night. The night-light at the bottom of the wall must have been infrared. A chime rang somewhere after he had taken two or three steps. A pallid, skinny, foxlike middle-aged woman appeared in the night and blood, eating a *takoyaki*.*

"A short time?"

"No."

"Overnight?"

"Yes."

---

*Snack of fried dough with pieces of octopus in it.—TRANS.

"Are you alone?"

"Yes. Do you have a quiet room?"

The woman looked sharply up and down at Mr. Ashida for a few minutes and seemed to be reassured. She crammed her mouth with another *takoyaki* that had been hidden in her hand. It must have been hot; she touched her earlobe in a hurry to cool her fingers. She shrugged and, signaling Mr. Ashida to follow her, disappeared soundlessly into the night and blood. She must have decided there was no fear of his committing suicide, common among the single guests. Speaking for the first time since the day before in more than monosyllables, Mr. Ashida was somehow relieved. This was also his first experience in such a house, so he cautiously carried his shoes with him. The fox-woman noticed, gulped down her *takoyaki*, and yelled in her astonishingly hoarse voice.

"Good heavens! Don't you trust us? We don't cook your shoes and eat them, you know! Leave them at the entrance hall!"

Mr. Ashida was shocked and tottered back to the hall and timidly left his shoes in a corner of the small square paved with flagstones.

He followed the red carpet up the stairs into a very erotic Japanese room. There was a formal alcove along the wall and, for some kind of good luck, a scroll of Dharma was hanging and a television and a radio stood under it. As he casually pushed the sliding door mounted with indigo-cotton kimono fabric, the next room appeared before his eyes, with its already prepared bedding on the floor. The wall was sprayed with gold-green sand. A pair of pillows with fresh pink pillowcases were neatly placed. He tried the door along the wall and found a washroom decorated with navy-blue tiles. Pulling open the inner glass door, he found a kidney-shaped bathtub and pink-tiled ceiling and walls. How could they cram so much into such a small space! It was like a crossword puzzle! Amazed, Mr. Ashida was trying various switches and buttons when the fox-woman reappeared holding a teacup on a tray.

"Would you like to take a bath?"

"Do you have hot water at this hour?"

"We do."

"Then, draw bath water for me."

"Are you going to check the temperature yourself?"

"Yes, I will."

As soon as the woman left, Mr. Ashida stripped himself and immersed in the kidney-shaped bathtub. The hot water seeped into his tired skin and penetrated each vertebra in his spinal column. Mr. Ashida stretched luxuriously and closed his eyes. The feeling of dissolution he had had when leaving the movie house had already gone. In the interim, the fluids had returned to his body. He felt friendly toward the tile wall, bathtub, taps, and plastic water buckets. He had regained control of objects. He felt the nimble lightness return to his ears. Slightly puzzled by the red and blue illuminations periodically blinking in the bathtub, Mr. Ashida nevertheless felt a sense of well-being and poured warm water over his head, rinsed his mouth, and washed his body.

Returning to the bedroom, he flopped onto the bedding with a big thud and, from his horizontal position, casually pushed open a screen door on the wall. This house seemed to have all sorts of hidden devices. Although he had not been surprised much by the illuminated bathtub, he had not expected the same kind of devices that had been enjoyed by the Sun King at Versailles so close at hand. Behind the sliding door was a complete wall of mirror and, lo and behold, a middle-aged man, resting his head on the pink pillow, was sprawled out. Clad in a disheveled cotton kimono, his spindly legs and arms spread-eagled, he was gazing back intently at Mr. Ashida. Momentarily, Mr. Ashida was startled, but he looked back at the image unabashed. The man in the looking glass glared back at him with an after-bath glow on his forehead.

He muttered, and the man in the wall moved his lips. He seemed to have muttered the same word.

Mr. Ashida drew the door over the mirror, pulled the novel about the invisibles out of his briefcase and resumed his reading.

3

The author seems to be writing a rather undistinguished self-exile story. But, with this kind of hero, a despair or nihilism or rebellion of epic proportion is in no way possible. The author is not unaware of the need for fortitude and tenacity in solidly uneventful lives, like those of the nameless insects that will eventually dig channels and tunnels through walnut shells. The author respects and values them; for this reason, he is often intimidated into a helpless condition. Mr. Teruichi Ashida freed himself from all anchors and began to drift. The author has succeeded as far as setting him free from the Ochanomizu bridge. But no indulgence on your part will convince you that Ashida can be a Gauguin, a Rimbaud, or a Lawrence. The artist, the poet, and the revolutionary never for a moment forgot to maintain a never-ending dream, a high curve in their daily life. Thus they are identified with the grass of a South Sea island or a grain of desert sand, and they left a rainbow-colored inspiration for the millions of bookish young rebels to come after them. Is Mr. Ashida taking an undescending high curve or a never-stopping straight line? Seeing that he is muttering to the mirror in the shady hotel in Osaka, the author is quite confused as to what sort of line he should let him take. He doesn't know whether he should continue to write in his mysterious, unintelligible style, to unleash or diminish Ashida's passion for flight. First of all, did Ashida leave his home in order to expand or to shrink?

The quiet middle-aged gentleman began to drift on the streets of Osaka in his now slightly wrinkled gray flannel suit. He spent one night at the Alpine Villa and had the fox-woman bring a newspaper in the morning. He examined the apartment ads from cover to cover. In about two hours, he left the inn with his briefcase, never to return. Several hours later, he was seen at a small real-estate office in front of the suburban Takatsuki station. Then, in another hour, he was found paying cheerfully, in addition to the monthly rent, a series of mysterious charges labeled bond money, key money, gratuity, then settling in a room in a new two-story cinderblock apartment house next to a rice field. He was then seen stretching comfortably and reading the last chapter of his book on the art of being invisible. The four-and-a-half-mat room was filled with the aroma of new, green, rush mats. From the window, he could see the fields, high-voltage lines, steel structures, and the roof of an electric machine shop. The walls seemed not quite dry yet, and the bathroom walls in the corridor were studded with hardened drips of cement. The scent of wood was pervasive throughout, and the staircase creaked with newness and crude workmanship. The walls, pillars, corridors, windows, everything was square and white and emitted a fresh scent; there was no hint of dirt or grease. Mr. Ashida finished the novel and took a nap, and when he woke up, he gave some money to the caretaker downstairs and had him buy a quilt and blanket.

For about one week, he slept, every day until midday, then he read the newspaper in bed from cover to cover. He read about things he understood or did not understand: the government's tax policy, the Vietnam War, beef-stew recipes, obituaries. He did not skip a word. Running out of reading material, he read the newspaper publisher's address and telephone number. Flat on the fresh green mat and wrapped in a thin but fresh quilt and a fresh cotton kimono, he hung onto the newspaper for hours. His profile was peace itself, and he seemed to hate to finish the paper. When he finally relinquished his right to the paper and folded the bedding neatly and put it into the closet, he washed his face, brushed his teeth, and went into town. He strolled slowly in the sunshine of an early May afternoon, looking at the sky, the field, the directions into which the high-voltage wires ran, presenting an image completely foreign to the Japanese race. He had the image of a wealthy, purposeless, content stroller. People smelled in him a fresh, refined purposelessness as he walked under the ginkgo promenade in the Umeda District or on Shinsai Bridge Boulevard or on Midō Boulevard. He seemed to trail behind him a generous, transparent wake in the tumultuous, restless city crowds.

Mr. Ashida looked into the shop windows, at the shining opals, at the hands of sushi makers fluttering like birds in treetops, and inhaled the aroma of freshly ground powdered green tea at the tea shop. He bought some fruit or a cake, and once he even asked for men's cologne at a cosmetic counter and selected a Givenchy cologne after trying samples. He would not go into a mah-jongg shop or a *go* club filled with dust and odors, but instead visited a deserted basement poolroom like an aquarium. He liked to feel its desolation and sobriety in the echoes of ivory balls.

It had become his habit to bring fruit or cake for the girl attendant, so, as soon as she saw through the glass door the legs of Mr. Ashida descending the lonely staircase, she would dash to open the door for him. A girl with a face like a potato adorned with parsley snips, she had a habit of transfixing herself against the wall and nibbling her nails down to the quick. Customers seldom dropped in, so she had nothing to do. She would bite into one of the apples Mr. Ashida had given her and, like a squirrel, leave sharp teeth marks on it.

While Mr. Ashida shot pool, the girl would eagerly open the cake box and begin to eat a piece ravenously. If she asked him questions, he generously laughed and answered in the Osaka accent.

"What kind of cake is this?"

"It's a German cake."

"It looks like a tree stump."

"You're pretty sharp. It's called *Baum Kuchen*. It means tree cake in German, too."

"What do you do, sir?"

"I'm a rich man's son."

"You're always loafing, aren't you?"

"I have nothing else to do."

"Oh, lucky you! You can loaf and play clumsy pool all day. You have it made! I wish I were in your shoes."

"I was born clumsy."

"You really are clumsy!"

"You don't have to be so frank about it."

"I just said it. I didn't really mean it."

Pong!

"Oh, you hit the ball!"

"How unusual!"

"Isn't it though!" the girl said.

After playing pool for about two hours, Mr. Ashida resumed his fresh, refined, unpurposeful stroll. Sometimes he saw movies, some other times he attended the Shōchiku comedy theater. In the evening, he looked for a restaurant. Purposely, he always selected a small dirty place in an alley. He enjoyed being sometimes right and sometimes wrong in his intuition about where to get good or bad food. After the meal, he walked a little more, then returned to his apartment in Takatsuki with its green scent of tatami mats. Sometimes, he stood in the back of a burlesque theater to watch a striptease. One night, he was watching a woman dance for a long time without making any attempt to remove the sinful triangle when an irritated spectator with a flushed face stood up and began to shout, "Hey, get down to business and do it right!"

A week or ten days later, Mr. Ashida awoke a little after noon as usual. His bed was surrounded by magazines, towels, a soap box, ashtrays, and a cologne bottle. Even though he was in flight, life was still life. A change had come to the room. Something transparent, light, and misty seemed to waft in the room. He had not seen anything two or three days before, but he now noticed the change clearly. All the objects in the room had been purchased in town, all fresh and newborn. They were scattered on the new, green, green-smelling, fresh mats. Until several days ago, the objects, shining hard like mine ore that had just been unearthed, were protesting against the green mats. Now the hardness was gone and the contours of the objects seemed to have softened, mellowed, and even fused slightly with the mats. The mats, too, seemed to have lost their firmness.

Mr. Ashida stretched his legs from the bed and with his toes pulled out the newspaper that had been inserted between the door and the sill. It was his new trick. He drew his leg to his chest and dropped the newspaper on his stomach. Then he held it in his hands above his face. After scanning the headlines on the first page, he dug into the contents, his eyes moving slightly up and down, following the dry prosaic sentences. Politics, editorials, local news, entertainment, housekeeping, recipes, fishing, chess . . . Then, his eyes began to search earnestly in the want ads. One at a time, from right to left, he traced the small, solidly packed columns that looked like a printer's font box. Finishing this action, he fell into deep thought but soon rose from the bed and put on his trousers.

He walked out in a pair of wooden clogs borrowed from the woman caretaker of the apartment. Contrary to his usual style, he hurried over to a stationery store in front of the station and bought five forms for personal resumés and a small bottle of ink. Back at the apartment, he lay flat on his stomach on the bedding and began to write his vita, flopping his legs to find a comfortable position. In his neat handwriting, he printed his new apartment number as his address, his date of birth, a summary of his education, and his job history.

As he reflected briefly on his past, everything seemed strangely remote. Why did he feel no stirring in his heart several hundred miles away from home? If he had run away several more hundred miles to some strange town, would he have felt something? In this apartment, he never even thought of his wife or of his daughter. The mercury lamp in the garden, his daughter's piano, and his wife bending over her painting till late at night—these images always lurked in a corner of his head, but they were no more than very distant flickering miniature pictures separated from him by some vast dusky space. He could remember, one after another, things like his office building in Nihonbashi, his teak desk, his secretary, board meetings, annual financial reports, balance sheets, prospectuses, bars at night where his young subordinates talked, sputtering words like race horses spitting foam, greens at the golf course, bankers who smiled with faces but never with eyes. But they were all distant, remote miniatures beyond the dusky vast space. Why were they so far away, so small, and so dark? And why did such a perfect and sudden revenge as his bring no satisfaction?

There was nothing that penetrated his skin. He did discover, it seemed, how ambiguous and ephemeral things such as "work," "relationship," and "home" were, but what of it? Was this a feeling akin to that of a scholar who has just discovered some harmless new bacteria? Did he feel vacuous because he lacked the happy madness of a scholar whose passion and energy were poured into the idea of discovery, rather than the thing discovered? Had he been so badly tired that he had decided to take this peculiar little vacation? Traveling a little, spending a little, tasting pleasure a little, and showing a little bit that he was master, and spending some 200,000 yen to recall his youth with a clumsy game of pool—was that all?

Mr. Ashida spent the next day loafing. He had left the neatly written resumés scattered on the floor. He would expose his plans to the sunshine and to the night air during his long walk, and if they could stand the test and did not putrefy or rust, then he would carry them out. He bought a bottle of cheap perfume for the girl, went to the poolroom, walked on Shinsaibashi Boulevard twice and Midō Boulevard once, peeped into a beautiful but unintelligible French film, then ate a rice dish and clam stew. Toward nine o'clock, he returned to his apartment feeling rather tired. He slept soundly, and when he awoke the next morning he read not the newspaper but his resumé. He read it slowly, word by word, but did not detect any putrefaction or rust. He put his resumés and the ad clippings that had given him some ideas in his jacket breast pocket. He shaved carefully, brushed his teeth thoroughly, and put a drop of Givenchy behind his ears. Soon, there appeared on the road to the station a dignified man with a smile, fresh, competent and experienced looking, soft but sharp eyed, a man who seemed, rather than a cheerful stroller with no purpose, a man devoted to running a business as smoothly as well-oiled gears.

On this day, Mr. Ashida, with his resumé, had interviews at three second-rate cabarets, one high-class restaurant, and one medium-size belt-manufacturing plant. They had all advertised in the newspaper for an "expert manager." The belt-manufacturing shop was a shabby, small place smeared with machine oil. After talking for thirty minutes with him, the owner rebuffed him before he had the chance to bring up the matter of his salary. "Let me think about it," the owner said, smiling wryly and scratching his head. He probably thought that Mr. Ashida's appearance and deportment were too elegant and that he could not afford him.

Ashida thought it over and decided to use the Osaka accent for the next interview. He also decided to say that he was looking for a job because the wholesale industrial-chemical business he had owned with a friend had gone bankrupt because of bad accounts. Nevertheless, the restaurant and cabaret managers who interviewed him were suspicious, looking at him uneasily as though at an elegant crane that had alighted in a dust bin. "We'll get in touch with you," or "We aren't in the position to hire you." They offered these answers with overly sweet orange drinks.

The last cabaret he visited was built strictly for a nighttime appearance, and the sunlight exposed the cracks in the thin mortar walls and the maps made by rains that had leaked in. The matchboxes said, "Dance Palace, *Sans Souci*," printed on cheap paper, pasted hurriedly and wrinkled. He walked in from the back entrance, where the gutters vomited mud. He climbed the narrow, worn-out, boarded staircase, feeling as though creeping into a pore of a completely dried-out sponge. But Mr. Ashida eagerly went into the telephone-box office of the owner and began to speak in his fluent Osaka accent.

The owner, with a face like a pale earthworm from a barren land, seemed to be thinking of something else while listening. Mr. Ashida looked into his eyes, buried in a mesh of little wrinkles, but could not fathom what lurked beyond them. On the office wall was an advertisement for lowest-grade saké. On the wall of a cabaret! Not a glass of orange drink, coffee, or even water was offered. The earthworm looked at the middle-aged gentleman who had come into the dustbin trailing the fragrance of Givenchy. He glared from his rotating chair on which a broken spring protruded. He said abruptly, "I pay very little." Mr. Ashida looked at the undernourished man with a big head and began to think that a man like this was sometimes an unsuspected lady-killer, with a big tool, greedy, stingy enough to wring a dry rag. He would be living in the slum, pleading poverty, but actually he would have stashed away plenty. Mr. Ashida's imagination had grown terribly vulgar, probably because of his alienated drifting.

"I don't know whether you are good at management. I want you to look at my books and analyze them. I'll make the decision after that. I'll put my cards on the table, and I want you to do the same. Then, we'll talk."

"You are pretty straightforward," said Mr. Ashida.

"I don't like to hear gripes afterward."

As he thumbed through the ledger handed over by the worm-man, Mr. Ashida could see in less than twenty minutes the quagmire and its depth and the shabbiness of the life this man had got himself into. Mr. Ashida had a rare gift for seeing men in columns of figures. He could judge that the owner of this cabaret was not particularly avaricious, not a bastard. He only needed money badly and was in bad straits. That was all. It was obvious that he sweated over his book trying to make ends meet, and what he needed was someone else who would take charge of the book and do all the detail work for him.

"All right."

"Did you understand?"

"Yes, I did."

"Do you think you would like to work for me?"

"I think so."

Looking up at the face of Mr. Ashida, who had unwittingly

slipped back into the Tokyo accent, the earthworm who had seemed a wheeler-dealer suddenly broke up his face like a happy child. Mr. Ashida felt uneasy, imagining that a wet floor-mop had suddenly broken into explosive laughter.

"And the salary?"

The worm-man glanced at Mr. Ashida and did a strange thing. He took Ashida's hand and let it wrap around his own fingers. His desiccated yet clammy, bony fingers wriggled in Mr. Ashida's palm. Is this how contracts were made in this area? The man kept his fingers in Mr. Ashida's hand and talked with a simpering coquetry.

"Will this do?"

Mr. Ashida could not answer.

"I've put my cards on the table, so you know how my business is. I can't pretend and make you angry. Will you agree to this?"

He shook Mr. Ashida's hand lightly several times. This unexpected behavior caught Mr. Ashida completely off guard, and he was speechless for a minute. He had not been aware that such a way of persuading existed. He felt as though a dead animal that he had been poking with a stick had suddenly come to life and attacked him. To make it worse, it was not a haphazard attack, but seemed to aim at Ashida's weakness. He was ruffled for the first time since his flight. Without any idea how many fingers were in his palm, he mumbled hesitantly.

"How about just a little more?"

"You are a haggler."

The man whispered as though he had seen through Ashida. His eyes glistened. His insidious voice seemed to hide some violent power. He glared at Ashida and withdrew his other fingers, but with his little finger, he nudged Ashida's palm lightly several times.

"That's it!" he said.

Ashida had lost his poise and failed to detect how many fingers were involved. He muttered, "That will do."

From the next day, Mr. Ashida commuted to the cabaret and worked diligently for two months. He came to his office early

in the evening and sat at the desk in the telephone-box office
and straightened the ledger and the bills. After 11:30, when the
cabaret closed, he descended the staircase to the street. In the
office, he worked in shirt-sleeves, wiping perspiration, turning
the pages of the ledger, plucking an abacus, writing figures on
scratch pads, catching figures that escaped, and digging out figures that hid their heads but stuck out their tails and transplant-
ing them to the right column. He contemplated, scrutinized,
pondered, and clicked his tongue. He totaled and sorted out,
and after each examination, he called the worm-man and asked
for explanations.

The worm-man, who had had to chew his poverty for a long
time like the sole of an old shoe, would praise Mr. Ashida's
financial acumen and diligence, and say that the cabaret began
to wear a halo. To explain his difficulties, he would rattle off
complicated excuses in a small voice and blame his female employees' slovenliness in a loud voice. He flashed forth with sharpness and violence sometimes, and fell into a hopeless sand hole
of sloth and obsequiousness other times. Mr. Ashida did not
know whether such a thing as a honeyed whip existed, or even
if it did what purpose it would serve. But this worm-man reminded him of a whip dipped in thick honey. Sometimes it would
thrash out, whipping the air; at other times it would stick to some
worthless object and wrap itself around it for days on end and
would not let go.

The worm-man scolded and coaxed his dancers who came
begging for wages he owed them, in the end succeeding in turning them down. Yet, if a snack vendor came asking him to clear
the 230 yen in his credit account, he apologized good-naturedly
and opened his wallet. His masterly performance in soliciting
pity would have melted the heart of a veteran loan shark who
could chisel money out of rocks. Yet he once stayed home three
or four days without contacting his office, and when Mr. Ashida
asked what he had been doing, he answered that he had been
in bed trying to solve a chess problem for a roadside chess gambler. Every night, the tiny office shook with the deafening sounds

of the band through the paper-thin wall. One after another, women came asking for their wages, entreating, threatening, swearing, sneering, seducing, play-acting, guffawing, sobbing— to be subjected to them was enough to make anyone's skin grow as thick as an elephant's.

Leaving the cabaret at 11:30, an exhausted Ashida would walk through the tawdry, neon-polluted, trash-strewn desert, feeling that only three or four frazzled nerves remained in his head.

For two months, Mr. Ashida never went back to the poolroom, nor did he buy a German pastry or cologne. He was never bedazzled by the sparkling of an opal or lured by the aroma of ground green tea. He never saw a French film or a Shōchiku comedy. He slept longer and got up later than before, and he read only the headlines in the newspaper. The light gray flannel suit was now stained as though he had dropped some strong liquid chemical on it, and the wrinkles on it were ineradicable. A small jungle of objects grew at his bedside as he never threw away anything and never cleaned the room. He used his room only for sleeping. Bills, ledger sheets, calling cards, matchboxes, half-eaten sandwiches, napkins, forks, and knives were now among the ashtrays and the soapbox. Cigarettes burned holes through the mats, and the fresh green smell of the rush mats diminished. All objects were glued down to the mats the minute they were left there; they fused into the scene. New things and old things became indistinguishable. Buried in them, he slept away while days and weeks melted into each other, and he forgot what day of what month it was the moment after he looked at the newspaper.

Sounds also became indistinguishable. He would probably not know the difference between the ivory balls colliding and echoing in the basement poolroom and a bucket falling somewhere. Since his flight, his daily vocabulary had become limited, but recently it had become further diminished in the extreme. Every evening, the collectors showed up furtively like hyenas, or ran up the steps boisterously, but Mr. Ashida kept his head down, silently smoking. Hyenas gone, he would turn to his desk and transfer the figures like a typesetter. Every night, after work, his tongue felt as it if had grown spiny like a swollen centipede.

One early summer night, God looked down and saw at the Osaka station a late-middle-aged man creep into a second-class sleeper of an express train to Tokyo. The man had in his cerebral cortex such words and expressions as *stuff, dealer, knifing, broad, making it, squealing, Lothario, giving one's mark, crow-money,** and phrases such as "What're you gonna do for me?" "No go," "I gotta buy milk for my baby . . ." "She's dead, dead!" "Will think about it. . . ." Such words and phrases could never be reduced to any smaller elements no matter how one might try to grind them down.

He bought a rice-ball lunch with sesame, condiments, and tea and crept into his berth, taking off his suit quickly. His perfectly clear but vacant eyes had no love, no hatred, but only light fatigue. He heaved a small, meaningless sigh and ate his food and drank his tea. He flopped into bed after eating and did not open his eyes until he arrived at Tokyo the next morning.

While he slept in the train, in the back-street cabaret in Osaka, saxophones sobbed sweetly, sourly, and sharply. A thirty-year-old mother of a baby with a hood for a husband suddenly began to laugh hoarsely in a dark booth, shouting, "I gotta disease in you know what!" and stared darkly at the ceiling.

The worm-man with a bow tie was desperately trying to solve a problem at a refuge camp–like chess club filled with tobacco smoke. In an apartment in Takatsuki, the objects that had accumulated because a man had lived in it briefly, half drifting, half settling, all expired where they had fused onto the scene: an empty bottle of Givenchy, an empty bowl from a take-out kitchen, and the like.

---

*Crow-money is a short-term loan made in the morning and returned in the evening, with interest; so-called because it leaves and returns to its nest when the crows do.—TRANS.

God looked down on Tokyo from somewhere on high and noticed a gray flannel suit disappear under the roof of 4-8-14 Igusa, in the Suginami District, and heard the piercing cries of a middle-aged woman and a little girl. The girl's voice soon stopped and was followed by the cheerful, loud sound of the piano practicing Bach's inversion, which wafted out to the tiny lawn.

"You are lying, lying! . . . I know you didn't embezzle the company money! . . . I don't believe it! . . . You're not a delinquent boy any more! . . . What made you go off like that! . . . There must have been a woman! . . . You are so peculiar! . . . Well . . . it's all right, since you've come back. . . . I know I'm not mature enough. . . . Men are all the same. . . . Is life simply 'playing house'? . . . I know, I know. . . . I won't say another word. . . . Yes, yes, it's all cleaned up. . . . So, the saying is true that the husband isn't as popular as the wife suspects. . . . After this, I want to know it beforehand. . . . Shall I prepare a bath for you? . . . Shall we do it? . . . Is *takoyaki* good in Osaka? . . . Why do you suppose they put the mirror in the whole wall?"

The woman's voice continued to rise and fall from eleven o'clock in the morning until late that night. Mr. Ashida responded to every question with straight facts in his unchanging soft voice, in contrast to his wife's frenzied high voice. His tone was not at all different from that of his daily comments on the staleness of raw fish fillets or on his craving for cucumber-and-fish-skin salad.

Late that night, the swooning moans of a woman emanated from the dark window of the second floor and dispersed over the fields outside, but God was too old to hear.

Several days later, Mr. Ashida had a visitor sitting in front of his teak desk in his Nihonbashi office. How the visitor had got wind of the news was unknown, but he was a radio news reporter who had come to interview Mr. Ashida. The reporter asked about Ashida's motivations for the flight, and about his life during his self-exile. Mr. Ashida asked how he had found out about it, but the interviewer simply laughed and did not answer.

"About five thousand men disappeared last year. Of them, about sixteen hundred have come back to date. Only a small number ran away because of economic reasons or because of the intolerable noise level of cities. The majority of people had no reason. A baker went out on his motorcycle to collect accounts payable and ran away. He just took off and never came back."

"I see." Mr. Ashida nodded.

"When we investigate people who fled mysteriously and then returned, it never is another woman or an embezzlement."

"I see."

"The strange thing is that the majority of people lead the same sort of life before and after running away. Bakers work at bakeries, white-collar workers work as salaried workers at the desk, most of them seriously and industriously. I would like to ask you about the psychology of a runaway. We will ask the opinions of authoritative psychologists also. I have also contacted some sociologists. But more than anything else, we would like to hear the actual voices of people who have experienced self-exile. Well, that's more or less the reason I am here today. In short, we are planning a thirty-minute documentary program called 'Modern Impulses.' "

Mr. Ashida sat gracefully in a steel armchair on the sunny side of the room and, with a soft smile rounding his cheeks, looked at the interviewer. The young man had horn-rimmed, wraparound eyeglasses on his flat nose. Holding out a stick microphone to Ashida, he restlessly shot his glances all around, really looking at nothing. Once in a while, his eyes collided with Mr. Ashida's, and he swiftly turned his away. After this happened two or three times, he became sulky and stared rudely at Mr. Ashida. Mr. Ashida felt as though he were being stared at by a humpback fish in a Hong Kong shirt and a bow tie. Those were tenacious, pale, wet eyes that saw nothing. They were eyes that could not sustain observation. Rather, they were exhausted just by looking: two small, viscous balls that had nothing to do with the face—clear and efficient decadence revealed in broad daylight.

But who could blame him?

Mr. Ashida smiled gently. "Well, well," he mumbled. He smiled and mumbled again. "Well, yes. Well, well." The young man was content and nodded many times. And?

That was all.

Festivities by the River

1 · Stifling Night

At six o'clock, Kuse walked over to Café Brouillard on Tu Do Boulevard. Women were haggling on the roadside. Children begged coins everywhere. American soldiers were being carried away in tricycle cabs, jolted limply, guns across their knees.

It was the time of day when languid evening oozed out of people and tree trunks like droplets of perspiration. With the piercing white sunlight of the afternoon now gone, sticky porridgelike heat pervaded the promenade. The odor of putrid fish guts stagnated everywhere. The entire city was turning into a hot garbage pail.

Café Broullard was French in style, and the air inside was always freezing. As Kuse pushed the glass door, the film of perspiration peeled off instantly from his neck and arms. From the jukebox, Brassens was murmuring some ironical song in his dark, husky voice. Two American newspapermen Kuse knew by sight were eating hamburgers and drinking beer. The big, wet maps on their olive-green combat uniforms told that they had just returned from the front.

"Hi!" Kuse called to them, and they returned a gruff monosyllable without stopping to eat.

This café and another, Café Chez-nous, were the two hangouts for foreign correspondents in Saigon, and everyone stopped here at least once a day. Kuse usually had two beers or one dry martini here. Sipping a martini, he would sometimes talk about women and war with other Japanese reporters, exchanging information with them, or sometimes just killing time reading a newspaper. Everyone diagnosed news and rumors as if he were a member of the War Office, analyzing the war like a game of chess, making prognoses for which no one had any basis or conviction. Kuse could not bear to stay in his room in the evening. He lived on an alley off Nguyen Van Hué Boulevard, in a hot, dark, and malodorous second-floor room over a barber shop. A small lamp was its only lighting. Wall lizards came to eat insects on the wall and around the lamp, but they could not exterminate the proliferating bedbugs entirely. Once the sun was down, a man in Saigon had nothing to do but sleep or roam about the town. When Kuse returned late at night, the wall would be perspiring, and the girl next door would be coughing like an old woman. Here, one out of five had tuberculosis. Once they had contracted the disease, the Saigonese were helpless, no cure yet available to them. Sometimes the sound of eroding lungs was overpowered by the reverberation of artillery, but the young woman continued to wheeze long after the firing stopped.

The middle-aged Vietnamese waiter returned. "*Voilà, un martini sec.*" He pushed the glass with his bony fingers.

The balloon glass was well chilled and covered with condensation. A fresh fragrance of gin brushed his lips. His hot, tired intestines and their very wrinkles seemed to quiver and sizzle as crystal drops of gin seeped into them. The subtle bitterness of a peel of lemon. The cool breeze moving in the glass. Kuse loved this moment. The day was not yet worn out; rather, the hour had just risen from a long siesta, filled with fresh milk. Kuse, too, was still free from the pollution of his own words.

Nothing big had happened today. Shortly after noon, the new prime minister gave his inauguration speech at Independence Palace. That was all. His appointment was finally made official today, after the usual rumors about the behind-the-scenes negotiations circulated and after it was agreed that the new prime minister was to be selected from the Great Vietnamese Nationalist Socialist Party. The government officials seemed to have felt that some dramatic presentation was necessary for disclaiming the corruption that had festered in the land since the Stone Age. The new prime minister seemed to have understood this. When Kuse walked into the white-walled press-conference room, a small man of late middle age appeared with a ledger under his arm. He was introduced as president of the National Bank. The banker busily turned the pages of the ledger before the microphone and read out figures from the prime minister's accounts, testifying to the honest poverty and integrity of the man. Then, the prime minister made his speech, avouching his determination to continue the war effort against Communism. The press conference was over quickly. The reporters were all veterans from around the world, but the simplicity of the speech took the wind out of their sails and they failed to ask any questions. After that, Kuse stopped at the Central China Restaurant and had a leisurely lunch, returned to his rooming house for a long nap, then wrote a short article.

When the bottom of his glass began to show, he saw a boy by the name of Tanaka came into the café. Tanaka smiled when he saw Kuse at the counter and approached. Kuse noticed that the youth was wearing a muddy old pair of buckskin shoes on his bare feet and that his shirt reeked of rancid sweat. The odors of perspiration, fruit juice, rotten fish intestine, and a whiff of gutter clung to him. Tanaka worked at a bicycle shop, and his body emitted the odors of town and labor all around him.

Kuse took out a card from his billfold and handed it to Tanaka, saying, "I've got it for you."

The boy's eyes sparkled, but he said simply, "Thanks."

When Kuse had gone to the central post office to telegraph the article in the afternoon, he had stopped at the United States Information Service and secured a field-work permit for Tanaka. He had previously taken the boy to the USIS and let him sign the application, so the procedure was simple. He had said that Tanaka was his assistant, and Lt. Calvert, an acquaintance, had typed the permit right away. All he had to do was paste Tanaka's photograph in one corner. On the way out, he had gone to the next room and asked Lt. Col. Walker for two reservations on the eight o'clock helicopter for the next morning. The destination mattered little as long as it was one of the farthest outposts; he would leave it to the colonel. After a thought, the colonel had selected an outpost facing the Dong Nai River. Kuse had accepted it and left the office.

"We have two more days before the New Year, but I'm going tomorrow. Three days after the New Year, I'm coming back. The cease-fire is for seventy-two hours, exactly three days. Probably nothing will happen. Do you still want to go?"

"Yes. That's OK."

"You know that you won't see any war?"

"That's all right."

"We fly tomorrow morning at eight. Come to my place at seven. I'll let you borrow my camera and you can put it around your neck. All you have to do is follow me, looking like a cameraman. You don't have to speak English."

"I can speak a few words. When I was in Hong Kong, I was a guide for a travel agency. I learned it a little bit. I've lived in Taipei, too, so I can say something in Chinese. And I'm studying Vietnamese now."

His eyes twinkling, the boy carefully put the card in his pocket. The photograph on the permit was of a high school youth with round cheeks, at an age when he was absorbed in preparations for college entrance examinations. But the boy in front of Kuse was haggard, suntanned, angular. Now the jaw was stronger, and dark whiskers sprouted there at odd angles. Virility was emerging, solidifying into the young man's face. But in some unconscious moments, his eyes assumed the absent clarity of a child just awakening from a nap, still pursuing the torn bits of a dream. He might be loved by older women, Kuse thought.

"Do you want to go to Cholon?" Kuse asked.

"Oh, yes!"

"Since we have to eat American food after tomorrow."

"That doesn't bother me."

"I want to eat noodles at least once a day."

"How 'bout spaghetti?"

"Don't like spaghetti."

The boy jumped off the bar stool nimbly and walked out, swaying his smelly body. Kuse put money for the drink on the counter and followed him.

He had told Lt. Calvert that Tanaka was his assistant, but he was not. Kuse's employer was a small newspaper in western Japan with a branch office in Tokyo. The management had to hold many meetings before deciding to send Kuse to Vietnam. An assistant was out of the question. The reporters from the five major papers in Tokyo always stayed at the air-conditioned hotels, hired local assistants and sometimes even limousines to go after news. Kuse stayed in his room over a barber shop, seldom permitting himself the luxury of a taxi. Most of the time he hitchhiked or used a pedicab. He worked alone.

When Tanaka begged to be taken to the front, Kuse promised he would take him. He did not expect the boy to be able to take photographs.

It was by accident that he had picked up Tanaka. There was a man at a corner of Le Loi Boulevard who sold cats and *kyongs* in birdcages. Kuse always stopped to look at them on his way to the wire services to check the five o'clock news. He met the boy by the birdcages. Tanaka looked only a shade better than a beggar. Squatting on the roadside, he was holding a small *kyong* in the palms of his hands and feeding it some green vegetable from his mouth. A *kyong* never grows any larger than a yearling deer. It is not a deer, but its shape is that of a grown deer. Every time he saw it, Kuse wondered how such a delicate animal could live in the jungle. The tame animal walked out of the birdcage, got on the boy's hand, and pulled the vegetable out of his mouth and ate it, showing no sign of running away.

The boy gave a sigh of affection. "What a cute animal!" he said.

"He's like a tame paddy bird, isn't he?" Kuse commented.

Tanaka narrowed his eyes and answered, "I've never seen anything like this."

The middle-aged Vietnamese vendor squatted on the street, his bottom flat on the ground. Smiling, he tenderly stroked the animal's smooth back.

"Barbecue, nice, nice," he said.

After that, Kuse saw the boy several times, and he began to treat him to coconut milk or Chinese noodles at vendors' counters. Tanaka told Kuse he was working at a bicycle shop behind the central market. He was a repairman for blown-out tire tubes. He had earned a living by his skill in Taipei and in Hong Kong. Bicycles were being used for sports and leisure in Japan, but they were still a necessity of life in this part of the world. A man who could repair blown-out tires was a technician of sorts. He could travel around leisurely without hot patches, but with just an old-fashioned pumice stone to rub on tires and rubber cement. After graduating from high school in Kyūshū, Tanaka went to Tokyo and worked at a laundry, at a Chinese noodle shop, and at a bicycle shop. Inspired by an article in a cheap weekly magazine, he begged his father for one hundred thousand yen to supplement his own savings, and with no thought or plan he left Japan. He went to Taipei by freighter and found out that a skill for repairing punctured tires was a valuable commodity there. Then he crossed over to Hong Kong and again traded his skill, working as a guide for Japanese tourists on the side. He then met an American television reporter on his way to Vietnam and was hired as camera porter. Four days after their arrival in Saigon, a telegram recalled the American to New York, and Tanaka was left alone. He went to the Japanese Embassy and was introduced to an association of Japanese citizens, who handed him over to the bicycle shop. Again, he had to work with a pumice stone and rubber cement. The bicycle shop owner, pleased to have a dexterous and hard-working Japanese, took him into the family and taught him a few words of Vietnamese. He was impressed by the boy's diligence and wanted him to stay, but Tanaka's next destination was Bangkok. Eventually he wanted to go to India, to Karachi, Cairo, Istanbul—as far as he could go. Asked for an opinion, Kuse answered, "You can probably work your way to Istanbul by repairing tires, to the end of the Orient. I would say it's a good idea. Cycling is popular in Europe, too, so repairmen are probably needed. But work may be a lot harder to come by in Europe."

Tanaka was sipping coconut milk pensively, his eyes wide open. His young fingers lighting a cigarette with the flame from a Zippo lighter were coarse, and the nails were packed with black grease and dirt. Kuse was moved by the strange mixture of maturity and innocence, the boldness and delicacy of his jaw.

Several evenings before, Kuse and Tanaka were squatting on the roadside in Cholon after a day's work, sipping porridge made of animal intestines. The food was so hot it was difficult to hold the bowl. Kuse liked the gluey chaos of the porridge. The Chinese district was crowded; gongs were clanging and incense sticks were smouldering. A holiday atmosphere was already in the air. Crouched behind the vendor's cart, Kuse wiped the perspiration that burned his eyes and told the boy he was going to the front over the New Year holidays. There was nothing to do in Saigon. Tanaka put the bowl on the ground and began to plead with him. He had no plans in Saigon for the holidays. His boss was going to take his family to the delta country over the holidays. He would do anything to get to see the front. "I was born after the war and I don't know anything about war, so the grown-ups look down on me. It burns me up when they tease me. I've always wanted to see a war. If you think I'm in your way, I'll get lost any time. Just tell me, I'll split right away."

"My paper's poor," Kuse muttered. "They can't pay you." In the pale light of the vendor's acetylene lamp, Tanaka looked at him, insulted and angry. "Who's asking for money!" he shouted. "Money, my boss gives me. I've got some money stashed away, too."

His face was so naked and sincere that Kuse was moved. He promised he would think about it. The boy looked reassured and picked up the bowl from the ground.

Cholon was again filled with noisy crowds tonight. It was teeming with grubbiness and nourishment. Theaters were shaking with the clangor of gongs. On the streets, barefoot children in tattered pajamas were setting crickets in a sand-filled earthenware dish to fight, cheering, "Hao! Hao!" In the food shop's soiled window, shiny thighs and intestines of pigs and steers, painted in bright red, hung from large hooks. Vendors hawked their wares and pedestrians swarmed around carts to eat. They spat, they blew off their snot, and they shuffled around aimlessly. The great throngs appeared as if they might move eastward carried by a quiet landslide, enter the Sea of South China, and bury the ocean with their great mass, until the capes, islands, and the continent might finally disappear.

Starved, purged, and decimated, the masses still propagated. Asia expanded endlessly. Kuse saw evidence of this in Canton and Shanghai. In Hong Kong, clusters of people reached the top of rocky hills that might crumble and roll down at any moment. Singapore was packed with people all the way to the harbor. The night of Djakarta was rustling with the blindly moving, endless carpet of moss—the moss André Malraux had spoken of. How far would they proliferate? In this huge river of nameless masses, the revolutionaries and antirevolutionaries also probably had to struggle not to be drowned. Kuse had once seen a bar that had just been bombed by the terrorists. The walls were ripped off, the glasses were shattered into snowflakes, and the blood of American soldiers and Vietnamese women gushed out freely. White blood and yellow blood had spattered and had dyed the torn ceiling as though it had been sprayed by a compressor, and drops of blood trickled slowly like melting butter from the clinging pieces of flesh. Yet, within the hour, the crowd returned to the bar and everything was back to normal. Twenty-four hours later, only the holes on the wall remained, and crowds just as large as before strolled on the street. Women cackled and laughed beside their bamboo baskets filled with papayas and sugarcanes. Babies were laughing, rolling in muddy puddles. Pushed by the crowd, Kuse stepped over the baskets, crossed over the babies, and continued to walk.

They reached a small restaurant behind the Don Kan Bar and ate pigeons and chicken. Long after Kuse finished eating, Tanaka still lingered over his plate. Kuse lit a cigarette and poured beer over crushed ice in his glass and drank it before it was diluted. He kept pouring the beer, spitting bits of rice husks that remained on his tongue onto the floor. The boy was absorbed in licking the bones. He had picked all the bones, but sucked on each once again until it was clean white. He carefully and regretfully arranged the bones one by one on the border of the plate.

"How about quitting?" Kuse asked.

"Are you going home already?"

"No, not yet."

"Pigeons are so flavorful, even the bones."

"I'm talking about a girl."

"Oh, I see, I see."

"That's what I meant."

"I didn't know."

"Don't make me spell out everything."

"Yes, sir!"

The boy wiped his fingers on his trousers and happily stood up. He smiled warmly as though going to the seashore or mountains on a vacation. His age probably had a cleansing effect on him no matter what he did. His tanned face was unmarked: no pockmark, no blemish, no scratches, no smudges.

The two men left the cavelike dark restaurant and stopped a pedicab on the boulevard. A thick, steamy heat stagnated and filled the night. From the sky, the river, the promenade, and the darkness, great waves of hot breath came blowing. Bleary-eyed with food and soaked in perspiraiton, the two men panted as they were wheeled away. No matter how far they went, the air was filled with young women's moans and clinging nasal wailings. Last month, it was the song about a young girl who walked through an empty arcade where winds strayed. This month, it was the song of a young widow in black, gathering hibiscus flowers. Morning and night, this city sang incessantly.

"I'd weep instead of commanding troops," Kuse said.

"The bullets will grow moldy, too."

"They couldn't possibly fight wars in this country."

"God! They like sad songs here!"

"I would run away if I were a soldier."

"Yeah. I think I'll buy that record," Tanaka said.

They got off the pedicab near the river. There was no neon light or street lamp on the road. Blinking red dots moved across the sky. The artillery boomed, and high branches of coconut palms gleamed white in the flares from time to time, but the darkness remained, crowded with straw huts. The huts were more like the earth's tumors than human habitats. Pigs waddled in slush and chickens trotted around. A baby's whimper wafted from somewhere, followed by a slow, soothing lullaby. Odors of urine, garbage, and gutter refuse made the two men dizzy as they walked into a dark alley. They walked slowly, anticipating someone to stop them. The calls came soon enough. A muted, soft voice came from one hut and a similar voice from the next. The two men halted in the dark. Kuse fumbled in his pocket and folded a small round object into Tanaka's fingers. The boy chuckled.

"I'll see you later at the entrance of the hamlet."

Tanaka said, "Yes."

"Don't be hasty."

"What?"

"Count to twenty if you start to come."

"Okay."

Tanaka walked over to the next hut and disappeared. A woman's voice greeted him, and his cheerful voice responded. Kuse wiped off dripping perspiration from his chin and entered the nearly collapsing palm hut.

The ceiling was propped up by four bamboo poles. The only lamp in the room hung from a pole, quietly blinking. Besides a hard, wooden bed covered by a wrinkled mosquito net, a pan and a bowl in a corner of the floor were the only objects in the room. The girl, her grandfather, and a baby seemed to be the only inhabitants. As Kuse entered, the old man stealthily picked up the baby from the bed and walked out of the door. He would wait outside while Kuse was inside. An amiable, modest smile appeared on the old man's weather-beaten cheeks as he passed by Kuse. He whispered "Good evening" and disappeared.

The girl emerged from the dark and turned up the net to make a place on the bed. Her gesture invited him. Kuse sat quietly and lit a cigarette. "Good evening," he said.

She smiled furtively and whispered back, "Good evening."

The lamp shimmered, and house lizards squeaked sharply to each other. The odor of waterweeds and mud wafted into the hut. A creek seemed to be flowing behind the hut. Since the summer heat had not putrefied the waterweed, a quiet, fresh scent rose straight from the stream. The girl's lungs were probably eroding like so many other womens'. She did not cough, but her hard, thin ribs stood in relief like the hoops of a birdcage. She was too young to be a mother. There was still the air of a young girl around her cheeks. She was gentle and quiet, yet for some reason she reminded Kuse of a ripe papaya. The flesh of the fruit was inside the bush between her legs, which was no more than a few simple light strokes of ink-and-brush drawing. Kuse sank into the core of the fruit that breathed in and out the dense, damp night of the tropics. When the perspiration stood in his eyes, the dim lamp glinted harshly like the flare. She was guileless and humble like a young tree. Kuse wanted her to assume a posture he felt quite natural, but she was shy and firmly rejected him. The sorrow in her virginal eyes and cheeks drove him to decadent cruelty, and he forced himself into her.

After a while, she narrowed her shoulders and slipped away from his arms and went out of the hut. The artillery noise had stopped. A secret sound of urinating came from the creek behind. She returned and, crouching over the basin, washed herself, making the sound of water. Kuse was drenched with perspiration and lay in the mosquito net. He lit a soldier's bitter, black-leaf cigarette. Lying in the midst of naked poverty that could not be covered with his hands, he listened to the squeaks of house lizards and the showers of machine guns beyond the river. Over there was violent death, but here, the oil lamp sizzled and the scent of waterweeds drifted.

The girl sat on the bed and, slapping her hands together accurately and loudly, killed mosquitoes one by one. It was a sluggish, slow motion, but a thoroughly practiced and solid gesture.

"Would you like something to drink?" she asked.

"No, it's all right."

"A Coca? Or Sequi?"

"I don't want anything."

"Are you Chinese?"

"No, Japanese. I'm a newspaperman."

"You come from Hong Kong?"

"No, Tokyo."

"Yes?"

"Do you understand?"

"Yes."

Sending the smooth, slow air of a palm-leaf fan to him, the girl murmured "Tokyo" a couple of times in her mouth. In her whisper, Kuse sensed a placidness filtered through and through by sorrow. There was an indestructibility in her that was beyond anyone's touch. He was very much tempted to ask about her absent husband, but he controlled himself.

"Oh, the pig!"

He looked up at her cry and saw a black pig just entering the door. It passed, almost brushing against Kuse's nose, and went toward the back door. She laughed generously. He was shocked. He had never seen a pig's face so closely in his life. As it crossed the dim lamplight, its small eyes burned blood red like rapacious greed itself. Clawed and fanged, a carnivorous beast of the primeval forest had suddenly appeared, swollen by anger. It was beyond his understanding that the slovenly domestic animal that rolled in offal could have had such cruel eyes. Kuse sat upright, holding his breath, and stared at the back of the pig as it disappeared.

He waited for Tanaka at the entrance to the hamlet. Artillery began to roar again, and the earth's crust quivered. But through the din, Kuse heard crude music and young laughter wafting in the air. The instrument was a viol made of a coconut shell, and the loud laughter was unmistakably Tanaka's. A young woman seemed to be laughing with him. The voices died down. Kuse lit a cigarette and paced back and forth.

The boy did not appear for a long time.

2 · *Happy New Year!*

It was a very hot last day of the year.

At nine in the morning, the two men were carried to the front in an armed helicopter, "the chopper." A river flowed through large rice paddies surrounded by jungle and groves of rubber trees. The outpost was on the river bank. It was one of those

triangular bases seen everywhere in this country, with a small
lookout tower and a gunbase at each of the three points. On
these bases American and Vietnamese soldiers lived in huts with
corrugated tin roofs. Kuse and Tanaka were introduced to Captain Seagram, commander of the American forces here. They
requested that they be permitted to stay until after the New Year,
and the captain gladly gave permission right away. He took them
to his own hut and handed them hammocks and explained the
state of affairs.

The outpost was surrounded by the Vietcong and by the "twilight" villages, or the contested zones, some of which had two
chiefs, a government supporter during the day and a Vietcong
chief at night. The Vietcong never attempted a suicide attack
on the triangular base through the mine fields, but they had
frequently ambushed the American and the government forces
outside the base. Moreover, mortar shells regularly came flying
from the opposite side of the river. Strategically, the Americans
were free to go out of the base for an offensive move, but they
were virtually surrounded. The highways were torn up by mines,
and one never knew when to expect an ambush. The supplies
had to be carried in by heavily armed, large convoys. Various
"pacification plans" had been programmed to win the popular
support but with little success. During the three-day holiday of
New Year, the Americans planned to send a band into the Vietcong villages on the opposite bank. The captain explained that
his soldiers had chipped in and gone to Saigon to purchase a
drum, a saxophone, a trumpet, and even an accordion. "When
they return tomorrow morning," he said, "those with some experience will organize a band and cross the river."

"Can you defeat the Vietcong with musical instruments?" Kuse
asked.

"It's a battle without arms." Captain Seagram spoke calmly.
He was cheerful, straightforward, and very serious. He seemed
to have mulled over this for many days.

"There are all kinds of wars," he added, smiling.

The captain took the two Japanese on a tour of the base from one end to the other, then they had a lunch of hamburger and macaroni. Beside their table the Vietnamese soldiers squatted, bending over their wash basins, and ate their rats and catfish. Kuse tried their food a little and was amazed by the tenderness and tastiness of the rat meat.

"Will you be all right?" Tanaka looked worried.

"It's not bad at all. You might even say it's good. They say the rats from the rice fields are free of pest germs. They sell boxfuls of these at Saigon markets. The rats squeak and call the customers from the boxes like girls, you see. Don't you want to sample some?"

"I don't think I'm obliged to try that hard," Tanaka said, but asked for a piece from the basin and ate it timidly. He did not spit it out but swallowed without a word.

Kuse tried to take a nap in the hammock but the tin-roof hut was too hot. He decided to bathe in the sun in his shorts. He and Tanaka smeared Captain Seagram's suntan lotion all over their bodies and climbed to the top of the trench. They rolled out a straw mat and lay down. American soldiers lounged all around, some of them from the famous Special Forces, known for their fierceness, all baking their bodies in their red, green, or yellow shorts. There was an air of Miami or Waikiki Beach. As Tanaka turned his camera to them, they shook their hands, declining to be photographed.

The sun filled the sky behind the castlelike column of white clouds, and transparent flames of heat beat down in waves. The grass withered, the earth crumbled, and Kuse's bare skin smarted. The sun penetrated his closed, thin eyelids, and glaring light flared in the twilight of his retina. Roasted by the sky and by the ground, his skin oozed perspiration like a squeezed sponge, but it dried as soon as it sweated, and salt crystallized on the pores that had shrunk. The heat and the brilliance of the tropics were thorough and merciless. There was intense pleasure in excreting the gray indolence accumulated in the lazy Saigon life. The pale sludge secreted by alcohol, discussion, books, and sex now dissolved, dampened the straw mat and disappeared.

The Vietnamese soldiers, clad in shorts, played volleyball over the net stretched between two 155mm cannon barrels. The ball bounced slowly or flew rapidly back and forth over the net. Some distance away, in front of a hut, two American soldiers and three Vietnamese officers were seen playing horseshoes, looking like men of Brobdingnag and Lilliput. During the French occupation, this must have been a game of *pétanque*. The military tactics of securing a large enclave on the shore and encroaching gradually inland was called the "ink-spot" strategy by the Americans. The French expedition must have called it *tache d'huile* in its days. Monsieur changed to mister; *pétanque* changed to horseshoes; the oil changed to ink; *le capitaine* to the captain.

Tanaka narrowed his eyes sleepily and raised his face from his angular shoulders. He shifted his sight from the volleyball to the horseshoes, then to the Special Forces men who were turning over and over, undecided between well-done and medium-rare.

"War is a lot of do-nothing, isn't it?" he muttered, looking puzzled.

Kuse answered, floating in his comfortable indolence, "This is the last day of the year."

"Is it always like this?"

"More or less."

"Did you ever see a real battle, Mr. Kuse?"

"No."

"I didn't know they had so little to do."

"But death is instantaneous."

"Have you ever been dead, Mr. Kuse?"

"No, but it looks like I might be soon."

"What a strange war!"

Kuse turned over on his half-done stomach and began to bake his back. Briefly he recounted various episodes of this war to the boy. One early morning last December, a new coffin painted in red had been found on the bank of the Danang River. A military policeman opened the lid, and it exploded in his face. . . . The American soldiers dropped a bomb with "A Merry Christmas"

written on it. . . . The Vietcong and the government soldiers
played a friendly game of soccer in some village. . . . A platoon
of government soldiers put in a request for air transportation
and the Americans complied. Behind the deplaned soldiers was
a piece of paper that read: "Thanks for the ride. We work for
Ho Chi Minh. . . ." They were Vietcong in government uniforms. But several days later, a statement appeared in the paper
disclaiming the episode, saying the message in the plane was
planted by a mischievous American soldier.

"How much of it is true?"

"I don't know. But there are so many incidents that if such a
story is manufactured, it doesn't surprise anyone. So, don't just
say it's only a story. You should collect this kind of material. You
don't find out what's really happening if you read only the editorials, but if you read about crimes and tragedies and gossip,
you learn a little more about the country. Take bicycle repair—
it's a good job to be in if you want to become a journalist. Don't
read important people's speeches. They are space fillers for papers and magazines. Trash."

"Is that what they are?"

"More or less."

"I wonder why the Vietcong played such a hoax."

"I don't know."

"Did they think they were having a picnic?"

"They probably wanted to see how far they could fool the
Americans. Generally, the Vietnamese think the Americans are
too kind and too naive. It's too easy to swindle them, so it's no
fun."

"I ask my boss at the bicycle shop which side he is on, but he
says nothing. He teaches me everything about women and drinking places, but he clams up when I ask him about the war."

"I can believe it."

"But he said once, 'If you kill one Vietcong, there will be five
more the next day. If you kill five, ten will be born for each.'"

"Does he like the Vietcong?"

"No, I don't think so. But he doesn't seem to hate them, either.

I guess he just doesn't worry about the Vietcong or the Americans. He's busy with the repair work. It doesn't matter to him."

"Most people seem to be that way."

Kuse turned over slowly like a contented animal and looked around with his half-open eyes. The space between the trench and the bank was a field of barbed wire and mines, and the riverbed was covered with spiked electric wires, special explosives, and electric currents. Any object caught in the wire would set off an alarm throughout the base. Frequent attacks of machine guns from the opposite side had left visible traces on the sandbags. The sand spilled out from the bullet holes in the green-linen bags, and the wooden frames of the crenelles were chipped and torn. Beyond the river bank lay a vast field of rice plants, tranquil in the vacant whiteness of midday. On the gray marshland near the opposite bank, three children were seen searching for fish, buried up to their hips in the large mud hole they had dug out. The river flowed from the haze of the northeastern jungles, washed one side of the triangular base, and continued to course southwestward. It was a thick, potagelike body of yellow water that moved slowly. In the paddies that had recently been harvested, bamboo groves and thatched-roof huts of peasants stood like islets, but there was no shadow of buffaloes or child cowkeepers, nor any peasant women tramping on rice husks. Extraordinary tension and ennui filled the modest bucolic scene of Asia.

About five o'clock, Kuse returned to the tin hut, lay down in a hammock and, half asleep, began to read *Gulliver's Travels*. Tanaka ran in flustered, holding the camera around his neck.

"Big news, Mr. Kuse!"

"What's the matter?"

Covered with perspiration, Tanaka panted out, "Corpses, a lot of them!"

Kuse was puzzled.

"The government forces were ambushed. They came back with a truckful of bodies. They are all over the place. All of them dead!"

The boy spoke fast and dashed out again. Kuse put down the book, rose from the hammock and lit a cigarette. The entire camp suddenly awoke and began to buzz with the birdlike cries of the Vietnamese and the short, snapping shouts of the Americans. Footsteps rushed by. After smoking almost half the cigarette, Kuse finally stood on his feet, put on shoes and walked out, but he was still hesitant.

The bodies were laid on the red earth peculiar to the rubber groves. Two military doctors, a Vietnamese and an American, moved among the wounded who also lay or crouched near the bodies. Captain Seagram was working alertly, helping the wounded to rise or aiding them in putting on bandages. His T-shirt and trousers smeared with blood, he did not stop for a moment, lighting cigarettes and placing them in the mouths of the soldiers on the right and on the left between injections and bandaging, ignoring the sweat that dripped from his jaw and elbows.

"Chin up!". . . . "You were very lucky, you know?". . . . "A helicopter will be here for you very soon."

Distributing the cigarettes one after another, he encouraged and consoled soldiers who understood no English.

There were twelve bodies. This was serious damage to a patrol consisting of two platoons. The bodies on the red ground were all young, tanned, and small like a bunch of junior high school boys. Some were clean and others were atrocious deaths. There were hands tightly clenched over intestines that had spilled out of lacerated abdomens, and there were faces half smashed. Kuse had learned that small, modern firearms were highly destructive and, shot in a close distance, their power and speed exploded the human body into bits. The transfigured bodies of boys and young men testified to a sudden attack from a close proximity. None of the bullet holes was a simple mark of pencil size; every laceration curled back, large and deep, revealing the bones inside. Blood had ceased to flow and had coagulated on the grayish flesh, and the rigid wrinkles had begun to appear on the fingers of the dead. Putrefaction was fast in the tropics, and that familiar, sweet, almost obscene odor of corpses was already surfacing.

Each looked as if he had frozen in the midst of questioning, amazed how this could have happened to his body. Eyes, nostrils, lips, and wounds were already swarming with flies.

"Cruel!" Tanaka groaned at Kuse's ear and walked off. The boy's lips were dry and his eyes dark and older. He skirted stealthily behind the silent, crouching Vietnamese and American soldiers, and clicked the shutter. He might have been fighting off the onslaught of death with the lens, but could he have possibly shut off the feeling of humiliating the dead by an apparatus composed of pieces of glass and metal?

Two young women were sobbing loudly some yards apart. One was holding a newborn baby. They both pressed their faces against the red earth, shaking their tied hair and bodies, moaning intermittently, *"Troi-oi, troi-oi!"* They were poor. A curious custom of the Vietnamese Army permitted its soldiers to have their wives and children accompany them to the absolute limit of frontline safety. In this triangular base, too, the families lived right behind the trenches. They constructed something like an insect's habitat, digging holes, erecting artillery shells or bamboo poles on the ground and hanging rags over them. They had brought one brazier and one pot with them. Behind the trench mortar, machine guns, ammunition boxes, and grenade boxes, old women, wives, and children moved in and out of their habitats. Exposed to the glittering heat of midday, the old women slept, the wives mended, and the children sucked on sugarcanes. While the pot on the brazier cooked porridge, dogs ran from one hole to another, and a pregnant woman dozed, her head resting on a bucket. These people starved and multiplied, killed and multiplied, and were killed and multiplied.

Though the dead looked like high school boys, at least two of them were already heads of families. Two women were squatting among the bodies, sobbing and showering wails upon the widely spread, protruding legs of their husbands, one with open eyes, the other with a crushed head.

Kuse lowered his eyes to the ground and perspired. What will these women do after tomorrow? They will have to move out of the base sooner or later; but where could they go, carrying the brazier and pot on their heads? He knew now that the girl from the night before, who lived with a pig, was better off than these women. She at least had a roof over her head. If these women tried to return to their parents' home, they would most likely find the home village long since burned to the ground and abandoned. Not even the foundations of their thatched huts would remain. Roaming around the town with her baby, will the young mother sleep under a tree by day and try to sell her body door to door by night?

A middle-aged American soldier muttered, as he walked away, "It's not easy being a soldier."

After a dinner with Captain Seagram, Kuse returned to the hut. Tanaka was coiled in the hammock like a shrimp, lost in thought. He had not come to dinner. Kuse left him alone and went out. He peered into the Vietnamese soldiers' huts and saw some of them playing chess, others staging cricket fights. Quietly at play, the men pursed lips and smoked their precious cigarettes until their fingers burned. After finishing a cigarette, a soldier would stare at the smoldering butt on the ground and then go back to the game. If he lost a game, he would mumble something and withdraw into the shadowy part of their quarters. As Kuse moved from one barrack to another in the humid density of the night, the fragrance of incense came wafting from somewhere. There were no more sobbing voices of women. The two young widows must be huddling like animals in dark holes somewhere. Or were they crouching by the crushed head of the young husband, burning incense sticks and repeating prayers? Mixed in with the viscous odor of the corpses that had quietly but unmistakably begun to decompose, strains of chanting floated: "*Na mo aa mi da phat.*" (Save us, O merciful Lord Buddha.)

When Kuse returned to the hut, Tanaka was sitting up in his hammock, smoking a cigarette. He looked at Kuse and said, "It looks like they are going to go ahead and do it tomorrow."

"Do what?"

"I went to ask Seagram a short while ago. He says the band

is going to Vietcong villages tomorrow. He's serious. He means business. But he said we must be on our guard tonight."

"I guess so."

"If they shoot, we shoot back, but don't shoot until we are shot, he said. The Charlies are going to be up all night in the trench."

Tanaka spoke in a calm, detached voice, rose from the hammock, and took out a Coca-Cola from the refrigerator in the corner.

Kuse pulled his field bag toward him and took out his pocket-size cognac bottle. The smooth, fragrant liquid streamed down his throat, leaving a hint of bitterness on his tongue. But the next mouthful did not leave bitterness. After taking another swig from it, he handed the bottle to Tanaka. Rolling the liquid on his tongue, he lay on the hammock and resumed his reading of *Gulliver's Travels*.

His eyes followed the printed words, but his thoughts did not. The incense, the odor of death, and the young woman's prayer gripped him and did not let go. What he saw today was nothing new to him on his news-gathering rounds. But, no matter how many times Kuse had seen death, he could never get used to it. His determination always evaporated. Death always tripped him up, sending him reeling. Today, he was again shocked by the atrocity, and the fact that he was shocked forced him to realize that he was still a stranger to both parties, a mere outsider. He had no excuse for, nor hatred of, the incident. He only felt its primitive cruelty and was overpowered. He thought of no words such as "for the sake of people's independence" or "for the defense of democracy." Either slogan was too abstract in the face of the heavy, viscous, hot odor of the corpses. Neither "It was by an order" nor "Kill so that we won't get killed" appeared to explain the act. The entire system of morality and discipline was cast to the winds. A pipe without a safety valve was suddenly deluged by water. Every time he came upon this scene, he felt he was a man in the spectator's seat at a bullfight ring, peering down at the death of a bull. Grief, atrocity, whatever he witnessed, he could not be any part of it, other than a third party, a bystander. How could the people, who were born, raised and are going to die in this country, embrace a man who holds a return air ticket in his pocket? The moment he pronounced the words "I understand," most of it evaporated in the air; it was almost an insult. Being in this country resembled jumping into a river with one's hands tied behind one's back: one could not help, fight, nor till the land. All Kuse could do was to search for words clumsily, his fingers fumbling on the typewriter keys. He had made up his mind not to think, but only to feel. A man who was floating down the river should not fight, should not struggle, but yield his body to the flow of water and keep his eyes wide open. There was no role Kuse could play but for that of a spectator. He was a man who licked the edge of a glass and believed he had drunk the liquor.

"Wall lizards have cute faces," Tanaka said.

Kuse did not answer.

"They look like goby."

No answer.

"They have intelligent eyes."

"How about roasting them?"

"What for?"

"They used to say wall lizards are a good aphrodisiac."

"The first I ever heard of that."

Tanaka had caught a small lizard that had fallen from the beam of the tin roof and was scrutinizing it. Kuse disliked the fact that cognac made him perspire immediately, but he took swigs as he stretched out on the hammock, slapping mosquitoes on his stomach.

The next morning, Kuse had breakfast, with Captain Seagram and the Special Forces soldiers, of corn flakes and skim milk, bacon, and the eggs that Vietcong villagers came to sell. The captain asked whether Kuse wanted to go over to the opposite bank with the "choir operatives." He did.

"In two hours," Seagram said, "the chopper will bring the instruments. Then we can leave."

He said that he had thought of playing the Vietnamese national anthem, but didn't want to irritate the Vietcong. After a considerable amount of thinking last night, he had decided to put on a program of "Happy Birthday," "Home on the Range," "When the Saints Come Marching In," et cetera. The rough men of the Special Forces smiled wryly as the captain described his plans, but voiced no objection.

It was a pleasant New Year. The air was cool and crisp until about nine, and the breeze felt pleasant on the skin. The grass was wet and alive in the dew. The corpses were gone; only ashes and broken pieces of incense sticks were scattered on the damp, red earth. Kuse walked over to the trench. The mangrove charcoal gave off a pungent odor from the brazier over which a pot of porridge cooked. Dogs were barking, babies were crying, and old women and wives were working busily in and out of the holes. The husbands were sitting on the edge of the trench, looking at their families proudly. Kuse looked for the two bereaved women, but they were nowhere to be seen.

Tanaka approached in quick steps.

"Mr. Kuse, a strange boat is coming."

"What strange boat?"

"It looks like a Vietcong boat. It's coming downstream flying a flag. It looks suspicious, like the Cong gentlemen."

Fumbling the camera, Tanaka scuttled toward the river.

Kuse walked over to the bank. A number of Americans were sitting on the top of the trench, looking upstream. On the slow-moving yellow water, a sampan, laden heavily with people, approached gradually, flying a flag at the bow. Chugging lightly with its hot-rod engine, the boat created ripples in its wake.

"Look, look, look, they are the Congs, aren't they?" cried Tanaka.

"Wait. Don't get excited."

"That's a Vietcong flag!"

Kuse opened his eyes wide. It was unmistakably the blue and red flag with a yellow star in the center that fluttered on the flagpole. They have finally made their appearance! They have emerged from the jungle in the north-northeast, having changed their black shirts into holiday finery to make their entrance into Saigon in a sampan. Is this journey being made simply for a drink of the New Year's wine?

The American soldiers began to buzz, whisper, laugh, hoot.

"VC, VC, oh, VeeCee!"

"Charlie, Charlie!"

"Victor Charlie, oh!"

Two or three soldiers cheered and others joined. The sampan was overflowing with passengers.

They were in short pants, white shirts, jungle hats. Some let their long hair blow in the wind. Some held onto the flagpole, and others crouched and gazed up at the sky.

Suddenly Tanaka laughed and cried out, "Happy New Year!"

Older men on the boat did not even move, their backs turned to the Americans. But several boys responded to Tanaka with smiles and waves, squinting in the sun.

One of them cupped his hands over his mouth and shouted.

"Hallllllloooooo Charllllllllliiieeeeee!"

3 · When the Saints Come Marching In

They crossed the river back and forth for three days.

On New Year's Day, those who had gone to Saigon to buy musical instruments returned by chopper in the morning. They had purchased a trumpet, a guitar, and a couple of maracas. Though some soldiers could play the drums or the accordion, such instruments were too expensive. The instruments were bought with the funds collected among themselves, so no one was expecting a combo of professional caliber. Captain Seagram distributed the instruments among the soldiers, and then they boarded a pontoon to cross the river. Landing on the opposite bank, they marched in a single file on a ridge between rice paddies into a village. They had neither helmets nor bulletproof jackets; they were armed only with a can opener. There was a soldier carrying a boxful of rations on his shoulder. Kuse and

Tanaka followed the group from village to village. They listened to music, drank the native white wine with the villagers, and took a nap in the afternoon. In the setting sun at the end of the day, they retraced the ridge between paddies and returned to their base.

There was no guarantee for the ceasefire. Neither had the two sides held a talk, nor was there supervision by international monitors. The United Nations merely sanctioned the ceasefire attempts and the Hague International Court of Justice kept its silence. From somewhere in the jungle, a message on the radio announced a three-day armistice, and Saigon caught the signal and returned a wire in agreement. The southern European custom of the three-hour siesta persisted in this country, and during the prescribed time of day no bullet flew and no landlord was murdered. They had been fighting for many years with three hours of ceasefire each day. The holidays went one step beyond the siesta toward the unsigned treaty. Yet, there was no assurance that no one would be shot at. If someone happened to be shot and protests were made during the three days, all one could expect was a quick retort, "*C'est la guerre.*"

On New Year's Day, Kuse had questioned Captain Seagram at breakfast about the reliability of the ceasefire as he ate the bananas that had been purchased from Vietcong villagers. The captain said that both sides generally kept their word. He had checked with the provincial headquarters after midnight on New Year's Eve and confirmed that the firing had stopped along the frontline. After a few localized firefights, everything had quieted down completely. This strengthened the captain's conviction, and he had decided to gamble on crossing the river unarmed. The Vietcong knew the villagers would not be pleased if unarmed men with musical instruments were shot while entertaining them. They were cruel but intelligent, the captain said. This lean, small, blond man from Montana was unyielding once he made up his mind. He was slow in making decisions, but once on a course he had the determination to complete the task, come what may. Kuse felt unadulterated stubbornness hidden under the captain's soft surface.

"We should have done something like this a long time ago. You've got to win the support of the villagers. It may even be too late. But if the Commies do everything they can, we, too, have got to do everything we can."

The captain told Kuse that a "Pacification Plan" had once been tried out in this district. Vietnamese operatives came from Saigon and visited villages, propagandizing the cruelty of the Vietcong. They spoke of the village chiefs and landlords and teachers who were vivisected and showed photographs of blown-up buses and mutilated bodies of passengers. They distributed pamphlets and told dramatized stories with cardboard pictures. But they were afraid of assassins and returned to Saigon at night, leaving the villagers behind. No matter how much they talked, the villagers chose to ignore them. It was a well-known fact that the government itself was totally corrupt. The Vietnamese government also had the decisive disadvantage of not having a legendary leader like Ho Chi Minh. Then the agricultural advisers came from the United States. They put on black pajamas, slept with the villagers in the straw huts, ate with them, and worked with them. They taught the natives to boil water before drinking it, how to raise pigs more effectively, and how to use chemical fertilizers. They were "Ugly Americans" who worked hard, drenched in sweat. They ate worse food than the Vietnamese and forgot sleep. But soon they had to leave the peasants for their next assignment, for Bangkok, or to return to the United States. Then the war itself spread into the paddies and groves, and everything went down the drain.

"The Vietcong are like needles in a haystack," said the captain. "They must be pulled out with a tweezer, and that's a job for infantrymen and political workers, because the war here is an infantry's war. But the ARVN [the Vietnamese government soldiers] tried to exterminate them with bulldozers—tanks, 155 millimeters, and armed convoys. We helped them, too. So the untouched hay all turned into needles. That was a mistake. Everyone makes a mistake, but we certainly made a big one."

Speaking quietly, the captain showed acute regret in his eyes. But in spite of all evidence to the contrary, Kuse felt the American officer was still unhurt, unscathed. Though his body had been covered by blood only yesterday, inside, he stayed completely uncontaminated. His story, too, was only another version of the ones repeated by numerous American officers. Kuse wanted to argue some points but decided that the captain did not need a newspaperman's opinion and kept silent. In general, the farther removed from the battle front, the higher and louder the voices of arguments. Kuse's daily life in Saigon was filled with those discussions. His hands tied, floating downriver, he could do nothing but argue. He was tired of the demeaning bitterness he invariably felt after such debates. Furthermore, his personal analyses and prognoses for the war had been by now all soiled with the fingerprints and saliva of introspection. There has been no new creative view for peasants' movements in Asia since the Chinese revolution. There was no way of preventing a revolution unless antirevolutioanries changed into revolutionaries. It had come to the point where a paradox had turned around and become truth.

The American soldiers got off the boat and, with Captain Seagram and an interpreter at the head, formed a noisy single file on the path between dry paddies, blowing the trumpet and strumming the guitar. Giggling, ARVN officers and soldiers followed them. Kuse and Tanaka brought up the rear.

"What a weird war!" Tanaka said.

"How many times do you have to say that?"

"I've never heard of such a war!"

"This sort of thing has gone on more often than you think."

"Really?"

"Sure. In China, the Japanese Army's pacification unit carted around more than a band. Comedians and popular storytellers and magicians cruised from village to village. Don't look at this war as something special. They call it an 'ugly war' every time they open their mouths, but I'd like to see an un-ugly war."

"Still . . . it's strange, really strange."

With bewilderment and delight mixed on his face, Tanaka followed the band, chuckling and taking pictures. His eyes laughed in the glorious sunshine and showed none of the gloom of the day before as they gazed at the corpses. Had he forgotten them or had they submerged deeper into his memory?

Some villages were surrounded by bamboo groves and others had black sticks of napalm-burned coconut trees. The clay walls had turned into honeycombs of bullet holes. Thatched huts looked as if they had stood there since the Stone Age. Some hamlets were inhabited by many and others by few. The band was received by hostile stares in some villages and in others, met by round-eyed children flocking around. Captain Seagram called out the village chief in every community he came to, and with the help of the interpreter, requested permission to make a little music in celebrating the New Year. He never talked politics. Some chiefs were perplexed. Some just stood there rubbing their hands. But when the children, boys, girls, young women, and old women congregated, vacant-eyed or with eyes warped with hatred, the chief no longer knew what to do and reluctantly joined the audience. Captain Seagram led the band to the border of the village and let the soldiers play trumpet and guitar, surrounded by spectators. The soldiers were high-spirited though looking quite serious, and concentrated on blowing and plucking, quite out of tune. Those who had no talent for instruments just shook the maracas or sang.

The program was always the same. They started out with "Happy Birthday," then became sentimental with "Home on the Range," and then revitalized themselves with "When the Saints Come Marching In." Sometimes they threw in an innocent note of "Twinkle, Twinkle, Little Star," and the finishing touch was added always by a solemn rendition of "Auld Lang Syne." They were universally appealing pieces, and Kuse was touched by the thought that must have gone into programming. He spoke of it to the captain who had retired behind the band to listen and watch the reaction of the audience. He nodded deeply and answered, "Yes, this is all internationally known music."

The American soldiers sang:

> *Happy Birthday to you,*
> *Happy Birthday to you,*
> *Happy Birthday, dear children,*
> *Happy Birthday to All!*

There was a little hut under a banana tree and the graffiti on the white wall in red paint said, *"Da dao de quo'c My"* (Down with American Imperialism).

The villagers had the interpreter translate the verses of the songs and listened, crouching or standing. The children laughed happily when the soldier blew the trumpet with comical gestures, but their fathers, mothers, and grandparents were as rigid as mud effigies. Kuse could not read any expression on their blank faces. The wrinkled faces, ravaged by the sun, slashed by the leaves of rice plants and dragged through the mud by buffaloes showed sphynxlike silent withdrawal. They had the quietude of a swamp that had swallowed everything without a single ripple on the surface. Kuse felt he was an unwelcome intruder. The expressions in the villagers' eyes were no different whether they looked at Charlies or at him. Several pairs of eyes flared in hatred as they stared. Such eyes flashed momentarily behind the spectators, disappearing now and reappearing later on. They probably belonged to men who had returned from the jungle on the previous night.

Captain Seagram stood applauding, then shouted, "OK, let's go to the next!"

Kuse was surprised by the merriment in one village. The community had an old small temple for Kuan Yü, the third-century Chinese hero. The structure was weather-beaten and was on the verge of collapsing. Peering through the latticed door, Kuse saw in the dusty darkness a statue of Kuan Yü with his long beard down to the ground, his crude, angry stare frozen. Whether the festivity had anything to do with the temple was uncertain, but when the group marched in playing music, the village was in the throes of a gay dance.

Two masked children were dancing in the center of the spectators' circle. The masks were those of monkeys, painted in red, black, and yellow, in lacquer or gouache. A man was beating an old drum, another striking a gong that looked old enough to be of the Shang or Chou period, and the children were jumping about wildly. The spectators sometimes laughed gently or applauded. Two grown men began to dance, their heads covered with large papier-mâché objects looking like Dharma statues. Kuse soon realized that they were not Dharma, but a monkey and a tiger. As they tottered around in drunken steps, the audience rocked with laughter. The girls giggled, putting their hands on their mouths. Kuse was moved. These were the medieval comic dance and the lion dance of Japan. Only here they were a monkey and a tiger. The ancient inhabitants of the Japanese archipelago had not encountered tigers, so they deified the imaginary beast, the lion, enjoying and fearing it. In his childhood, did he not recoil from the lion dancers when they suddenly tumbled into the hushed, clean entrance of his house on New Year's Day, shaking their red and gold manes? And at the same time, was he not mesmerized, unable to take his eyes off them? The sumptuous explosion of those intruders, their violence and exquisiteness, suddenly came back to him at this most unlikely place. As if a geyser had spurted out, music of memory rang through his body, and Kuse opened his eyes and stared in amazement.

When the band began to play "Home on the Range," the masked children cried out in their treble voices and began swaying like waterweeds, though momentarily confused by the unfamiliar music. They soon began to sway with agility, moving their bodies smoothly in tune with the loud, sour notes of the trumpet. One boy frolicked around the circle and, approaching the long legs of the trumpeter, knocked against one leg with his angular shoulder. Then he took off his mask and grinned broadly, showing his decayed teeth.

The American took the trumpet off his mouth and cried, "What a groovy kid!"

He tousled the child's hair and laughed, shaking his paunch, and resumed his out-of-tune melody with renewed earnestness. The child put on his mask and began to dance in a drunken reel.

At lunchtime, the Vietnamese officers and soldiers went into the peasants' houses and ate their simple meal and then lay down to take a nap. Captain Seagram forbade his men to enter any house and made them remain under the eaves and trees. The soldiers were obedient. They had all burned raw in the sun but they never complained. The captain took his ration, looking for some peasant who might be willing to accept it in exchange for New Year's dishes. He came back with a pleased look on his face, holding rice and pork wrapped in a banana leaf. He ate his food sitting under a tree. When the children came visiting, he opened up a ration and offered canned food or a package of cookies to each one of them.

Flat on his stomach, arm wrestling with a youngster, the captain whispered to Kuse, "A kid like this can throw a grenade or lay a mine. It happens quite often. So we look for children first, when we come to a village on a maneuver. If there are no children or if they run away from us, you can bet your bottom dollar old Joes are hiding somewhere close."

"Do you think chocolate will stop the grenades?" Kuse asked.

"Not really. A kid like this can blow up anything when he wants to. Even a tank! A tank!" The captain suddenly turned to the child and slapped on the ground, shouting cheerfully, "Come on, come on!"

On the third day, Kuse was dozing late in the afternoon in an empty thatched hut. The band had moved a great deal that day, performing in many hamlets. Tanaka gave the camera to Kuse and joined in the circle of villagers, dancing and cartwheeling.

Kuse stuffed himself with rats for lunch and bought a bottle of native white liquor from a peasant. The low-grade liquor in a flyblown bottle was like water, yet gave him a heavy blow on his head. When Kuse invited the peasant who had sold him the liquor to drink it with him, he was offered roasted rats. Kuse had urged Tanaka to join in this feast but the boy had run away. Captain Seagram, a confirmed nondrinker and nonsmoker, broke his abstention and drained two glasses of the liquor, just to be with the peasants. Supplementing his pidgin Vietnamese with gestures and hand signs, Kuse drank with them. Muddled and dizzy, he repeated, "I'm Japanese, don't kill me," to which the peasants smiled politely.

"Do you have any books?" Kuse asked, growing dizzier.

Searching his hut, a peasant produced a worn-out lunar calendar. Printed in Vietnamese and Chinese, it was packed with information: days of the year, omens for each day, sowing time, harvesting time, procedures for family ceremonies of coming of age, weddings, funerals, and ancestral worship. Kuse began to read from the first day of the year, but he was overcome by the effect of alcohol and the words melted into chaos. When he came to, he was lying in an empty hut with no bottle, no calendar.

The solid ground felt good to his skin. Secret odors rose from the pleasantly moist earth, cooling his liquor-soaked brain. He was not sure where the occupants of the hut had gone. The nipa-palm roof and bamboo poles, especially three of the poles, bore numerous bullet holes. There was no bench, no pot, nothing but the earthen floor. In his stupor, Kuse wondered how many times human hands had to touch the bamboo poles before they could take on such a shiny texture, and how many times human feet had to stomp on the earth before it could become so solid. There was no odor of fire or urine, and the earth was smooth, black, and unctuous, like the surface of a coal. Even the brain burning with residual alcohol could judge that it was a monumental work. Energy enough to build a pyramid must have gone into this hut.

A buzz of voices hovered outside. It was Captain Seagram and a Vietnamese. Only officers and noncommissioned officers could speak English, so it must be one of the ARVNs who came with the choir, now speaking with the Captain. They were probably squatting under the eaves. As stumbling English hesitantly sounded, smooth English responded slowly to help the other. Kuse remained on the ground and listened, half dozing. One said artillery . . . the other corrected the pronunciation. Artillery . . . infantry . . . the voice corrected, infantry. . . . Paratroop. Motor. Recoiless. Howitzer. Weapon carrier. Chopper. Tit for tat. Ambush. Contact. Body count. Platoon. Regiment.

The hesitant voice mumbled, "English, difficult. . . ."

The smooth voice spoke patiently, "I will teach you."

The uncertain voice said, after a pause, "New Year finish today."

The smooth voice replied, "Yes, it ends today."

"VC come back."

"The VCs are here."

"Yes, VCs are here."

"We danced with the VCs, didn't we?" said the Captain.

"Only children."

"Yes, only the children danced."

"We come. VC go away. We go away, VC return. Always same. Tonight this village, VC go to jungle. We return to outpost."

"It's like hide-and-seek."

"What you say?"

"Hide-and-seek."

"Yes. Hide-and-seek. But I think. After New Year, I think VC will be quiet."

"Why?"

"Captain Seagram, here."

"Oh, dear, dear!"

"I think VC lie to peasants. After VC take Saigon, they make village fighting zone once more. If they don't fight, they kill. They take tax, they take soldier. Same as now. Now VC say to peasants, everything will be all right. After they win war and Americans go home, everything will be all right. But they take tax, they take soldier. I think all government same. They all lie. They don't keep promises."

"Yes, you must think about it very carefully."

"I think every day."

"In the United States, if you don't like the president, you can go to Washington and say, 'Hey, you are *Numbah ten*,' but if the VCs take over, it will become just as you say. That's true."

"They say, when peasants revolted in north, People's Army came and put down in 1956. Many peasants killed. Peasants in south don't know it. People's Army killed peasants six thousand. I'm scared."

"The South Vietnamese don't believe anybody, do they?"

"No, nobody. Don't know anything, anyone. That's why VC become stronger. People in this village don't know VC, I think."

"That's the problem."

"You smoke Bastos?"

"Thank you, but I don't smoke cigarettes."

"I see."

The conversation ended there. The two spoke no more. They didn't seem to go back to practicing pronunciations either. Kuse quietly lit a cigarette, keeping the sound of the Zippo down. The stumbling voice had spoken, selecting a word at a time, like the water dripping from a keg. Kuse had been moved by the dark gloom hidden in the voice. There was no hatred or hostility. The Vietnamese was relaxed and only speaking of his vague premonitions, yet his tone seemed to have a note of conviction. Eavesdropping always made one feel lonely. But this slow, uncertain voice made Kuse feel something more, something heartbreaking. It was a young voice, but its mature bitterness was born of early hardships.

The holidays were over. The birds had flown away from the marsh.

At five o'clock, the corps gathered at the edge of the village for the return trip. The American soldiers and Vietnamese officers emerged from the coconut groves and thatched huts, and without being told, formed a single file and marched into the bush. When they had entered the grove in the morning, they had made a loud noise with the trumpet and with the rattle of maràcas, but now everyone was glumly silent. The instruments hung heavily from their inert hands. Sunburned and perspiring, the Americans walked with their chins dropped, withdrawn into some dark anger. The Vietnamese officers crept along the ridge, long leaves of grass drooping from their mouths, or cigarettes dangling from their lips. A transformation seemed to have streamed into the village, riding on the tide of the evening.

When the troops awakened from their nap, the crowds that had surrounded them with their toothy smiles and whispers had all vanished. The soldiers looked under the eaves and into the huts one by one in passing, but they only saw old women moving in the dark, young girls dandling the babies, and men sitting on the edge of benches. No one turned around to look at the visitors. No one smiled. The children were absently kneading mud. Tanaka, who had been teaching the children how to stand on their heads and how to make finger dolls, was now having a hard time keeping up with the group. The village sat with the lonely visage of a widow.

They trekked through the bush, plodded across large paddies, and came to the river. The boats were moored some distance away down the river. As far as they could see, the woods defoliated by chemicals had turned into a red desert in the evening glow, and the dead trees protruded like the bones of dinosaurs. Fragile dead leaves were crushed under the shoes, making shell-like sounds. Over the vast dried-up rice paddies, the wide skidding marks of burning napalm remained black, and houses stood stripped down to their stucco walls, their roofs blown off by the artillery.

When they reached the bank, Kuse asked, "Do you think you had any results?"

Captain Seagram wiped his perspiring brow with the back of his hand, and after a few silent steps, answered that he never thought about the results. A little farther on, he added that he only did what he had to do. He walked quickly down toward the wide belt of yellow water.

4 · *The Boat Returns*

"Want to take a walk?"

"It's too dark."

"Let's go and cool off," Tanaka coaxed. Kuse had lain in the hammock after dinner and begun to read his *Gulliver*, but now he put the book face down. He was having a hard time finishing it.

They strolled within the limits of their small triangular base. Kuse felt like an animal pacing in a cage. It was now completely dark. The huts were lit up and the American soldiers' radios were playing jazz. The members of the band were languidly playing poker. The Vietnamese soldiers were, as usual, either at chess matches or cricket fights under the candlelight. Wives and old women were in and out of the trenches. Like animals, they seemed to be able to see in the dark. Pots were sizzling in wash basins filled with glowing charcoal. Here, a wash basin was an all-purpose utensil. Women used one basin for boiling tea, for serving cooked rice, for making fire, for frying bananas, for washing children, and for still other purposes.

The two men climbed up the trench and sat down on the top and smoked cigarettes. Kuse knew it was still safe, but by force of habit he covered the cigarette light with his hand. It was a good target for the snipers. The splashing sound in the river was probably catfish chasing frogs. Insects were creating the vast surf of noise. The secret, dense, humid, and at the same time cosmic, night pervaded the sky and the earth, and an immense body of water seemed to be moving below their feet. Yet there was not even a lapping sound. One detected the river only by the catfishes' occasional splashes.

Tanaka murmured, "It's so quiet."

Kuse answered, "The rivers here are all like this. The Mekong and the Basac, they are all oily and smooth. The Perfume River in Hué is blue and clear, but that's also quiet. It made a nice picture with hills and bamboo groves in the background. When I was there, *crachin* was coming down."

"What's that?"

"It's a drizzle, so cold and penetrating and clinging, it feels like your bones might rot away. They had that sort of rain in that part of the tropics. Very silent and very chilly."

No light was visible across the river and upstream. The villages through which the soldiers had passed for three days, singing, tooting, and dancing, had now fused into darkness. There in the groves, the political committeemen probably gathered boys for lectures and songs, and the women were probably making rice balls for their sons who were about to depart. Passwords must be flying back and forth, weapons clicking, dead leaves crushing underfoot, and the chorus of *"Da Dao De Quo'c My!"* must be echoing in the jungles. But Kuse could not hear or see anything except a sky full of stardust scattered all around.

Tanaka said, "I don't want to go to Bangkok any more. You know, Mr. Kuse, I think I'll stay here a little longer. I've been really thinking for the last several days. You understand, don't you?"

"Sort of."

"My boss at the bike shop wants me to stay, because I'm good at repairs. Everybody's so nice to me. I had no special purpose when I skipped Japan. I feel I can stay here a little longer."

"I envy you."

"I learned a lot even in these three days. I realize that I really didn't know anything before. I'll start learning from the basics. I'll read more books, too. Will you teach me things?"

"You don't need books to study the fundamentals."

"But I don't know anything."

"You just watch out for *congais*."

"But the *congais* are so nice. They're so sweet."

Kuse was silent.

"The other night, she scratched the back of my balls. I was embarrassed as hell, but it was so nice. That gave me shivers. You never touch a place like that usually, you know. I was impressed as hell she knew about it. She knew my body better than my mother."

Kuse was taken aback, and he silently smoked the cigarette cupped in his hands. He had not heard such a voice for a long time. It was so innocent that he felt sorrowful. He wanted to look into the boy's eyes.

"Ah, the fireflies!" Tanaka said.

"Where?"

"The usual place."

On the bank, at the end of the mine field, was a tree in which fireflies congregated every night. A cluster of tens of thousands of fireflies covering entire branches would shine for a while and then suddenly disappear. They were not like the Japanese fireflies that gleamed rhythmically, one by one. Here, they seemed to have a special habit: a group leader sparkled as though giving a signal, and instantly the total mass began to glint in a fluorescent blue, and just as suddenly sink back to a total darkness. It was just like turning off of a Christmas tree. The moment during which the brilliance changed into darkness or the darkness into brilliance at the will of one firefly, one could almost hear the great clamorous whoops. This was another manifestation of the profligacy of energy by tropical nature, which accepted no control. Nightly, Kuse looked at this spectacle and began to imagine the collapse of cities and the caving-in of continents. The moment the myriads of cold glimmerings appeared in the dark, one city collapsed, and the moment they disappeared, one continent vanished. And, no matter how many times he had watched this spectacle of light and dark, he still could not predict when the great torch would be lit or extinguished. He felt it on his shoulders as if it were an actual weight, this enormous energy filling the night. As he watched the mass of lights reaching the irretrievable moment of darkness, he sensed a pandemonial chorus rising. It was like a crescendo of great homage to nature, and at the same time like a cold sneer of nature.

Tanaka cried out in the dark, "It's gone! All gone!"

A few minutes later, Kuse rose, climbed down the trench wall, and returned to his tin hut lit by a pitiful lamp.

The boat returned about nine o'clock.

Kuse was lying listlessly in the hammock, observing a Special Forces lieutenant polishing his AR-15 rifle. Captain Seagram was constantly in and out of the hut and the telegraph office. Kuse had believed that the Special Forces was composed of roughnecks, but the lieutenant was a slender dandy who sported a brush mustache and looked like a lover in the old films. He did not look like a man who could sneak into a jungle at night to fight hand-to-hand in order to gouge out the enemy's guts. Nevertheless, he must have been picked out after careful screening to be a member of the Special Forces. This elite soldier had taken out two portraits before he began polishing his rifle and propped them against the wall. One was his wife's photograph in color, and the other was a copy of it in watercolor on silk, with cotton balls on the back bulging out to emphasize her curves. It was probably the work of a Saigon souvenir artist. The watercolor was crude and in the worst taste, but the lieutenant had placed it carefully next to the color photgraph. After gazing from one picture to the other, he let out a small sigh and began to polish the rifle.

Kuse asked, "Which do you like better?"

The officer did not crack a smile. "They are both my wife," he said.

The reason for the sigh seemed quite other than what Kuse had suspected.

Just then, Tanaka came running in.

"The boat is back, Mr. Kuse!"

"What boat?"

"The Vietcong boat. Remember? The boat that went down on New Year's Day."

Kuse jumped out of the hammock, thrust his feet into his shoes, and scurried out of the hut without tying his shoelaces.

They ran to the trench in the dark. From the watchtowers of two of the triangular points, searchlights swept over the river and focused on a sampan approaching with the popping sound of an engine. Crowds of Americans and Vietnamese watched it from the trench. Kuse and the boy pushed through to the front. Slow eddies of yellow water glinted at the pale white fingers of the searchlight. The sampan moved upstream slowly, loaded with passengers just as it was three days ago, deeply immersed by its full capacity. Jungle hats, open-neck shirts, short pants, black pajamas, Ho Chi Minh sandals, young men, boys . . . an assortment of forms was on the boat where, at the stern, the red and blue flag with a yellow star fluttered. All watched solemnly, no one uttering a sound. Tanaka stood with both arms hanging limp. He seemed to have no intention of calling to the boat as he had the other day. The men on the boat had covered their faces with their hands in the full spotlight, stubbornly silent. Only the chugging of the engine echoed across the river.

Suddenly a sharp Vietnamese voice cried out from the watchtower.

Immediately an answer was shot back from the boat.

Kuse nudged Tanaka and asked what they had said.

"He told them to stop, and they answered it's still New Year's Day," said Tanaka.

Another shout from the lookout tower rang through.

"*Di! Di! Di!*" the words sounded to Kuse. "Go! Go! Go!" Tanaka said.

The voice darted like the cries of a waterfowl, and instantly the lights were turned off. Darkness returned. The sampan, the flag, everything was obliterated; and only the puffing noise moved slowly upstream. The voice from the watchtower, could it have been that officer, Kuse wondered, the man who was talking with Captain Seagram this afternoon outside the thatched hut? Wasn't it that quiet-voiced man?

Back in the room, the lieutenant was still polishing the rifle.

"When are you going to infiltrate?"

"After midnight," the officer answered and continued to polish the weapon, softly whistling a tune from *South Pacific*.

Tanaka returned minutes later. Kuse was lying on his hammock, sipping the native liquor drop by drop from the bottle. Tanaka told him all the stories he had gathered here and there. An ARVN officer said that the VC's supply lines for rice and ammunition had been kept active through the holidays. Tanaka had asked how they knew this and was told that spies were all over the area. Captain Seagram announced that the lights were to be turned off at ten o'clock tonight. At twelve midnight, all American soldiers would enter the trenches, completely armed. The Special Forces of both the ARVNs and the Americans were to depart the base at midnight. The VCs had already started their movement at various points.

"That's what I heard," said Tanaka.

"Thank you," Kuse said.

"This place may get dangerous, too."

"Is the information accurate?"

"I don't know. I asked them, but they didn't answer. That must be a top secret. Seagram said we should be ready to run for shelter at any moment."

"Stan'by, huh?"

"Yes, stan'by."

Tanaka unbuttoned his shirt but kept his trousers and shoes on and threw himself into his hammock. Kuse noticed that firmness and weight seemed to have set in on his tanned jaw.

"Do you want a drink?"

"No, thanks. I'm fine," Tanaka answered sleepily and closed his eyes, resting his hands on his chest. Kuse glanced at the profile. Was it the night or the desolateness of the hut that made the face, condensed in the dim light, no longer that of a boy or of a young man? Tired, drenched in perspiration, a mature man was quietly enduring life. For three days, the boy's expression had been changing constantly, momentarily appearing then melting into blankness, before Kuse had a chance to understand his true feelings. The face in the hammock was now glued down and immobile. Kuse rested his bottle on the floor and gazed into the face. He was amazed how fast the boy had to grow up, peering into the eyes of the dead. There was nothing Kuse could teach him now. There was never anything he could have taught Tanaka. Kuse felt a tinge of loneliness similar to that at the end of a journey.

Captain Seagram stood at the entrance.

"Will you go back to Saigon tomorrow?"

"Yes, I think so," Kuse answered.

"The milk-run will be here at ten," the captain said politely and reached over and turned off the light. Then he walked away. The dark descended soundlessly and engulfed the hut. Drowning in it, Kuse lit a cigarette. The lieutenant had disappeared, unnoticed.

Tockay lizards screeched. Tanaka was snoring. The odor of barracks, perspiration, and saddle soap drifted in the air. The cigarette light flickered. The smoke he could not see tasted only bitter. Kuse turned over and the hammock swung, squeaking the nails on the wall. His neck, his chest, his abdomen, his thighs, his shirt, the hammock, the walls, everything that his fingers could touch was sweating. The scintillating fireflies, the voices that echoed over the water, the loud wailing of the trumpet, and the chanting of young women that wafted like smoke in the dark . . . he tried to remember them, but even they had clouded with perspiration and turned sour. In the tropics, everything got soiled with fingerprints immediately, drooped limp and perished. The only things that did not putrefy were Captain Seagram and the political committeemen in the jungle. Kuse licked his bitter lips and picked off the dry skin with his teeth. He imagined the tens of thousands of bodies buried in the rice paddies, in the rushes, and in the mountains, slowly disintegrating, secretly murmuring in the dark earth. The peasants here had the custom of digging graves in the rice paddies. In the countryside one could see old and new mounds mingling among rice plants. If the two dinosaurs of the world continued to fight until their backbones were broken, the rice paddies would disappear from this country and only a vast field of mounds would remain. Still they would continue to fight. They had already wedged their fangs deeply into each other's body. The more they struggled, the deeper the entanglement.

Kuse remembered a turncoat he had met at a POW camp. About thirty years of age, the man was wearing the black pajamas of the peasants, but his prominent forehead had an air of superior intelligence and willpower. The circumstances of his defection were unknown, but he was said to have been a battalion commander of the People's Army. He held his head high and did not hide his disdain for the barbed-wire fence, for the gourd water containers scattered on the ground of the army base, and for the permeating odor of excretion.

"Why did you defect?" Kuse had asked.

"I did not defect. I parted with them."

He answered sharply in a slow, accurate English as though to assault. He had little of the hissing sibilance that usually accompanied Vietnamese English.

"I'm absolutely opposed to the policies of the United States. I'm also completely against the Government of South Vietnam. The Front is correct in their thinking, but if we go on with the present situation, the Vietnamese will be exterminated. This is that kind of war. So I parted company with them. If you are a Japanese, you should understand this." He answered concisely, carefully selecting each word. Having spoken, he slowly walked away, led by the arm. In the beating sun, Kuse watched the figure walking away calmly with the guard. The sincere conviction in the man's eyes was shrouded by a melancholic gentleness, and Kuse had to hold his breath. He could not dismiss the impact the man had made on him.

The tockay lizard shrieked. The perspiration odor hung in the air.

Kuse wiped his face and neck with his wet shirt. He recalled the words of Lu Hsün,* perhaps because of the memory of the officer who had defected. No other words gripped him like his. Every time Kuse faced the harsh realities of this country, he remembered Lu Hsün's words and chewed on them like bitter cud. But he hesitated to talk about it. That man, the turncoat officer, might have smiled hearing Lu Hsün's words. Kuse had wanted to speak of the words but part of him rejected the idea. Not having experienced the poignant grief of these people, what right did he have to quote Lu Hsün?

Revolution, antirevolution, nonrevolution.
A revolutionary is killed by antirevolutionaries. An antirevolutionary is killed by revolutionaries. A nonrevolutionary is killed either by antirevolutionaries because he is suspected of being a revolutionary, or by revolutionaries because he is regarded as an antirevolutionary. Or else he is killed either by revolutionaries or by antirevolutionaries because he is neither.
Revolution, re-revolution, re-re-revolution, re-re-re-re . . .

He opened his eyes wide in the dark and suddenly longed for a sip of dry martini from a cold glass covered with dew. Then his chin dropped and he fell asleep.

It was about eight in the morning when he was shaken by the shoulder. The sunlight had lanced through the holes in the tin roof and he had thought he was still drifting in the bright, warm water of dreams, when actually he had already slipped into the warm morning.

"Mr. Kuse, killing again!"
Kuse could not answer.
"Don't you want to see?"

*Lu Hsün (1881–1936), father of Chinese revolutionary thought, studied in Japan from 1902 to 1909 and became an idol of the literary leftists in both China and Japan.—TRANS.

"Who killed whom?"

"They paid back. This time, the ARVN killed the VCs. They carried the bodies back in the same truck. The Vietcong made a boo-boo. They are counting the bodies now."

"How can I look at the bodies without brushing my teeth?"

"Are you drunk?"

Kuse forced his glued-together eyes open and saw Tanaka leaving the hut swinging his hips efficiently and accurately. Kuse's mouth was like a garbage can coated with nicotine and the residue of local liquor. He scraped off the fur on the back of his teeth with the tip of his swollen tongue and began to put on his shoes.

Loose, disjointed bags were abandoned under the banyan trees. There were nine of them, all skin and bone, aged about sixteen to eighteen at most. One of them could not possibly be more than fourteen. Looking at the innocent face of a boy with a rice sack still on his shoulder, Kuse remembered the youngster who had danced with a monkey mask on his face. These thin legs were those of the boy who had frolicked to the rhythm of drum and gong. But the disfigured face was totally unfamiliar. Kuse tried hard to recall the faces of the young spectators in the village, but the vacant cold faces on the ground brought back no memories. These faces were pressed into the ground or looked up, the shoulders hunched, the elbows bent. Some appeared to be taking a nap, others praying. The bullet holes had stopped bleeding, and the death odor was not yet present, but flies were already crawling over the fresh wounds, busily moving about in the dry, open eyes. Kuse's eyes twitched. He had to turn away.

Rice bags, grenades, letters, photographs, ammunition belts, all the belongings were removed, and the dead were left with their shirts and pants, just as they were on the day of festivity. A young Vietnamese officer gave a command in a strident voice. Soldiers as young as the dead moved slowly. They grasped the arms and dragged the bodies to the river bank, where a battered boat was moored. The officer ordered the men to load the boat with the bodies. Someone kicked the boat and it glided into the midst of the yellow current, swaying. It sat low in the water and began to move slowly downstream. The corpses were more like a mound of excretion with navels than a pile of rags. The protruding childish hands and feet in rubber sandals dipped into the water as if paddling every time the boat tilted, creating small ripples.

"What for? What for?"

Kuse involuntarily stepped out two, then three steps and cried to the officer. The cleanly shaven small face turned slowly and looked at him. It was a face he had never seen before. The placid, light brown eyes were filled with strange power. Met by the cold, wet eyes, Kuse felt as though slapped on the face. The mighty air of a veteran was there. But the man was obviously bored with the whole business and this fact bewildered Kuse. Again, something began to crumble inside him.

"It's nothing," the officer said in his tottering English. "What the VC do, we do."

Someone touched Kuse's arm. Tanaka, carrying a camera around his neck, nudged him to go. The two began to walk. The red clay was slippery and they had to stamp the ground firmly step by step. Kuse's cheeks were burning, flushed, his back was roasting, his eyes smarting with perspiration. He stopped at the top of the trench and turned to give a last look. The boat was teetering in the middle of the river, then began to move southwestward. Tall columns of summer clouds stood in the blue sky, which was hazy with heat. Kuse lit a cigarette and gazed into the floating boat, narrowing his eyes.

Another hot day was beginning.